Words of Praise for

Harlequin®

SPECIAL EDITION

from *New York Times* and *USA TODAY* bestselling authors

"When I started writing for Special Edition,
I was delighted by the length of the books,
which allowed the freedom to create,
and develop more within each character and
their romance. I have always been a fan of
Special Edition! I hope to write for it for many years
to come. Long live Special Edition!
—Diana Palmer

"My career began in Special Edition.
I remember my excitement when the SEs
were introduced, because the stories were so rich and
different, and every month when the books came out
I beat a path to the bookstore to get every one of them.
Here's to you, SE; live long, and prosper!"
—Linda Howard

"Congratulations, Special Edition,
on thirty years of publishing first-class romance!"
—Linda Lael Miller

"I owe a great deal to the Special Edition line for allowing me to grow as a writer. Special Edition did that, not only for me but for countless other authors over the past thirty years. It continues to offer compelling stories, with heroes and heroines readers love— and authors they've come to trust."
—Debbie Macomber

"Special Edition books always touch my heart. They are wonderful stories with the perfect happy ending."
—Susan Mallery

"How could I not love a series devoted to my favorite things—complex families and deep friendships? I'm so proud to have been a part of this wonderful tradition at Special Edition."
—Sherryl Woods

HUSBAND FOR A WEEKEND

GINA WILKINS

ISBN-13: 978-0-373-65665-3

Recycling programs for this product may not exist in your area.

HUSBAND FOR A WEEKEND

THE ANNIVERSARY PARTY

The publisher acknowledges the following writers who contributed to THE ANNIVERSARY PARTY: RaeAnne Thayne, Christine Rimmer, Susan Crosby, Christyne Butler, Gina Wilkins and Cindy Kirk.

This edition published by arrangement with Harlequin Books S.A.

For questions and comments about the quality of this book please contact us at Customer_eCare@Harlequin.ca.

www.Harlequin.com

Printed in U.S.A.

CONTENTS

Books by Gina Wilkins

Harlequin Special Edition

†*A Home for the M.D.* #2123
†*Doctors in the Wedding* #2163
Husband for a Weekend #2183

Silhouette Special Edition

**The Family Plan* #1525
**Conflict of Interest* #1531
**Faith, Hope and Family* #1538
Make-Believe Mistletoe #1583
Countdown to Baby #1592
The Homecoming #1652
‡*Adding to the Family* #1712
‡*The Borrowed Ring* #1717
‡*The Road to Reunion* #1735
The Date Next Door #1799
The Bridesmaid's Gifts #1809
Finding Family #1892
The Man Next Door #1905
The Texan's Tennessee Romance #1954
††*Diagnosis: Daddy* #1990
††*Private Partners* #2027
††*The Doctor's Undoing* #2057
††*Prognosis: Romance* #2069
†*The M.D. Next Door* #2092

Harlequin Books

Special Edition Bonus Story:
The Anniversary Party—
Chapter Five

Silhouette Books

Mother's Day Collection 1995
Three Mothers and a Cradle
"Beginnings"

World's Most Eligible Bachelors
Doctor in Disguise

Logan's Legacy
The Secret Heir

‡Family Found
*The McClouds of Mississippi
††Doctors in Training
†Doctors in the Family

Other titles by this author
available in ebook format.

GINA WILKINS

is a bestselling and award-winning author who has written more than seventy novels for Harlequin Books. She credits her successful career in romance to her long, happy marriage and her three "extraordinary" children.

A lifelong resident of central Arkansas, Ms. Wilkins sold her first book to Harlequin in 1987 and has been writing full-time since. She has appeared on the Waldenbooks, B. Dalton and *USA TODAY* bestseller lists. She is a three-time recipient of a Maggie Award for Excellence, sponsored by Georgia Romance Writers, and has won several awards from the reviewers of *RT Book Reviews.*

Dear Reader,

There are a few standard romance "themes" I just love to experiment with occasionally, to see how I can present them in a fresh way. I played with a few of those themes in this story—friends who become lovers, a single mom and a commitment-wary man, a "pretend" marriage—and I had a wonderful time twisting those ideas in a slightly different manner than I'd used them before.

Kim Banks comes from a dysfunctional background that has left her with the belief that everyone will leave her eventually. Though his own family was a much more traditional one, Tate Price has resisted commitments until he has established his fledging business and is certain he has found someone he wants to spend the rest of his life with. Combined with their wariness about destroying the friendship that has become so important to them both, those obstacles seem to be too daunting to overcome when it comes to the attraction that simmers between them. When they are persuaded unexpectedly to pose as husband and wife for the sake of Kim's eccentric mother and ailing grandmother, they find themselves getting carried away with make-believe…and tempted to try to turn it into reality.

Special Edition has given us thirty years of heartwarming romances, and I've been so fortunate to have a chance to be a part of this wonderful tradition. Happy anniversary, Special Edition, and a big thank-you from me as both a writer and a grateful reader.

Gina

For my writing friend and sprint partner, Elle James.
Thanks for helping me stay on track!

HUSBAND FOR A WEEKEND

Chapter One

"You don't think I could make it work?" Tate Price asked his friend and business partner, Evan Daugherty.

Evan shook his head, his mouth quirking into a faint smile. "No. For an hour or so, maybe. But not for an entire weekend."

"Want to make a bet on that?"

Kim Banks shifted uncomfortably in her seat. "Um, guys?"

The two men in the party of five at the restaurant table ignored her, even though she was the one who had unwittingly initiated this good-natured confrontation.

"I'll take that bet," Evan said, his gaze locked with Tate's smiling amber eyes. "Say, a hundred bucks?"

Tate's firm chin lifted in response to the provocation. "You're on."

"Seriously, guys. We're not doing this. My mother will just have to be disappointed in me—again."

Kim might as well not have spoken at all, for the reaction she received from her regular Wednesday lunch mates.

"I tend to agree with Evan." Kim's coworker Emma Grainger absently speared bamboo chopsticks into the noodles on her plate as she focused on the conversation. "I'm not at all sure this scheme would work."

Before Tate could reply his sister, Lynette Price, another coworker of Kim's, jumped in. "Tate could definitely do it. He's, like, the king of practical jokes."

Emma tucked a strand of dark hair behind her ear and shook her head. "Married people give off a certain—well, vibe. Tate and Kim just don't have it."

"Because they haven't tried for us," Lynette countered logically.

Growing increasingly uncomfortable with this line of talk, and hardly able to even look at Tate now, Kim cleared her throat. Maybe she should not have told her friends about the bizarre appeal her eccentric, five-times-married mother had made during an out-of-the-blue phone call last night. It turned out that, unbeknownst to Kim, her mother had been lying for more than a year that Kim was happily married to the father of her nine-month-old daughter. Now her nutty mom had asked Kim to bring the baby—as well as someone pretending to be Kim's husband—to an upcoming family reunion.

Kim had learned years earlier to shrug off Betsy Dyess Banks Cavenaugh O'Hara Vanlandingham Shaw's antics, because she would drive herself as crazy as her mom if she took it all too seriously. Humor and avoidance had become her two weapons of choice against her mother's periodic campaigns to draw Kim back into the chaos from which she had escaped nine years earlier, as soon as she had turned eighteen and graduated high school. Though Kim had assured her amused friends that she had no intention of complying with this latest wacky request, somehow the conversation had wound around to whether anyone—specifically Tate—could hoodwink Kim's extended, estranged family into believing he'd been married to Kim for some eighteen months.

She shot a quick look at Tate then. Despite the incredible twist their conversation had taken, he lounged comfortably in his seat, looking as fit and undeniably hot as ever. Seeing her looking at him, he winked, and she dropped her gaze quickly to her plate, feeling her cheeks warm. For the past five months, Kim had been trying to hide her attraction to Tate from her friends, and she thought she'd done so successfully. She'd tried just as hard to deny it to herself, but that had been a much more futile effort.

"Tate would also have to convince them he's her kid's dad," Evan pointed out. "So not only would he have to pretend to be in love with Kim, he'd have to look comfortable with her kid. Having the kid shriek every time he picks her up would hardly help his case."

"Her name is Daryn," Kim muttered. "And I—"

"That wouldn't be an issue," Tate said with a chuckle. "I just wouldn't pick her up. Kim could be the hovering mom who doesn't give anyone else a chance to take the baby."

"And it's not like Daryn is old enough to talk, so she wouldn't be a problem," Lynette agreed.

Emma propped an elbow on the table as she looked at the men with a contemplative frown. "This still doesn't sound like a very good bet for you, Evan. Why would anyone openly challenge Kim about whether she and Tate were really married? You'd need a more definitive sign to prove Tate was able to convince Kim's family that he's her loving husband."

Evan looked intrigued. "Like what?"

"Grandma's ring," Lynette chimed in eagerly.

Kim choked. "Oh, now that's going too far."

She had confided in her friends that her long-widowed maternal grandmother was disgusted with her children's and grandchildren's dismissive attitudes toward their marriage vows, resulting in an appalling number of divorces among them. Grandma Dyess had informed everyone that the first of her grandchildren who entered into a union that Grandma herself believed would last would receive her diamond engagement ring. So far Grandma had refused to endorse any of her grandchildren's choices, and rightly so, since only one of the seven was currently married and Kim had heard that union was a shaky one. Still…

Lynette waved a hand dismissively in response to Kim's protest. "I didn't say you should take the ring under false pretenses. Obviously, that would be wrong. But if you and Tate could convince Grandma to offer it to you, that would mean he'd won the bet."

"And that's not wrong at all," Kim murmured sarcastically.

Lynette just beamed at her, visibly pleased with herself for coming up with such a perfect solution.

"That would definitely work," Emma agreed. "If Grandma offers the ring, it would be clear that Tate pulled off the charade."

"That would be the ultimate proof," Evan conceded.

"But I still say if anyone—grandmother or other relative—expresses doubt, the bet would be lost."

"Well, since you won't be there, how would you know if anyone expressed doubt?" Emma asked. "Tate wouldn't have to tell you if they did."

Both Lynette and Evan looked offended by Emma's naive question.

"Tate wouldn't lie to me to win a bet," Evan disputed loyally.

"He'd only lie to my entire family," Kim said with a shake of her head, both exasperated and reluctantly amused by this insane conversation.

"Well, yeah," Lynette agreed matter-of-factly. "That's the challenge, right?"

Setting down her chopsticks, Kim looked from one of her friends to the other with a frown of disbelief, her gaze sliding rather quickly past Tate. "Are you guys really serious? You're actually suggesting Tate should accompany me to my family reunion in Missouri and pretend to be my husband? My daughter's father?"

"You said you wouldn't mind seeing your ailing grandmother one more time," Lynette reminded her. "And that your mother would never forgive you if you exposed her as a liar to her entire family. Seems like the perfect solution."

"The perfect solution is for me to skip the reunion altogether, which is what I told my mother I plan to do. Just as I've missed the past three Dyess family reunions."

"Lynette's right, this would give you a chance to see your grandmother without permanently alienating your mother. And if he can make it work, Tate's a hundred bucks ahead," Evan agreed with an uncharacteristically mischievous laugh.

Tate shrugged, his smile easy, his eyes inscrutable as he looked across the table at Kim. "No one's given you any say in all this."

"It's about time someone acknowledged that."

He chuckled. "It's a crazy idea, of course. Would probably get awkward as all get-out. But if you want to give it a shot, I'm in."

She blinked. "You would really do this?"

"Sure. I could use the extra hundred bucks," he added with a quick grin toward Evan.

Kim wasn't fooled that the money had anything to do with his offer, but she was not quite certain how to read the expression in Tate's amber-brown eyes. She'd had lunch with him almost every Wednesday for the past five months, but there were still times she couldn't tell what he was thinking.

Kim, Lynette and Emma had started the Wednesday lunch outing six months ago as a little break from their usual, frugal practice of brown-bagging. A month later, Lynette had impulsively invited her brother to join them when he'd mentioned that he would be in the area. He had brought his business partner, Evan, and somehow Chinese Wednesday had evolved into a weekly ritual after that. Occasionally other people came along, and sometimes one or more of the core group had other obligations, but most Wednesdays found the five of them gathered around a table in this popular Little Rock, Arkansas, restaurant. They ate, chatted casually about a variety of topics—usually work-related—then Kim, Lynette and Emma returned to the medical rehabilitation center where they all worked as therapists and Tate and Evan left to check on their ongoing landscape projects.

Kim always looked forward to these get-togethers. She told herself she needed the break from work and deserved the weekly splurge. The conversation was always lively and sprinkled with lots of laughter, a nice midweek pick-me-up. During the almost seven months since she'd started working with them, Lynette and Emma had become her friends, and she considered Tate and Evan friends, as well. They all carefully avoided any intra-group drama, which meant no real flirting between any of them. It was nice to just be pals without complications.

Which didn't mean she was unaware of exactly how attractive Tate and Evan were. She had no intention of getting involved with either of them, but she was far from oblivious to their appeal. Especially Tate, she had to admit, if only privately. If she were looking for someone with whom to have a toe-curling fling—which, as a hardworking single mother, she had neither the time nor the inclination for—brown-haired, tanned and fit Tate Price would most definitely qualify as a candidate. Evan was a great-looking guy, too, with his thick, near-black hair and gleaming, solemn dark eyes, but there had always been something special about Tate....

Not that she would want to hook up with the brother of a good friend anyway, she always assured herself hastily. Way too much potential for awkwardness involved there. And Tate had stated on more than one occasion that he had no interest in any commitment until he and Evan were comfortable that their fledgling landscape design business was established and successful.

His business was just about the only thing Tate took seriously.

Lynette bounced a little in her seat, all but clapping her hands in excitement. "You should do it, Kim. It's not like anyone would be hurt by the game. And in a way, it would serve your mother right if she has to scramble to keep up the ruse she started."

Lynette thought of this as a game? Having Tate pretend to be a husband and father?

"It *would* be kind of funny," Emma murmured, her almond-shaped dark eyes crinkling with a smile as she looked from Kim to Tate and back again. "I would love to see you towing Tate around like a bossy wife."

Tate eyed Kim in teasing appraisal. "You think she'd be a bossy wife?"

Emma giggled. "No, I just think it would be funny if she acted like one toward you."

"I have no interest in being any kind of wife," Kim reminded them, aware that embarrassment made her sound more cross than she intended. "Daryn and I get along quite nicely by ourselves."

Lynette's smile faded. "I know your father and stepfathers all left you eventually, but that doesn't mean all men abandon their families, Kim. I could name lots of couples who have been together for a long time, including my parents. You'll meet someone someday who'll always want to be there for you and Daryn."

Kim shrugged, having no intention of discussing any baggage she carried from her past with her lunch companions. "You know what they say—if it ain't broke, don't fix it. I'm quite content with the life I have. Now if only I could convince my mother of that."

"She'd never understand it," Emma said perceptively.

"Not if she's the type who always has to have a man in her life to feel complete."

"Bingo," Kim murmured.

"Then maybe you should just skip the reunion rather than risk a permanent falling-out with your mother," Evan remarked. "Besides, I still believe it would be hard to fool everyone. Even for Tate."

"Maybe Kim's the one who doesn't think she could make it work," Tate said, his ego still piqued, apparently, by his partner's doubts. "She said she didn't want to go to the reunion and pretend to be married because she's a terrible actor."

"I said I'm a bad liar. It's not necessarily the same thing as being a bad actor. And that's not the only reason I don't want to get involved in this."

"Of course not."

She frowned at him, trying to decide if he was patronizing her.

"Well?" Lynette prodded impatiently. "Are you going to at least think about doing what your mother asked? Especially if Tate's willing to go along?"

Feeling everyone's gaze focused on her, Kim bit her lip, warning herself not to let her friends sweep her into this impulsive plot. "I'll think about it. But I'm still inclined to say no, even if it makes Mother mad. She'll get over it. Probably."

Lynette's dimples flashed again. "You take your time deciding."

Something told Kim that Lynette would do her best to help with the decision—and by help, she meant persuade. Studying Tate's rather challenging smile through her lashes, Kim felt a sudden surge of nerves, wondering if she was insane for even considering this reckless scheme.

She had to admit that there'd been a time when she would have jumped at the chance to pull a practical joke of this magnitude on her annoying family—but that was before she'd grown into a responsible, serious-natured single mom, she reminded herself. Her impetuous, adventurous, wild-oats-sowing days were behind her now.

But maybe she could indulge in one last, reckless escapade before settling into a maturely circumspect future?

"Tate, why don't you give Kim a kiss? We'll tell you if it looks natural." Emma made the suggestion as if it were perfectly reasonable, then looked vaguely surprised when Kim spun to gape at her. "What? You want this to work, don't you?"

Kim wasn't sure why Emma, Lynette and Evan had gathered at her house at noon on Friday, nine days after that fateful lunch, before she and Tate departed for the four-hour drive to Springfield, Missouri. Kim and Tate had both taken the afternoon off work for the trip, but the others had wasted their lunch break for this. Evan, apparently, was there primarily to make fun of his partner. Emma and Lynette had shown up presumably to make sure Kim didn't back out at the last minute. Which, she admitted privately, was a definite possibility.

She had spent the past nine days changing her mind so often she now had a dull headache. Even standing outside her house preparing to start the drive, she dithered about whether she should risk any future contact with her mother and just call off this whole crazy scheme. Tate was still taking the situation as a big joke, even as he loaded his suitcase into the back of Kim's hatchback, stuffing it among the numerous bags and miscellaneous accessories necessary for traveling with a nine-month-old.

"Kiss her?" Closing the hatchback with a snap, he turned to respond to Emma. "You mean, now?"

Always the ultraorganized, detail-oriented member of the group, Emma nodded thoughtfully. "It wouldn't hurt to practice before you leave."

Tate grinned. "I don't think I need practice kissing."

Kim would just bet he didn't. Even the thought of kissing Tate made her toes curl.

Emma rolled her dark eyes in response to Tate's quip, but continued seriously. "I'm assuming you haven't kissed Kim before. If your first time is in front of her family, it could be awkward."

Kim nearly choked. As if this weren't already awkward enough! "Even if Tate and I really were married, I doubt we'd be kissing in front of my family. I tend to be private with that sort of thing."

Looking up from the baby she was holding and cooing to, Lynette gave a little shrug. "Emma's right. You two have to look comfortable together if you're going to make this work. And frankly, Kim, you're the one who needs the practice. You keep looking at Tate today as if you've never seen him before."

While the others laughed, Kim felt her cheeks warm, and it had little to do with the stifling early-August heat. The truth was, she did feel almost as if Tate were a stranger to her today.

Prior to last week, she'd believed she knew him quite

well, that he was one of her good friends—her inconvenient attraction to him notwithstanding. Now, with him preparing to accompany her to her family reunion—as her husband, no less—she wasn't sure she knew him at all. For example, she couldn't figure out exactly why he'd agreed to participate in this crazy charade. It certainly wasn't because he needed the hundred dollars from his business partner.

"I still don't understand why your mother felt the need to lie to everyone," Evan mused, his thoughts apparently similar to hers, if for another reason. "It's not like being a single mom is considered all that shameful these days."

"You'd have to know my mother and her sister to understand," Kim said with a wry shrug. "They just can't comprehend how a woman could be happy without a man in her life. Which explains why Aunt Treva just ended her third marriage and Mom's on her fifth. The minute one loser leaves, Mom hooks up with another one. Every time I talk to her, she reminds me that all three of her children were conceived within wedlock—even if it was by three different husbands. She said she had to tell her mother and her sister I was married or she would never be able to hold her head up in the family again."

"Bizarre," Emma agreed, "but still, if you're going to convince your family that you and Tate are a settled-in couple, you're going to have to work at it a little."

"You know, this is really getting out of hand," Kim said abruptly, shaking her head. "I don't know what I was thinking. Let's just forget the whole thing, okay? Thanks, Tate, but I won't be needing you this weekend, after all."

Emma and Lynette swapped a look as if they'd predicted this moment. Lynette shifted the wide-eyed baby on her hip. "You can't back out now, Kim. You want to see your grandmother, remember? And you wanted her to see Daryn at least once."

"So, I'll go alone. I'll tell the truth—that I never married and that Daryn's father isn't a part of our lives."

"And expose your mother's lies to everyone?" Sympathy for Kim's plight reflected in Lynette's green eyes. "She would never forgive you. I know you've had a rocky relationship with her, but are you really ready to burn all your bridges with her?"

Hearing her own concerns put into words, Kim sighed. "I don't know. Situations like this one have made me keep my distance from her, but she is my mother…."

"Exactly."

"So, I'll go along with the fabrication, but I'll tell everyone my husband had to work or something and couldn't join me this weekend."

"You'd never get away with it," Evan predicted with a wry smile. "You said yourself, you're a terrible liar."

"How bad could it be if I accompany you?" Tate asked. "We'll show up for the reunion, I'll stand close to you and smile a lot, you introduce your grandmother to your daughter and then we'll make an excuse to leave early. Your mother will owe you an enormous favor and you can hold it over her head forever to make sure she never drags you into a mess like this again."

He made it all sound almost logical. Kim shook her head in bemusement, thinking insanity must be contagious. She didn't know if Tate had caught it from her, who'd been infected by her mother—or if both she and

Tate were being influenced by the three friends standing nearby and enjoying this spectacle. *Easy enough for them,* she thought with a frown.

"Tate's bag is already in your car." Lynette spoke as if that were the deciding factor, as if the bag couldn't be removed quite easily. "You might as well go through with it now."

"Apparently, she'd rather call the whole thing off than kiss Tate," Evan commented, his eyes gleaming. "Not that I blame you for that," he added with a half smile.

This situation seemed to have brought out a roguish side of Evan that Kim hadn't seen much before. She'd always thought of him as the serious, disciplined partner.

"I'm thinking y'all made your bet with the wrong person," Tate murmured, eyeing Kim with lifted eyebrows. "Kim seems to be the one who doesn't believe she has the talent—or maybe the nerve—to go through with this. Actually, I'd be willing to make a fifty-dollar side bet that Kim's the one who'll blow our cover before I do."

Even though she knew she shouldn't let his mild taunt pique her ego, Kim still felt her hackles rise. The others watched her speculatively, and she wondered if they agreed with Tate that she was the weak link in this impromptu partnership.

She reminded herself that none of them had known her prior to her new life as a quiet-living, hardworking single mom. She'd started working at the rehab clinic after her maternity leave, and they hadn't known her when she'd worked at another facility in a different, nearby Arkansas town, so they couldn't be aware that this was exactly the kind of escapade she once would have thrown herself into with impish gusto. She wasn't that person any longer—but it still irked that they so obviously doubted her.

She sighed gustily and let her youthful recklessness reassert itself—but only temporarily, she vowed. "I'll take that bet."

She reached out to grab Tate's navy polo shirt and yank him toward her. Before he could finish his sputtered laugh, she pressed her mouth to his.

Chapter Two

Fireworks. Trumpets. Operatic voices bursting into song. Were there any clichés that did *not* spin through Kim's mind when Tate wrapped his arms around her and responded enthusiastically to the spur-of-the-moment kiss?

She had always appreciated his lean but solid build, figuring the manual labor he did outdoors in his landscape design business built muscles and burned calories. Now she felt the strength in those tanned arms, the rock-hardness of chest and thighs.

She had always thought he had a sexy mouth with shallow indentions at the corners that could almost be called dimples. Now he demonstrated just how skillfully he used those warm, firm lips.

She wanted to believe she was the one who brought the kiss to an end, but she suspected Tate drew back first. She was too dazed to be certain. She blinked at him, wondering if she saw a similarly stunned look in his narrowed eyes before he masked any reaction behind his usual easy grin.

"Well?" he asked the others. "Did we pass?"

Lynette lifted an eyebrow as she studied Kim's face. "Either you're a better actor than you claimed, Kim, or Tate made that kiss work, because…wow."

Kim's chin lifted again in response to the implication that Tate had been in control of the kiss, regardless of whether it might just be true. Acting once more on the impulsiveness that had so often gotten her into trouble in the past, she turned to Evan. Catching the collar of his cotton shirt in both hands, she planted a kiss directly on his lips.

No fireworks this time, she noted with some dismay. No trumpets or other clichés. Evan was a good-looking, well-built guy and it was a nice kiss—but it didn't shake her to her toenails the way kissing Tate had. Deciding she didn't want to analyze the difference just then, she pushed Evan away and turned almost defiantly toward the others. "Any more comments about my acting abilities?"

Evan cleared his throat rather loudly. "So, maybe *I* should be the one to accompany you this weekend," he said with a teasing leer, reaching for Kim again.

Emma and Lynette laughed as she dodged him, and Kim was satisfied that her unexpected move had derailed their sudden speculation about whether she was a little too attracted to Tate.

What might have been a slight frown on Tate's face smoothed quickly into a grin. "Too late, pal. My bag's already in the car. Speaking of which, shouldn't we be on the road, Kim? And don't the rest of you guys have to get back to work?"

Emma glanced at her watch. "We do, actually. Have fun, you two—and remember, we're going to want to hear all the details."

Lynette turned toward her brother. "Do you want to put the baby in her seat? It would be good practice for you."

Tate held up both hands and backed off. "No. I said I'm not using Daryn to help me win this bet. You know babies scare me. If Kim needs my help with anything, she only has to ask, but Daryn isn't a prop for me to rehearse with."

Kim appreciated several things about Tate's words, most especially the fact that he'd used Daryn's name, rather than calling her "the kid," as Evan was prone to do. She stepped forward to take her daughter from Lynette. Adorable in a red-and-white gingham-checked romper, with a red-and-white stretchy headband festooned with a white fabric daisy circling her fine, light brown hair, Daryn kicked and babbled, enjoying the attention. She gave Kim a slobbery, two-toothed grin and, as always, Kim's heart melted. She'd made quite a few mistakes in her life, but she would never classify Daryn in that way. A surprise, yes, but never a mistake.

Kim fastened Daryn securely into her rear-facing car seat, then handed her the soft, stuffed monkey that accompanied the child everywhere. Settling in contentedly, Daryn kicked her feet and waved the toy enthusiastically to elicit jingly chimes from the bells inside. Kim was used to the sound, but she wasn't sure how Tate would feel about listening to it for the next four-plus hours. Fortunately, Daryn tended to sleep during car rides, so the jingling would be sporadic.

"Would you like me to drive?" Tate offered, nodding toward the driver's door of her car. "That would free you to take care of the baby."

She deliberated only a moment before tossing him the keys. "Sure, why not? You might as well make yourself useful."

Tate winked at Emma. "You're right. She is a bossy wife."

Everyone laughed, including Kim, though she felt a funny little jolt at hearing Tate refer to her as a "wife." As she opened the front passenger door, she reminded herself that she'd better get used to it—at least for the next day or so.

"Oh, wait!" Lynette made a show of hitting herself in the head with the palm of her hand. "I can't believe I almost forgot."

Kim lifted her eyebrows in question. "Forgot what?"

Lynette dug into her pocket and pulled out a gold band. "I brought this for you," she said to Kim. "You and I wear about the same size in rings, I'd think, and this fits me. Tate, did you bring yours, like I told you to?"

Tate held up his left hand, demonstrating that he was already wearing a band on the ring finger. Kim hadn't even noticed, and it took her aback to see it there. She hadn't thought about rings, which only proved how little prepared she was for this weekend.

"Whose ring is this?" she asked as Lynette pressed the other band into her hand.

"It was our grandmother's. Tate's wearing our grandfather's ring. We inherited them when they passed away. I realized last night that you'd need rings to convince your family you're married, so I called Tate and told him to bring his and I'd let you borrow mine."

Swallowing hard, Kim shook her head. "I don't want to take responsibility for your grandmother's ring. I'm sure I have something that will work. I have a silver band somewhere, I think."

"What can happen to it on your hand?" Lynette asked matter-of-factly. "Besides, it's more believable with a matching set. You can return it to me when you get back. I'm going to want to hear all the details, anyway."

"Maybe Tate should put it on for you," Evan suggested with another wicked grin.

Wondering what had gotten into her usually serious-minded friend, Kim frowned at him and quickly shoved the ring onto her finger. It was a little tight, which was a good thing, since she didn't want to risk having it fall off. "I've got it. Now, you guys had better get back to work. Tate, if we're going through with this, let's get on the road."

He chuckled and opened the driver's door. "Yes, dear."

The others were still laughing when Kim closed herself into the car and reached for her seat belt. She couldn't quite share their amusement.

Hands on the wheel, Tate slanted a quick, sideways glance at Kim, who sat very straight and prim in the passenger seat of her car, her face turned away from him as she gazed out the side window. The car was so small their arms almost touched over the center console, but it might as well have been a yacht for all the emotional distance between them at that moment. She hadn't said a word since he'd driven away from her house ten minutes ago.

Was she regretting again that she'd become involved in this admittedly outlandish scheme? Probably she wondered why he'd allowed himself to be swept into the plan by his sister and friends. He'd had plenty of time to ask himself that question during the past nine days, and still hadn't come up with an answer that was entirely satisfactory. He'd decided to stop analyzing and just go with it, a philosophy that had always served him well in the past.

Was Kim anxious about what lay ahead? He couldn't blame her for that. He wasn't nervous, exactly, figuring the next couple of days would be interesting and provide plenty of funny stories for his friends, but he was aware of the challenges they could encounter. He hoped she wasn't uncomfortable being alone with him now—especially after that unexpectedly volatile kiss.

Surely she knew she could trust him not to let things get out of hand; just as he knew she wouldn't read too much into his behavior this weekend, since she had always been adamant that she wasn't looking for a relationship. He and Kim were friends, and he treasured that friendship. He had no intention of breaking that bond.

Okay, maybe there'd been times when he'd been tempted to carry their relationship beyond a casual acquaintance. Maybe there had been more than a few occasions when he'd looked at her laughing with her friends across the lunch table and felt a strong urge to have her all to himself. More than once, he'd considered asking her out, but he'd always dissuaded himself with the reasons that would not be a good idea. He didn't want to ruin their comfortable friendship. He had always been wary of dating single mothers. His sister would never forgive him if he did anything even unintentionally to hurt her friend. And then there was the fact that Kim had never given him any significant sign that she wanted him to ask her out, despite an occasional moment of what he thought of as heightened awareness between them. Even now, after a kiss that had shaken him to his bone marrow, Kim was as reserved and carefully cordial with him as ever.

Maybe the kiss hadn't been as stimulating for her as it had been for him. He'd thought he saw some of his own surprise and awareness mirrored in her eyes when she had pulled away, but then she'd turned and planted one on Evan. Which, Tate admitted privately now, had rather annoyed him. Just what purpose had that served in preparing her for the coming weekend?

A particularly enthusiastic round of tinkling and babbling came from the backseat as Daryn pumped her toy and kicked her feet. "She seems content back there," he said, figuring talk about the baby would set Kim more at ease.

She glanced over her shoulder. "She likes riding in the car. She'll probably fall asleep soon."

"She sure likes that monkey."

"Mr. Jingles," Kim informed him with a faint laugh. "A gift from her father."

Tate kept his eyes on the road and his tone casual. "Yeah? I thought you said he wasn't a part of your lives."

"Oh, he's not. He visited me in the hospital when

Daryn was born, left the monkey and a generous check, wished us both the best and walked out of our lives. Last I heard, he was living in Alaska where he's pursuing his dream to be a bush pilot."

It was the most he'd heard her say about her child's father. Perhaps she was simply acknowledging Tate's inevitable curiosity about the man whose role he was filling this weekend. Maybe she didn't want those questions to become the elephant in the car with them, so to speak.

"You don't sound bitter," he commented.

She shrugged. "Chris is a nice, fun guy, but he'd make a terrible husband and father, as he is the first to admit. We were together for a while, but I never expected it to last forever. Granted, Daryn was a surprise, but both Chris and I would have been miserable if we'd tried to stay together for her sake. Especially him, since he didn't really want a child. As for me, I consider myself blessed to have her, and I'll always think fondly of Chris because of her."

It didn't sound as though she received any support now from Daryn's father, but judging from the months Tate had known Kim that didn't surprise him. He'd always thought of her as very independent and self-sufficient. He admired that about her. Just as he appreciated her calm, quiet demeanor that didn't quite mask a delightfully dry sense of humor. And her ease with keeping their luncheon conversations flowing and interesting. Not to mention that she was certainly pleasant to look at with her wavy, shoulder-length chestnut hair, brown eyes the color of good whiskey, a cute smattering of freckles across an impishly tilted nose and a slightly crooked smile that always made his pulse jump into overdrive when aimed in his direction.

Another happy squeal and frantic clinking came from the backseat, reminding him of the main reason why he'd never done anything about that racing pulse. As loath as he was to compare himself to Kim's ex, Tate was in no better position to take on the massive responsibility of a child—especially now, when his long-planned business was just taking off.

"Do you mind if I turn on some music? Daryn drifts off to sleep more easily when there's music playing. She needs her nap."

Though he couldn't help wondering if Kim was trying to ward off any further conversation as much as soothe her baby, Tate shook his head. "Feel free. What does she like? Heavy metal? Acid rock? Please tell me it doesn't involve purple dinosaurs."

Kim laughed softly. "You're a little dated on kids' TV, not to mention rock genres, but there are no purple dinosaurs involved. I usually tune in to a pop or country radio station, but we're not picky."

"I'm a country fan, myself."

"I knew that," she reminded him, reaching for the radio buttons.

Of course she did. Just as he knew her favorite television programs because of their weekly chats over lunch. He hoped whatever happened this weekend didn't affect those easy conversations he'd always enjoyed so much. He supposed he hadn't thought that far ahead beyond this impulsive outing. As hard as it would be for him to state exactly why he had agreed in the first place, he knew he had to make certain that he and Kim remained friends afterward. She meant too much to him—on a platonic basis, of course—for him to risk not having her in his life, at least on a once-a-week basis.

After a brief stop halfway into the trip for a walk break, a diaper change for Daryn and ice-cream cones for Tate and Kim, they were back on the road toward Springfield. Kim had offered to drive the rest of the way, but Tate confided he was a restless passenger and would just as soon drive, if she didn't mind. Since she would rather ride and sightsee than negotiate the turns and traffic on the road clogged with tourists headed for Branson, Missouri, Kim was happy to agree.

Daryn fussed a little at being strapped back into her car seat so soon, but she fell asleep again within a few minutes on the road, to Kim's relief. For the most part, Daryn was an easygoing baby who rarely cried, but she'd thrown a few memorable fits in her time. Kim was glad this wasn't going to be one of those times.

A little more than an hour's drive lay ahead of them when they crossed the Arkansas/Missouri state line. Kim pointed that out to Tate, telling him she would guide him to her mother's house after they reached Springfield. She'd never been to this house, but she had been given detailed directions. Her mother had moved into a new place since Kim had last been persuaded to come for a visit.

"You know, it just occurred to me," Tate said with a sudden frown. "What has your mother been calling me? You said she's told everyone you've been married for more than a year. Did she give your imaginary husband a name?"

"She said she called him—er, you—Trey. You know,

as if you were Somebody the Third. She thought that sounded impressive, I guess."

"Hmm. That's rather a coincidence. Actually, I am the third Tate in my family. My mom's dad and his dad were both named Tate, though obviously there's no 'the third' in my name."

"Don't worry, I'll tell everyone you prefer answering to Tate. As to your last name, she said she never mentioned it and no one asked."

"Rather odd, isn't it?"

"Not in my family," she replied with a faint sigh. "As competitive as they all are, they wouldn't want to hear too many details about this perfect life Mom has concocted for me."

She saw him slant a look her way, and she could only imagine the thoughts going through his head. He and Lynette came from such a normal, stable family. Tate was in for a shock when he met Kim's relatives. It was just as well she wasn't bringing him home as a mate, even a potential one, she told herself. He'd be running in panic before the weekend was over rather than tie himself to anyone from the dysfunctional clan he was about to meet.

She checked the directions again as Tate turned onto the street where her mother lived. "Second house on the left," she said, checking the numbers. "Yes, this is it."

A car and a pickup truck were parked in the driveway of the buff-brick house, so Tate pulled up to the curb. "Nice place," he commented, studying the modestly middle-class house on the tidy street lined with similar homes. "Somewhat more… um, normal than I was expecting."

"It is quite average-looking, isn't it?" She eyed the

cheery flowers in the beds on either side of the small front porch. "Apparently, Mom is a suburban housewife these days."

"As opposed to...?"

"Her first husband, my father, was in the military, so she was an army wife living on base for a few years. They split when I was just two and he died in a motorcycle accident not long afterward. Her second husband, the father of my first half brother, Julian Cavenaugh, sang in a traveling bluegrass band based in Branson. We lived in a mobile home park and Mom threw pots and made macramé wall hangings to occupy herself while he was on the road. They divorced when I was eight, when the singer decided he made better music as a single act. Her third husband had a lot of money, so she was a society maven in St. Louis during that phase, when my younger half brother, Stuart O'Hara, was born. That marriage ended when I was thirteen, when Stuart's dad was caught in a tax fraud scheme and lost everything, including my mother."

Tate didn't say anything, so Kim finished her convoluted history quickly while reaching for her bag. "Her fourth husband was a cattle rancher in a little town about fifty miles from Springfield. Mom embraced country life, learning to bake and knit and raise chickens. I lived there until I was eighteen and left for college. I never went back—she and Stan split up before my first semester ended. She was involved with several men after that, but didn't marry again until three years ago. This latest one, Bob Shaw, is a tax accountant, a couple of years younger than Mom. She turned fifty earlier this year, though she wouldn't admit it under threat of torture. I've only seen Bob once. He seemed nice enough, if a little bland."

"Are you close to your brothers?"

"Not really. Stuart was just a little boy when I moved out, and I haven't seen him all that often since. Julian entered the military the day after he graduated from high school, married soon after that and was deployed overseas for the most part until he got out of the service and moved back to Missouri a few months ago, sans the wife. Apparently, she found new companionship while he was serving in the Middle East."

"Nice."

"Yeah. My brother and I share our mother's luck with romance, apparently."

She climbed out of the car without giving Tate a chance to ask any further questions. So far when she'd told him these stories about her family's past, he'd merely listened intently, then kept whatever reactions he'd had to himself. Perhaps he was too bemused to think of anything to say, since her background was so vastly different from what she'd heard of his and Lynette's.

She knew he would never look at her quite the same way after this escapade. She just hoped that when this weekend was over, they could at least still be comfortable as once-a-week lunch buddies.

Before she could even unbuckle Daryn from the car seat, the front door to the house opened and her mother rushed out to greet them. "Kimmie! Trey! I'm so glad you're here. Where's that grandchild of mine?"

Tate had time only to give Kim a look of startled amusement before Betsy descended on him. Her mother, Kim noted, had needed no rehearsal. No one watching would ever suspect that Betsy had never even met the man she was hugging so warmly.

Betsy gave Tate a smacking kiss on the cheek before drawing back to gaze up at him. "How was the drive?"

"Very nice, thank you. Um—have I met your husband?" Tate asked in a quiet voice meant only for Betsy's ears. Kim barely heard him, herself, as she approached them with Daryn in her arms.

"Not just yet, dear." Betsy smiled blandly as she replied. "Don't you remember, I came alone to visit you and Kim after Daryn was born?"

"Of course." Tate grinned, clearly charmed. "How could I have forgotten that?"

Betsy beamed. Kim noted that her mom had adopted her newest role with the same attention to detail as all the parts she'd played before. She looked every inch the middle-class homemaker with her blond-highlighted hair, red-plastic-framed glasses, yellow-print cotton top and ivory cropped pants. She barely resembled the woman who'd worn braids and tie-dye during her bohemian phase, or designer-labeled suits and heels to country club luncheons, or denim and gingham and boots on the ranch.

Betsy patted Tate's arm with a pink-manicured hand. "Funny and handsome. As I've said many times before, my daughter is so fortunate to be married to you."

Tate laughed softly.

Betsy turned to plant an air kiss near Kim's cheek. "Hello, darling. You look wonderful—though I did like your hair better a bit shorter. And look at my little Daryn. She's growing so fast! You'll want to be careful not to feed her too much, dear. Chubby babies grow into chubby adults, you know."

Reminding herself that quarreling with her mother was like arguing with a cat, Kim responded mildly, "Daryn falls right into the middle of the recommended size charts for her age, Mom. She's perfectly healthy."

It didn't surprise Kim that Betsy made no attempt to hold the wide-eyed baby, just kissed her soft cheek, then stepped quickly back. "Oh, I just love your wedding rings," she said in approval. "Yours looks a bit tight on your hand, Kim. As though maybe you've gained a little weight since your wedding day."

Kim had been all too aware of the unfamiliar ring on her finger during the drive here. She didn't really need her mother pointing out the flaws with it, especially since Kim was wearing it to satisfy her in the first place.

Betsy moved toward the house without waiting for a response. "Come inside. Everyone's eager to meet you, Trey."

"His name is Tate, Mom. He really prefers that."

"Tate Price," he murmured.

Betsy winked at him and linked her arm through his. "Of course."

Tate grinned over his shoulder at Kim when Betsy tugged him toward the house. "I'll come back later for the bags, honey," he said, his eyes gleaming a little too brightly.

Kim gave him a saccharine sweet smile in return. "That will be just fine, *sweetie*."

Feeling as though she were caught in a current she couldn't quite escape—a familiar sensation when her mother was around—Kim fell into step resignedly behind her mother and her "husband."

Chapter Three

As much as he disapproved what he'd heard of Betsy's maternal behavior—or lack of it—Tate couldn't help but be amused by her. Was she really as oblivious to reality as she acted? She was either one of the most natural actors he'd ever encountered, or she was a little delusional. Maybe both.

A seemingly compulsive flirt, she held his hand and twinkled up at him as she towed him into her house, leaving Kim to follow behind with the baby. He looked rather helplessly over his shoulder at her, but Kim merely wrinkled her nose and shrugged as if to remind him that she'd tried to warn him.

"Everyone, look who's here! Come say hello to Kim and Tate and precious little Daryn," Betsy called out as they entered the crisply air-conditioned interior of her home.

Tate wasn't one to pay much attention to interior

decor, but he got an impression of tidy, rather generic furnishings and framed prints in a neutral color scheme with touches of gold and green. And flowers. Lots of flowers, cheerily arranged in glass and ceramic vases displayed on nearly every surface. He might not know a lot about furniture, but he could name every bloom on display.

A young man with limp brown hair and a vaguely disgruntled frown looked up from the tablet computer he'd been fiddling with on the living room couch. "Tate? I thought you said his name was Trey."

"It's Tate the Third, obviously," Betsy replied without a pause. "He's decided he prefers Tate. Stand up and greet your sister and brother-in-law, Stuart. Where are Bob and Julian?"

"Bob wanted to show Julian something under the hood of his car," Stuart replied vaguely, remaining seated. "Hey, Kim."

She greeted him politely, and only a little more warmly. "Hi, Stuart. How's it going?"

"It's all good. Nice to meet you, Tate," he muttered in response to his mother's meaningfully cleared throat.

"Good to meet you, too, Stuart." Tate had forgotten to ask Kim if her stepfather and her brothers had been told the truth about her marital status; judging by Betsy's words to her younger son, Stuart, at least, was still in the dark.

The teen nodded, then redirected his attention to his computer.

Betsy sighed in exasperation, and turned to Tate with a little moue of apology. "Stuart's not much of a talker, I'm afraid. But I'm sure he's delighted to welcome you to the family."

Tate shared a baffled look with Kim. "Um. Okay."

Sounds from the doorway announced the arrival of the final two members of the family. Tate summed up the newcomers in a sweeping glance. Bob Shaw was a meek-looking man in his late forties with thinning, sandy hair, a ruddy face, a potbelly and a warm smile. Julian was of medium height and weight, somewhere in his mid-twenties, dressed in a red T-shirt and jeans.

Of Betsy's three offspring, Julian Cavanaugh bore the strongest resemblance to their mother. Dark blond hair spilled over his forehead, dipping into eyes the same clear blue as Betsy's. Kim and Stuart must have inherited their brown eyes from their fathers. Tate couldn't say whether Julian's smile, as well as his coloring, resembled his mother's. The way the guy was scowling now, it was hard to picture him smiling at all.

Betsy slipped a hand beneath her husband's elbow. "We're all here now. Isn't this lovely? Bob, Julian, this is Kimmie's husband, Tate Price the Third. And look how much our little Daryn has grown since the last photographs I showed you. Isn't she adorable?"

Bob kissed Kim's cheek, tickled Daryn, then stuck out a hand to Tate. "It's nice to finally meet you—Trey, is it?"

"Tate," he corrected. "I've decided I prefer to be called that."

Betsy giggled softly in response to his quote of her, and he winked at her.

Bob nodded knowingly. "Thanks for coming with Kim to the reunion, Tate. It means a lot to Betsy."

Apparently, Bob was in on the secret. "My pleasure."

Julian eyed Tate with open suspicion. "Took you long

enough to get around to meeting us. This is the first time Kim's been home since you got married."

So Betsy had lied to both of her sons. As amused as he was by the woman, Tate could understand why Kim had wanted to put some space between herself and her wacky mom. It had to be both frustrating and exhausting to try to keep up with Betsy's whims and schemes.

Kim didn't make it necessary for Tate to come up with a response to Julian's accusation. "That's not Tate's fault. I've been very busy. Between my work and the baby, I've had very little free time. This long weekend is the closest I've come to a vacation since the last time I saw you."

"That was at the reception for Mom and Bob," Stuart mumbled without looking up from his computer. "It was the day after my fifteenth birthday. We were going to have a cake for me at the reception but no one remembered to order one."

He didn't sound particularly resentful, Tate decided. More matter-of-fact, as though he were accustomed to being overlooked. Tate wondered if Stuart, too, would separate himself from his family as soon as he felt comfortable being on his own. It sounded as though Julian came around somewhat more often than Kim now that he'd gotten out of the service, but from what he'd observed thus far, Tate certainly didn't fault Kim for her different choice.

If Betsy even heard Stuart's comment, she gave no sign. Instead, she patted Bob's arm and said, "Sweetie, why don't you help Tate bring in their bags and show him to their room? The boys and I will catch up with Kim and Daryn until you get back."

Tate looked at Kim with a slightly lifted eyebrow,

but she nodded for him to go ahead. As he followed Bob from the room, it occurred to him that he and Kim would be sharing a room for the night. Of course her family would assume they shared a bed—besides, he doubted there would be an unfilled bedroom with the whole family here.

Bob seemed to follow the direction of his thoughts. "There are three bedrooms upstairs," he explained, motioning toward the staircase on their way out. "Ours and Stuart's and the guest room. Julian has an apartment not far from here, so he'll be sleeping there tonight. Betsy said you were bringing a portable crib for the baby?"

Remembering seeing the folded crib in the large trunk, Tate nodded. Daryn would bunk in the same room with them like a teeny-tiny chaperone, but it could still be awkward. He'd just have to do his best to put Kim at ease, even if it meant sleeping on the floor himself.

"There's a lot of stuff," he said, opening the back of the car. "I'll probably have to make a couple of trips. It's amazing how many supplies one little baby requires for only a weekend."

Bob chuckled. "I remember."

In response to Tate's questioning look, he explained, "I've got two kids of my own, both college-age now. They live with their mother, my ex-wife, in Texas, but I see them quite often."

"They won't be here this weekend, then?"

"No, they haven't exactly bonded with Betsy's family." He sighed lightly and gave a little shake of his head. "Can't really blame them for that."

Giving Tate a rueful little shrug, he reached into the

car and pulled out the travel crib and a heavy bag. "My in-laws are…complicated. It's no wonder my poor Betsy has to resort to rather extreme measures when dealing with them."

"Like inventing a husband for her daughter, you mean?"

"Well, yes. I must say, you're being a good sport about all of this."

Tate shrugged. "Just helping out a friend."

"Is that all you and Kim are? Friends? Because when you smiled at her, I thought maybe…"

Scooting around the older man, Tate grabbed a couple of bags and hefted them out of the car. "We should get these things inside. Kim might need something for the baby."

Bob took the hint immediately. Hefting his own load a bit higher, he turned toward the house. "I'll help you get the rest on the next trip."

Rather relieved, Tate followed with his own armload. The one thing he did not want to do before spending a night in the same bedroom with Kim was to overanalyze his feelings about her.

"Well?" Betsy demanded of her sons almost the minute Bob and Tate left the room. "What do you think of your brother-in-law? Didn't I tell you he was a great guy?"

Kim sighed and gave her mother a chiding look over Daryn's head. She saw no need to keep lying to her half brothers about this fake marriage—not that there was really any need for Betsy to lie to anyone about it, but especially not her own sons. At least she seemed to have told Bob the truth.

Still reluctant to humiliate her mother publicly, Kim vowed to draw her aside at the first possible opportunity and request that they find a way to let Julian and Stuart in on the secret. Maybe they could just call it a big joke on the rest of the family.

"He seemed okay." Stuart answered his mother's question with a shrug, again without looking up from his screen. "Better than I expected, I guess."

What was that supposed to mean?

Before Kim could ask for clarification, Julian spoke up. "Seems kind of cocky to me. Just because he's an architect or whatever doesn't mean he's any better than the rest of us."

"Tate isn't an architect, he's a landscape designer. A very talented one," Kim correctly mildly, though she felt her defenses rise in response to the criticism.

Stuart shot a look at their mother. "You told me, too, that he was an architect."

Was the game already over? Whatever else they might be, her brothers weren't dumb, and they'd already been taken aback by the apparent name change. Kim figured there was no way her mother was going to be able to cover all the fabrications she'd told them.

Betsy gave a sad sigh, and for a moment Kim thought her mother was actually going to come clean.

She should have known better.

"That was my mistake." Looking somewhat mournfully toward Kim, Betsy explained, "When Kim mentioned that Trey—I mean, Tate—was a landscape designer, I thought she meant an architect. I can be so scatterbrained sometimes."

When everyone merely nodded in response to that comment, she added, "I would have been corrected much sooner if my daughter ever found time to call—or better yet, to actually visit her mother occasionally."

Both her brothers looked at her somewhat reproachfully, and Kim scowled. All of a sudden, it was all her fault? How did Betsy keep getting away with these antics?

"Look," she said firmly, "there's something you need to—"

"So you married a gardener, not an architect?" Julian nodded in satisfaction, as if that explained something that had puzzled him. "That makes more sense."

Her frown deepened. "What do you mean?"

He shrugged. "Well, it just seemed odd that you'd be married to a successful architect and still be working all the time, rather than staying home with your daughter. I figured Mom had exaggerated some about your husband's financial success, but now I get it."

"You get what?" Kim asked, studying him through narrowed eyes.

Looking back down at his computer, Stuart mumbled, "He's saying you're probably supporting the guy while he plays around at being a 'landscape designer.'"

Kim gasped in response to Stuart's cynical translation. Before she could make an indignant response, Julian spoke again. "I figured something had to be keeping him around. You make pretty decent money as an occupational therapist, don't you?"

Kim had to clamp down on her tongue with her teeth to stop herself from saying things that were entirely inappropriate for her daughter's tender ears. She reminded herself that twenty-four-year-old Julian had recently been through an ugly divorce and was probably still bitter about it. Following their mother's repeated examples, he'd rushed into an impetuous, infatuation-based marriage, and it had been no surprise to anyone when the union ended in flames. Grandma Dyess had not offered her ring to the couple.

Still, Julian's resentment and disillusion was no excuse for him to attack her—and especially not Tate, who'd done nothing at all to deserve this level of cynicism.

She made herself speak with icy dignity. "I work because I love my job, and I'm good at it. As for Tate, he has a degree in urban horticulture and landscape design, and the business he and his partner established in Little Rock is doing very well. They're in growing demand, and they've already made quite a reputation for themselves in both residential and commercial circles. I'm very proud of what they have accomplished in a relatively short time."

"Why, thanks, honey. I'm proud of you, too."

Hearing Tate's amused drawl from behind her, Kim looked around with a strained smile. She hadn't intended for him to overhear, of course, but she had spoken quite honestly. She *was* impressed with how hard Tate and Evan had worked to establish their business, and with the success they had enjoyed thus far.

"We've brought in everything from the trunk," he said. "Is there anything else in the car I should grab?"

"No, that's all, thanks."

Daryn was beginning to fuss and chew her fist, which made a perfect excuse to escape for a while. "If you'll all excuse me, I'm going to feed Daryn. Tate, would you mind bringing her bag for me?"

She nodded toward the large, flowered bag sitting on the floor beside the diaper bag. She was capable of carrying both bags and her daughter, but she didn't want to leave Tate alone to her family's mercies.

"Of course."

"Do you need help?" Betsy made the offer rather vaguely, and Kim wasn't surprised that her mother didn't argue when assured that her assistance was not required.

The cheery, yellow-and-white kitchen sat at the back of the house, with a big window over the sink overlooking a nice-size backyard planted with more colorful flowers and an inviting patio designed for entertaining. Kim took in the details at a glance, then turned to Tate, who stood behind her, smiling sympathetically.

"Deep breath," he advised.

She filled her lungs and let the air out slowly, but the exercise did little to relieve her irritation.

"I was thinking my brothers deserved to be told the truth," she said in a low voice. "Maybe I've changed my mind. Judgmental brats."

"You looked annoyed when I came in. I heard you defending my business to them. I appreciate what you said, but you know you really don't have to leap to my defense with your brothers. I'm pretty good at standing up for myself."

"I know. It still made me mad." Balancing Daryn on her left hip, she warmed baby food in the microwave and filled a sippy cup with cold milk. Daryn was already reaching eagerly for the cup when Kim sat at the table with the baby on her knee. "They had no excuse for being so snotty about you when you were perfectly nice to them."

Sitting across the table, Tate shrugged as he watched her spoon strained peas into Daryn's open mouth. "No big deal, they don't know me. She puts that away pretty well, doesn't she?"

Kim wiped a smear of green from her daughter's chin with a paper towel. "She loves her veggies. And by the way, she is a very healthy weight."

She didn't know why she was letting her mother's little digs get to her. It didn't bother her so badly when they were aimed at her, but she found herself getting very defensive about her daughter. She would have to work on that.

Tate smiled at her in a way that made her suspect he knew exactly what she was thinking. "She looks perfect to me."

For only a moment, she was caught up in his warm amber gaze, her hand frozen with the spoon of peas halfway to her daughter's mouth. Daryn made a sound of impatience and Kim jerked her attention back to the task at hand, chiding herself for getting distracted by Tate's pretty eyes. This was no time to allow her thoughts to drift into that territory—not that there was ever a proper time for that, she reminded herself sharply.

Her mother swept into the kitchen on a faint cloud of floral perfume. "Honestly, Kim, couldn't you have offered Tate a cold drink? What can I get for you, Tate?"

He shook his head, the faintest of creases between his brows as if he were holding back a frown. "I'm fine, thank you."

"You're sure? I have fresh-squeezed lemonade in the fridge."

"Maybe I'll have some later."

Her hostess duties out of the way, Betsy turned again to Kim. "I should have thought to get a high chair. It would be much easier for you to feed her if you didn't have to hold her in your lap. I'll send Bob to buy one right now."

"That's not necessary, Mom. This is fine. Besides, we're only going to be here one night."

"For this visit, yes, but I was rather hoping you'd come back more often now."

Refusing to be swayed by Betsy's plaintive tone, Kim looked from her mother to Tate and back again. "You've made that rather difficult for me, haven't you? I can hardly drag Tate back after this. It's bad enough that I let you talk me into this crazy scheme this time."

Her mother glanced quickly toward the doorway, then looked relieved that no one was there to have overheard. "Your husband doesn't have to accompany every time you visit your family," she said carefully. "We all understand that he's quite busy with his business."

Betsy's next words reminded Kim why she wasn't likely to visit even without the awkwardness of the marriage lie. "I'm surprised to see you feeding the baby solid foods and milk from a cup. I nursed my babies for a full year, you know. It's a much healthier start than jars of commercial baby food and regular milk."

Because she didn't want to fight with her mother in front of Tate, Kim drew a deep, steadying breath before replying evenly, "I nursed and pumped for as long as I was able and still work full-time, Mother. I also prepare most of Daryn's food myself, using fresh fruits and vegetables and a food processor. Daryn's pediatrician recommended I start her on solid foods and whole milk a month ago when her weight was beginning to drop. She has thrived ever since."

She did not add that she well remembered her mother

bottle-feeding Stuart formula; Betsy had been too busy playing at being a high-society charitable volunteer to spend time nursing the baby who'd been raised by nannies until the acrimonious divorce had caused a drastic change in Betsy's financial standing. Kim doubted it would do any good to call her on the discrepancy. Her mother was so skilled at deception that she seemed to believe her own tales, and she would argue heatedly if disputed.

"You needn't worry about your granddaughter, Mrs. Shaw. Kim is an amazing mom. She always puts Daryn's needs first. She's totally committed to making sure Daryn has a good life. I've always admired that about her."

Kim felt her cheeks warm in response to the unexpected and very sincere-sounding compliment.

Eyeing Tate appraisingly, her mother said, "Please call me Betsy, dear. After all, we are family."

Kim rolled her eyes. Tate smiled, but she noted he didn't look quite as charmed as he had before.

After feeding Daryn, Kim decided to take her out for a walk, saying that the baby needed a daily dose of fresh air and Kim needed the exercise. Suspecting it was primarily an excuse to get away from her family for a bit, Tate offered to walk with her. He needed to stretch his legs, himself, after their car trip, he said.

Though Betsy seemed a little miffed that they were so eager to escape so soon after their arrival, she hadn't tried to detain them, though she had asked if her sons wanted to join the walk. Both Julian and Stuart had declined, to no one's surprise.

Tate and Kim spent a very pleasant hour walking the

sidewalks of the cozy neighborhood, with Kim pushing Daryn in a stroller. They admired a few especially nice lawns and savored the weather, which was lightly overcast and several degrees cooler than it had been back home. Tate was sorry for the nice outing to end, and he was pretty sure Kim felt the same way—though he couldn't have said whether it was because she had particularly enjoyed the time with him or was just that reluctant to return to her mother's house.

He suspected the latter.

After returning from the walk, they spent a half hour in the living room, watching a news broadcast while Daryn played with a couple of toys on a blanket spread on the floor. Bob and Betsy were in the kitchen, making final preparations for dinner. Betsy had effusively refused any assistance other than her husband's, insisting that Kim and Tate should take the time to chat with Julian and Stuart—which would have been difficult, since Julian immediately went back out to the garage to work on Bob's car and Stuart drifted off to his room with a vague mumble about needing to make some phone calls.

Watching Daryn rocking unsteadily on her hands and knees, Tate winced wryly when the baby plopped down on her tummy with an "oof" sound. Rather than fuss or try again, she lay there happily kicking and slamming Mr. Jingles against the blanket, causing the bells inside him to clatter noisily.

"I take it she's not crawling yet?"

"Not yet." Sitting cross-legged on the floor beside the blanket, Kim reached out to pat her daughter's diapered-and-rompered bottom. "She comes close, but hasn't quite put the moves all together. I'm sure Mom would say I'm doing something wrong that's holding Daryn back, even though the pediatrician assures me she's developing just fine."

He started to say something, but she stopped him by holding up a hand and shaking her head. "Sorry," she said with a grimace. "I guess I'm just overly sensitive when it comes to my parenting skills. Probably because I'm always so aware that Daryn's well-being is all on me."

"Then she's in very good hands. I'm sure your mother knows that, despite some of the things she blurts out."

"I hope you're right."

He shrugged. "I've never doubted that you're a very committed mom. That was one of the first things I learned about you."

Kim glanced at the doorway, as though aware that this wasn't exactly a private venue in which to have this conversation, but then she smiled at him. "Thanks, Tate. I needed that."

He winked at her, pleased that he'd been able to boost her bruised confidence. "Anytime."

Kim had just tucked Daryn into her travel crib upstairs when everyone was called to dinner. Betsy sat at one end of the dining room table, with Bob at the other end, Julian and Stuart on one side and Kim and Tate on the other. A portable baby monitor sat beside Kim's plate, though not a peep had issued from it.

Betsy served a simple fare of steaks, grilled corn on the cob, baked potatoes and a side salad. Bob had grilled the meat and corn, though Betsy hinted that she was exhausted from baking potatoes and making the salads and a cake for dessert. Tate made a few more silent observations about Kim's background as everyone filled their plates.

His own family was by no means perfect. He and his sister did their share of squabbling, though they'd grown closer since moving out on their own. His dad was a workaholic whose time had been stretched thin, but he loved his wife and kids and they'd known he would always be there if they needed him. His mother was a bit of a hypochondriac who tended to fret about her children's well-being, but she'd relaxed a little during the past few years, finally accepting—for the most part—that they were old enough to take care of themselves.

An average family, with average strengths and weaknesses. He loved them, drew strength from them. Knew they loved him, too.

Before dinner was half finished that evening, he could see that Kim's family had almost nothing in common with his own. She had very few bonds with her half brothers, perhaps because they had each been raised so differently. She barely knew her latest stepfather, though she seemed to like him well enough, considering this was only the second time she'd met him. As for her relationship with her mother—well, no wonder that was so strained. Frankly, Betsy was a nut.

Tate hadn't yet decided if there was a streak of malice beneath that beaming, scheming face. Betsy was undoubtedly self-centered, unapologetically deceitful, deliberately tactless—but was she aware that her thoughtlessness caused her daughter pain, or was she simply oblivious to consequences? He'd been amused by her until he'd become aware of her little digs at Kim. He hadn't found those in the least funny.

"Does anyone need more iced tea?" Betsy asked, filling a somewhat awkward silence that had fallen over the table once the standard compliments for the food had been exchanged. "Bob, sweetie, why don't you bring the pitcher and top off the glasses?"

Nodding congenially, Bob jumped up to fetch the tea pitcher. Not for the first time, Tate thought that even after three years of marriage, Bob seemed perfectly happy being ordered around by his wife. Tate wondered how much longer that satisfaction would last.

Betsy turned toward Kim with a slight frown. "Did I hear a fuss from Daryn?" she asked, cocking her head toward the baby monitor.

"No, Mom, she's sound asleep."

"You're sure you shouldn't go check on her? How do you know that thing is working?"

"It's working."

Unlike Bob, Kim was visibly losing patience with Betsy. Tate didn't blame her, but she really should learn to let her mother's little barbs deflect off her. Betsy didn't seem to dig at her sons in quite the same way. Was it a mother/daughter dynamic thing—or did Betsy know it was harder to push emotional buttons with Julian and Stuart?

Trying to take the attention off Kim, he spoke to her brothers. "We haven't had much chance to get to know each other yet. I understand you're recently out of the service, Julian. What do you do now?"

"Bob got me a job at his accounting firm," Julian answered without a great deal of enthusiasm. "I'm taking night classes toward getting a CPA."

Before Tate could respond, Stuart frowned. "Kim hasn't even told you what Julian does?"

Realizing his mistake, Tate suppressed a wince, but Kim rescued him that time.

"Tate's simply trying to make conversation, Stuart," she said evenly. "Besides which, I couldn't tell him much about either of you because I haven't heard what you've been up to lately."

Betsy cleared her throat. "Perhaps if you called more often…"

Tate spoke again quickly to her brothers. "Kim has talked about both of you, of course, but I thought we could get to know each other in person now."

He was going to have to do better than this if he didn't want to blow the whole marriage charade before the reunion even began tomorrow. "Tell me about yourself, Stuart. What have you been up to this summer?"

Stuart shrugged, but a look from his mother made him answer politely enough—for a teenager. "Just been hanging out. I have a part-time job at a video game store at the mall."

"Stuart starts college a week from Monday," Bob added as he refilled Tate's tea glass.

"Yeah? Where will you be going, Stuart?"

The teen muttered the name of a well-respected liberal arts college in Springfield.

"He's going to live here at home and commute," Betsy said. "I wasn't quite ready to send my baby away. That will come soon enough, won't it, Bob? We'll have to get used to an empty nest eventually."

When Bob merely smiled and nodded, and no one else responded, Tate tried to keep the conversation moving. "I've heard that's a very good school. Have you chosen a major yet?"

Stuart shrugged again. "I'm interested in mathematics and computer sciences."

"Good choices."

Stuart chomped down on his ear of corn to discourage further conversation.

"Tell Tate more about your new job, Julian," Betsy urged, picking delicately at the baked potato and salad in front of her. She'd passed on the steak and corn, saying that she was watching her weight. She'd looked archly at Kim's plate as she'd made the comment, but for once using a modicum of tact, hadn't remarked aloud about Kim's choice to have a reasonable serving of everything.

"I work in accounting, Mom," Julian replied curtly. "Hardly anything more to tell."

"What about your real love?" Bob asked Julian with a look that might have been sympathetic. "Restoring old cars?"

Julian slanted a look at his mother that was almost defensive. "It's a hobby, that's all."

"An obsession, you mean," Stuart mumbled. "At least, that's what your ex called it."

Julian scowled. "Yeah, well, she's a—"

"Julian," his mother interrupted quickly, with a pointed look at Tate, as if to remind her son they had company among them. "Tate, don't get the wrong impression. Julian isn't a mechanic, he's an up-and-coming financial advisor. He enjoyed tinkering with cars as a teenager, but he doesn't have nearly as much time for that now, isn't that right, Julian?"

"No," Julian said, and if he tried to hide the regret, he wasn't entirely successful. "I don't."

"What types of cars have you restored?" Tate asked, doggedly trying to keep the conversation moving.

"Couple of classic Mustangs. I'm working on a '69 Mach 1 now. It's in pretty bad shape, haven't had much time to work on it, but it's got great potential."

"Sixty-nine, huh? Nice. Which engine?"

For the first time since they'd been introduced, Tate saw a spark of enthusiasm in Julian's eyes. "Three fifty-one V8."

"Windsor or Cleveland?"

Beneath the table, Kim lightly tapped his leg, then gave a thumbs-up sign when he glanced down.

The spark in Julian's blue eyes flared into a flame of passion. "Windsor—not quite as easy to find the parts, but she's going to purr like a tiger when I've got her up and running."

"Shaker hood scoop?"

"Yes, of course. And I was thinking of—"

"Oh, there's no need to get all technical about the mechanical aspects," Betsy interrupted impatiently. "You don't want to bore our guest, Julian."

Julian subsided with a slight flush, looking down at his plate.

Tate was finding Betsy less amusing all the time. "Actually, I have a lot of admiration for a skilled mechanic, whether on a professional or recreational level."

"More challenging than gardening?" Stuart asked in a slightly mocking murmur.

Feeling Kim stiffen beside him, Tate laid his hand quickly on her thigh, silently assuring her that he didn't need her to jump to his defense. "In its own way," he agreed equably.

Betsy frowned reproachfully at her younger son.

"Tate is a landscape designer, Stuart. Didn't you hear Kim say he has a degree in the field? What do you think of my flower beds, Tate? Bob and I have worked quite hard on them this summer."

"They look great," he said, making an effort to speak as warmly as before. He was determined to keep this visit pleasant for Kim, though he was aware he had an uphill battle ahead if her family continued to snipe at each other this way. "Nice use of color."

"Thank you. I'm a member of a local gardening club. We meet once a week during the summers, and we visit each other's gardens. I had them here last month for lemonade and tea cakes in my backyard garden. Everyone was quite complimentary."

"Is that what you do, Tate?" Bob asked. "Design flower beds for homes and businesses?"

"Partially, though we specialize in adding water features to landscaping. We've also focused on urban food gardens recently. With the growing interest in healthy, locally grown organic foods, we've had quite a demand for ways to use limited areas of ground in a manner that is both productive and visually appealing."

"Perhaps you could come speak to our club soon," Betsy said on a sudden rush of inspiration. "I know my fellow gardeners would love to hear you speak."

"You'll have to contact his secretary and get on his waiting list," Kim said without waiting for Tate to respond. "Tate and his partner are in high demand as speakers, and they're working on a book about urban gardening, so they're quite busy. They charge a fee for their speaking engagements, of course."

Betsy blinked, then smiled brightly again. "Well, that's very impressive, Tate. Of course, I'm sure you can make an exception to do a favor for a member of the family. I'd be quite the hit with my garden club if you would volunteer a session for us."

Kim sighed gustily and opened her mouth to deliver what would likely have been a scathing response had she not been interrupted by a whimper from the baby monitor.

She pushed back her chair. "I'd better go check on Daryn."

"I'll come with you," Tate said quickly, jumping to his feet. "Just in case you need help with her."

"Hurry back, you two," Betsy called after them. "We haven't had dessert yet."

As much as Tate usually liked dessert, he could honestly say that this time he would just as soon skip it. Because he knew that wasn't going to happen, he merely nodded and followed Kim quickly out of the dining room, glad he had an excuse to escape the tension there for a least a few minutes.

Chapter Four

Just as Kim had expected, Daryn was sleeping soundly in her portable crib when Kim entered the bedroom with Tate at her heels. Kim had recognized the sound she'd heard through the monitor as just one of those little noises Daryn sometimes made in her sleep. Any other time, she'd have waited a bit to see if she needed to respond, but she'd leaped on the excuse to get away from her family for a few minutes—and so had Tate.

"Well?" she asked quietly as she turned toward him. "Now do you understand why I tend to avoid my family reunions? And you haven't even met the worst part of the family yet."

He groaned softly.

"You're the one who volunteered for this," she reminded him.

"Yes."

Was he second-guessing that impulse now? She

wouldn't blame him if he were. She certainly regretted that she'd let herself get swept into the scheme.

Tate glanced at the sleeping baby, speaking in a stage whisper. "She's okay?"

"She's fine. She's a sound sleeper, just makes little noises sometimes."

He nodded, then glanced at the queen-size bed that took up the majority of the floor. Automatically, she followed his gaze. Between the bed, a nightstand and dresser, a small reading chair, the portable crib, the bags holding their things and all the baby supplies, little space was left in the guest room.

Thinking of the night ahead, she swallowed. It was obvious that she and Tate were going to have to share that bed. There wasn't room on the floor for him to stretch out, even if she would allow him to make that gesture.

She trusted him, of course. In all the time she'd known Tate through his sister, he'd given her no reason to believe he was anything other than a decent, honorable guy. Commitment phobic, perhaps, but then that was a good thing in this case, since she'd made it clear that she felt the same way. He would anticipate no awkward expectations from her and vice versa. Friends. Pals. Lunch buddies.

Buddies who had somehow allowed themselves to be talked into playing husband and wife for a weekend.

"How long do you think we can hide in here?"

She smiled wryly in response to Tate's exaggeratedly stealthy question. "I suppose we'd better go have dessert."

Making sure Daryn was still sleeping, Kim left the

lamp on the dim setting when they left the room. She did not look at the bed again on her way out.

Because it was such a pleasant evening, Betsy insisted they have dessert and coffee on the patio, where she could show off her flower beds to Tate. Kim carried the baby monitor with her, setting it close by as she settled into one of the wrought-iron spring rockers grouped around a matching, round wrought-iron table. Tate sat beside her again. She noted that Julian took the seat next to Tate, though their mother looked a little peeved that Julian had beaten her to the chair.

Apparently, some of Julian's initial antipathy toward Tate had dissipated during the discussion of classic cars. She couldn't say Julian was exactly warm toward Tate now, but he seemed a bit more willing to give him a chance—especially after Tate told him his first car had been a restored '70s muscle car. They talked cars during dessert even though Betsy did her best to interrupt them every few minutes and redirect the conversation. Their mother had never approved of Julian's passion for classic cars—a love he shared with the nomadic musician father who had drifted sporadically through his life.

With Kim's father dead, Stuart's in prison, Julian's who-knew-where most of the time and their last stepfather completely out of their lives, it was no wonder they all had relationship issues, she thought wryly. As for herself, she had no intention of dragging a series of men through Daryn's life the way Betsy had done with her and her brothers.

Almost as soon as he'd swallowed the last bite of his cake, Stuart made an excuse to leave, saying he was meeting friends in town. Bob and Julian went back to the garage, leaving Kim and Tate outside with her mother.

"I wish everyone had stayed around to talk a bit longer," Betsy said with a slight pout. "But this will give us a chance to prepare for tomorrow."

"Prepare?" Kim eyed her mother warily. "What do you mean?"

"Oh, you know. Just chat." Her mother smiled blandly at Tate. "My mother and sister are…shall we say, rather difficult. I'm sure they'll love you, you're such a charming young man. But you should be on your guard tomorrow, anyway. If I could make just a few tiny suggestions…"

"Tate doesn't need your suggestions, Mom," Kim asserted flatly.

"Only a few little things. Like with Daryn, for example."

Tate raised an eyebrow, holding up a hand toward Kim to signal that he could take this one. "What about Daryn?"

"I haven't even seen you hold her, dear. Perhaps you could put a little more effort into your parenting."

Kim gasped in outrage. "You haven't even held Daryn, yourself, since we arrived! How dare you criticize Tate."

"You fed her, then took her for a walk, then played with her while I prepared dinner, and then you put her straight to bed. When would I have held her?"

"Don't give me that. You know you could have—"

"Besides, she doesn't even know me." Her mother's voice held an affecting little quiver now. "It would break my heart if I tried to take her and she cried."

Tate, at least, seemed to fall for the performance,

even if Kim remained cynical. "I wouldn't worry about that. I'm sure Daryn would love being held by you. She's an easygoing little thing, doesn't seem at all shy."

Betsy smiled at him tremulously. "Thank you, dear. Perhaps she'll let me play with her for a few minutes in the morning, if Kim will allow me a little time."

Rolling her eyes, Kim murmured, "You're welcome to play with her anytime you want."

"Thank you, dear. Now, about tomorrow, Tate..."

"That's enough, Mom. We don't plan to stay that long tomorrow, anyway. I'd like to see Grandma for a few minutes and introduce her to Daryn, but that was my only goal for this weekend. The sole reason I dragged poor Tate along was because you insisted I would ruin your life if I exposed the shenanigans you've been pulling with them. So don't tell him what to do tomorrow. You should be grateful to him for being here at all, not critical of anything he does while he's here."

"Well, of course I'm grateful. As you should be, of course. You're very fortunate to have such a good friend to help you when you need him."

"When *I* need him?"

"Well, yes. So you don't have to confess to your grandmother and aunt that you're—" Betsy paused to look around, then continued in a whisper "—an unwed mother."

"Oh, for—"

"Um, Kim, why don't we—"

Whatever hasty distraction Tate was going to suggest was interrupted when Bob came back outside. Perhaps sensing the tension in the garden, Bob looked quickly from his wife to their guests before saying, "The Cardinals game is getting pretty exciting in there. Julian's watching now. We thought you might like to join us for the final innings, Tate."

"Sure, I'm a Cards fan."

"So am I," Kim said, reaching for the baby monitor. "I'll join you."

The truth was, she couldn't care less about baseball, but she'd had enough of her mother's nonsense for now. At least in the den, she could pretend to be engrossed in the game, which would save her the effort of making more stilted conversation until it was a reasonable time to turn in.

Not that bedtime would be any easier, considering who she would be sharing a room with that night.

Deciding it would be less awkward if they didn't try to get ready at the same time, Kim slipped out of the living room fairly early to prepare for bed. She washed her face and changed in the guest bath across the hall from the bedroom. Remembering that her mother tended to keep the air conditioner turned down quite cool, she'd brought a pair of navy pajamas with a button-up top and loose, elastic-waist long pants. She couldn't have been dressed more modestly if she'd worn a turtleneck and overalls, she decided, appraising herself in the mirror. Which was exactly her intention.

She left the nightlight burning so that Tate had no trouble getting around in the room when he tiptoed stealthily in after she was in bed. Like her, he was basically fully dressed in a gray T-shirt and sleep pants striped in dark and light gray. She didn't try to pretend to be asleep when he stood awkwardly beside the bed, looking as though he didn't quite know what to do.

"I could curl up on the floor," he said, keeping his voice low so as not to disturb the still-sleeping baby.

"Don't be silly, there's not room even if you could be comfortable there. Just don't hog the covers, and we'll get along fine tonight."

She'd spoken lightly, treating the situation as no big deal. As if she were in the habit of sharing a bed platonically with male friends. She doubted Tate was fooled, but he seemed to relax a little in response to her easy tone.

He climbed into the bed, staying far to his side as he stretched out. "I don't hog the covers and I don't snore," he assured her. "But I have been known to break into show tunes in my sleep."

She lifted her head off the pillow. "Um—"

Chuckling, he rolled away from her. "Kidding. Good night, Kim."

Laughing softly, she twisted to her other side so that they lay back-to-back. "Good night, Tate."

Kim must have been very tired, or as a single mother she had learned to sleep when she could. Maybe both. As far as Tate could tell from his side of the bed, she was asleep almost as soon as her head hit the pillow.

He wished he could say the same for himself. Though he remained very quiet and still so as not to disturb Kim, he lay awake for a long time, watching numbers scroll past on the digital clock on the nightstand.

Even though they weren't touching, he was aware of every inch of Kim beside him. He was wryly aware that the pajamas she wore were modest enough to satisfy a nun, but that didn't stop him from finding her appealing in her jammies. He had no intention of doing anything about that attraction, of course—despite the urgings of certain parts of him. He was a healthy young male, after all, even if he was trying to be a gentleman during this often-awkward adventure.

To distract himself from thoughts of the sexy lady in bed with him, he focused his attention toward the crib. At first he went on alert whenever the baby squirmed or made a sound, but Kim slept on, and the baby quieted almost immediately each time. Normal nighttime noises, he decided. He guessed parents got used to them.

And then he found himself waiting for those noises, worrying when the baby was too quiet. Was she okay? She was still breathing over there, right? Scary stories drifted through his mind and he held his breath until he heard her sigh and wiggle again.

He thought of Kim's comment that she was somewhat sensitive about her parenting because the full responsibility for Daryn fell on her shoulders. Must be terrifying. He couldn't imagine having to make daily decisions about food and day care and medical choices for an infant. How did one decide about the best nutrition for a nine-month-old when there were so many conflicting opinions? How did she know the safest place for her child to stay during the weekday hours when Kim had to work to support them? How did she know when a sniffle was just a sniffle or a sign of something more serious? When a whimper in the night was something to respond to immediately or to let pass by?

This was exactly why he'd so far avoided parenthood. Even at thirty, he didn't feel qualified for that responsibility. He hadn't been around babies much, hadn't even held one in almost longer than he could remember and he'd been in no hurry to change that status. He'd had an unspoken rule against dating single mothers. Even really cute ones with pretty whiskey eyes and enchanting freckles.

Still, it felt a little too nice to have Kim lying beside him, snuggled into her pillow, her breathing slow and even. Should his ego be stung that she had found it so easy to ignore him and fall asleep? He thought it might be, at least a little.

He must have fallen asleep at some point, because he was jerked awake before dawn by a shriek from the crib. Startled and disoriented, he nearly leaped from the bed, his heart pounding in his chest, his eyes wide and blurry. "What?"

Softly illuminated by the bluish night light, Kim was already at the crib, patting her daughter and making soothing sounds.

"I'm sorry," she said in a low voice. "I guess she woke up and didn't know where she was."

"I know the feeling." Pushing a hand through his tousled hair, Tate sank back onto his pillow, drawing a deep breath to steady his pulse. "She's okay?"

"She's fine." Tentatively, Kim raised her hand and stepped back from the crib. Daryn gave a little sigh, but lay still, already asleep again.

Kim returned to the bed, sitting on her side and swinging her legs up before lying on her pillow again, carefully avoiding physical contact with him.

The way his body responded to having her beside him again, she might as well have wrapped herself around him. He shifted uncomfortably on the mattress. *Stupid male hormones,* he chided himself.

"I wasn't sure she'd go back to sleep," she whispered. "Sometimes when she wakes up like that she decides it's time for breakfast. But now she'll probably sleep another hour or so."

Forcing his attention to the conversation, Tate checked the time, seeing that it was just before 5:00 a.m. "Is she always awake by 6:00?"

"Usually. But she's been sleeping through the night since she was four months old, so I'm not complaining about her early rising."

She shifted on the mattress, and her foot just barely brushed his. She drew back quickly, but not before he felt the little shock of response from the contact. "I'm sorry she woke you. I hope you can go back to sleep."

He shrugged, accepting that as a lost cause. "I tend to be an early bird, myself. Comes from working outside in the South in summer—best to get out early before the heat sets in."

"I worked in the gardening center of a home improvement store the summer between my freshman and sophomore years of high school. My job was to keep the displayed plants tidy and watered. I remember how hot those afternoons got here in Missouri. This has been such a brutal summer in Arkansas, I can't help but feel sorry about anyone trying to work outside on those hundred-plus-degree days."

He rolled on his side, propping his head on one arm. "You never told me you worked in a gardening center."

"Only for one summer," she reminded him, one hand beneath her cheek as she lay facing him. "My gardening experience hardly seemed worth mentioning compared to your and Evan's horticulture degrees."

"Did I ever mention that I thought about being a physical therapist? That was sort of my plan during high school, until I got a summer job with a landscaper and realized how much I liked working outdoors. I've always suspected Lynette was influenced by my talk of therapy careers to look into occupational therapy."

She sounded intrigued by his confession. "I didn't know you were ever interested in therapy. Funny, as much as we've talked during our lunches, there's still quite a bit we don't know about each other, isn't there?"

Despite the very dim light in the predawn room, he could see her easy smile, which looked more natural than any smile he'd seen from her since they had arrived in Springfield. He couldn't say whether it was because they were away from her family, or because the quiet, shadowy room and the sleeping baby nearby relaxed her innate guardedness or just because she was growing more comfortable with him again. Maybe all of the above, but he didn't want to waste any more time sleeping when they could be enjoying their time together.

"There are still a lot of things I'd like to learn about you," he said, still in that low, for-her-ears-only voice. "What made you decide to go into occupational therapy, for example?"

She chuckled. "Well, after that summer, I knew I wanted an indoor, air-conditioned job."

He smiled, but prodded, "I'm sure there was more to it than that."

She shrugged against her pillow. "My stepfather—

the last stepfather before Bob," she added with a wry twist in her voice. "The rancher?"

He nodded to indicate he remembered the hasty background she'd recited for him when they'd arrived in Springfield. "Stan, wasn't it?"

"Right. Good memory. Anyway, the summer before my junior year in high school, Stan broke several bones in his left hand in a ranch accident. He had to have surgery, followed by a few weeks of therapy. I was only working part-time in a fast-food job that summer, so I drove him to therapy a few times and hung around to watch his sessions. After that, I just knew it was what I wanted to do."

"You still like it, don't you?"

"I love it," she answered simply. "I enjoyed rotating through pediatric OT, but I'm at my best with adults."

"Lynette enjoys her work, too. She talks about it all the time when we get together—though she's careful to remember privacy guidelines for her patients," he added quickly. "We enjoy hearing some of her stories during family dinners. She doesn't give personal details, but she tells us about some of her most rewarding cases."

Kim nodded. "We all cherish our personal victories, when we feel like we've really made a difference in someone's life. Whether it's something relatively minor, like recovering from hand surgery, or learning to eat and dress and perform other activities of daily living after a stroke or brain injury, there's always a sense of satisfaction in helping someone regain at least part of what they'd lost."

"There must be plenty of frustration, as well."

"Sometimes," she admitted. "When there's little more we can do, or when we know more progress could be made if the client would exert a little more effort or when financial limitations interfere with potential progress. But any job has its frustrations."

"True. I have to confess, it always surprises me that Lynette has the patience for the job. She's always so rushed and so impulsive outside of work."

Kim laughed softly. "Yes, but she's a wonderful therapist. Her clients love her. She's especially good in the inpatient setting, with patients who are still reeling from their injuries and loss. She has quite a knack for encouraging them and lifting their spirits."

"She has high praise for you, too. She said you're the most patient, most unrufflable of any therapist she's worked with."

"That's nice of her." Kim sounded a little self-conscious about the praise when she teased, "But *unrufflable?* Is that even a word?"

He grinned. "You know how Lynette likes to coin her own vocabulary."

"Yes, she does. I've grown very fond of your sister in the past six months of working with her. I consider her one of my best friends. Emma, too. We all meshed very well from the start."

"Lynette feels the same way. She has told me she's very glad you came to work in her department." Without thinking, he reached out to brush a wayward curl from Kim's sleep-softened face. "I'm glad, too. I've very much enjoyed getting to know you during our Wednesday lunches."

"I've enjoyed it, too," she murmured, her gaze locking with his.

Because she hadn't immediately drawn away from his impulsive touch, and because it felt so very good to do so, he drew his fingertips down the line of her jaw to the very faint indention in her chin. "We did kind of hit it off from the start, didn't we?"

He regretted speaking so unguardedly when he sensed the invisible wall immediately go up between them again. Kim seemed to draw into herself before murmuring in a much more stilted tone, "Yes, I've come to consider you and Evan good friends, too."

Tate noted that she had been careful to link his name and Evan's on an equal basis. Which reminded him of the way she had parted from Evan, a memory that still rather annoyed him. Looking at Kim's soft, unpainted mouth, he didn't like knowing that Evan's lips had touched hers since his had. The unexpected surge of possessiveness caught him by surprise, but also provoked him into a very unwise move. Without giving himself time to think about it, he leaned forward and pressed his lips to Kim's.

He was absolutely sure he felt her start to respond. Her lips moved just slightly beneath his, softening, warming. Being kissed by her in front of their friends had been surprisingly stimulating. Kissing her in the intimacy of a rumpled bed in the predawn shadows rocked him all the way to his bare toes.

Kim pulled back suddenly with a little gasp, nearly falling off the edge of the bed behind her. She caught herself before he could, then shoved herself upright. "What was that for?"

"Just giving my wife a good morning kiss," he said, hearing the slightly husky edge to his low voice.

"Save the acting for an audience," she advised

sternly, swinging her feet to the floor. "We've already agreed kissing isn't a part of this charade."

"Did we? Pity."

Studiously ignoring him, she dug into her suitcase. "I'm not going to be able to go back to sleep," she said with a glance at the still-snoozing baby. "I'll go take a quick shower before Daryn wakes up for breakfast. I don't think she'll stir before I get back, but if she does, you can just pat her back to let her know someone is here with her."

"Um—" He looked warily at the crib, frankly nervous about being left alone with the baby for even that short time. What if she took one look at him and screamed? He wouldn't have a clue how to shush her before she roused the entire household.

"She'll be fine. Try to go back to sleep yourself, if you want."

"Yeah, okay. Um, take your time, I can handle this."

He didn't miss that Kim rolled her eyes a little when she gathered her clothes and moved toward the door. So maybe he hadn't sounded as confident as he'd hoped. Maybe she thought of him as a coward when it came to one harmless, sleeping tot. It wasn't as if he was an old hand at this, like she was.

Maybe it was piqued pride that made him say, "Kim?"

She paused at the door. "Yes?"

"If we ever end up in a bed together again? It won't be quite so platonic. Just thought you should know."

She blinked a few times, then whirled and let herself quietly out of the room, closing the door almost silently behind her. So why did he have the feeling she would rather have slammed it?

Frowning in bemusement at his own odd behavior, he sat up against the headboard, giving up any possibility of sleep as he vigilantly guarded his temporary charge.

Towel-drying her hair into damp waves, Kim tiptoed across the hall to the bedroom after showering and dressing. Another hot afternoon lay ahead, so she wore a red cotton top with fluttery sleeves and colorful embroidery around the scooped neck and slim, cropped pants. Casual, but one of her favorite summer weekend outfits; she assumed it was suitable for a gathering at her grandmother's house.

She hadn't dawdled, but she'd been gone closer to fifteen minutes than the ten she'd promised. She had needed the extra few moments to compose herself after that unsettling interlude with Tate.

He'd been teasing. Of course he had, she had decided while standing beneath a deliberately chilly shower. Tate had a quirky sense of humor. He was probably getting back at her for everything he'd been put through with her family last night. He'd probably been amused that she'd been so flustered, and he would likely tease her about it later, maybe even in front of their friends.

As for that comment about the next time they were in a bed together—well, that had to have been part of the joke. Right?

At least, that was the way she was going to have to regard it if she was going to make it through the rest of this day with him. Once she was back in Little Rock, back in the privacy of her own home, she could acknowledge if only to herself that kissing Tate in that bed had almost turned her world upside down.

Tate sat on the edge of the bed when she slipped into the room, a pile of folded clothing beside him as he waited for his own chance at the shower. A quick glance assured her that Daryn hadn't stirred. That must have been a relief to Tate. He'd looked alarmed at the very prospect of having to actually interact with the baby, she reminded herself.

"Shower's free," she told him as she entered the room, her expression carefully bland.

"Thanks."

Though he didn't exactly bolt from the room, he wasted no time making his escape. Rubbing the towel over her hair one more time, Kim thought that Tate's careful lack of interaction with Daryn made it very clear he wasn't interested in taking on a ready-made family. Which was hardly relevant to her, of course, but it could be disappointing for any single mom who was naive enough to fall for his teasing flirtation.

She scowled and tossed the towel aside, wondering why she had allowed her thoughts to drift along those lines. She would not let one kiss scramble her carefully cultivated common sense, darn it. Okay, two kisses—she hadn't forgotten the unexpected effects of that first time. But still, kissing Tate was a mistake, and she wasn't going to forget that again.

Daryn was just starting to stir when Tate returned. Like Kim, he'd left his hair damp, finger-combed away from his freshly shaven face. Having been assured by her that the reunion was a very casual affair, he wore dark jeans with one of the short-sleeved polo shirts that seemed to make up most of his casual wardrobe, this one in a leaf-green that nicely complemented his tan.

He looked great, of course—but then, he always did.

She suspected her cousins would flirt like crazy with him that afternoon, as they did any attractive man who came within their reach, single or otherwise. Maybe she should warn him about Patty and Cara Lynn—or maybe he would just have to meet her extended family to believe what she would tell him about them.

"Just got a whiff of coffee brewing downstairs," he announced, stuffing his sleepwear into a bag. "Guess we're not the only early risers. Or maybe we woke someone with our stirring around."

Daryn opened her eyes with a couple of sleepy blinks, then grinned, babbled and kicked her feet when she saw Kim looking down at her.

"Good morning, sunshine." Smiling back at the child, Kim reached for the diaper bag.

Tate took a couple of steps closer to the crib, eyeing the baby curiously. "Does she always wake up so happy?"

Kim tickled Daryn's tummy to elicit a trill of giggles. "Almost always. She's really a very good baby."

"I've hardly heard her fuss since we left yesterday. My very limited experience with babies and toddlers on airplanes and in the supermarket made me think they're usually screaming about something."

"Babies cry to communicate. They're hungry or wet or frightened or overwhelmed or in pain. Some are naturally fussier than others, just as a result of personality differences. Parents learn from experience to interpret those cries, for the most part. As for toddlers—well, then you start getting into behavior that requires firmer guidelines. Those kids throwing themselves into the floor of the store and screaming because they've been told no? That's on the parents more than the kids."

"So you're saying little Daryn here isn't going to throw any of those I-want-it-I-want-it tantrums?"

"I'm sure she'll try a few times. I don't expect her to be a model child. But I figure my job as a mother is to teach her how to behave in polite society, and if I fail in that, then I've let her down."

Realizing she'd unwittingly climbed onto one of her favorite soapboxes while changing Daryn, she flushed a little as she picked up the baby. "I didn't mean to sound like the perfect parent. I'm sure most parents are doing the best they can."

"Mmm." Tate expressed quite a bit of skepticism with that brief murmur, but he let the subject drop. He seemed to become aware that Daryn was studying him intently. "Um, good morning, Daryn."

Bouncing in Kim's arms, Daryn babbled a happy, if unintelligible, response.

Tate chuckled. "Either she said 'Good morning to you, too,' or 'What the heck are you doing in my mom's bedroom before dawn?'"

"I think she said she's ready for her breakfast." Avoiding Tate's eyes, Kim carried Daryn past him toward the door. "Shall we go down and see who's brewing that coffee?"

Bob looked up from a cup of coffee and the morning newspaper with a smile when Kim carried Daryn into the room, followed by Tate. "Good morning. Help yourself to coffee, I just made it. Or I can brew tea for you, if you'd prefer."

"Coffee's good for me." Tate moved immediately toward the big pot already surrounded by cups waiting to be filled.

Bob set his paper aside and pushed away from the table. "There's fresh-squeezed orange juice in the fridge. I thought I'd make waffles for breakfast. The batter's already prepared, so all I have to do is pour it onto the waffle maker. We have sliced strawberries, maple syrup or honey for toppings. Or we have eggs and bacon, if anyone would prefer that. We won't wait for the others. Who knows when Stuart will be down. He's not much of a breakfast eater."

"Waffles sound delicious." Balancing Daryn on her left hip, Kim opened the fridge to pull out a carton of milk. "Where's Mom?"

"She'll be down soon. I told her to take her time getting ready this morning, that I'd handle breakfast."

Her mother was definitely being spoiled by this one, Kim mused, reaching for the jar of baby cereal she'd left on the counter last night. Maybe this marriage would actually last? She still wouldn't have been willing to bet real money on it, but after three years, the union was still looking surprisingly stable—mostly because Bob seemed to have the tolerance of a saint.

"Here, let me hold the baby for you while you prepare her breakfast," saintly Bob volunteered, reaching out to them. "I'm sure you're used to having only one hand free, but perhaps I can make it a bit easier for you."

Daryn dove happily into Bob's arms, patting his face and babbling when he grinned at her.

"Aren't you a little angel?" he crooned, clearly besotted. "Kim, do you mind if she calls me Grandpa? I'd be proud to claim her as a grandchild."

"Well, she isn't calling anyone anything yet," she replied lightly, rather touched by his request. Though she doubted that Daryn would be around Bob all that much in the future, even if the marriage to her mother should last, it was still kind of him to treat them like family. "But I have no objection to her getting to know you as her Grandpa."

She had regretted that Daryn would have little extended family in her life, considering the estrangement between Kim and her mother and brothers, and the fact that Daryn's biological father and his family weren't interested in getting to know her. Their loss, she always reminded herself. If Bob wanted to help fill some of that vacancy, she should be pleased, even though she couldn't help worrying that Daryn—and maybe she—would only be disappointed by him eventually.

"Do you want a cup of coffee, Kim?" Tate asked, looking at her with the carafe in hand. What might have been a slight grimace of apology twisted his mouth; maybe he'd become aware that he should have been the one offering to help with Daryn.

She smiled lightly at him to assure him she didn't mind. "Yes, please."

Carrying Daryn's breakfast to the table, she sat and reached for her daughter. "Thank you, Bob."

Bob brushed a light kiss across Daryn's thin, tousled brown hair before depositing her in Kim's lap. "My pleasure. I've always looked forward to being a grandpa, though my own kids are still a few years away from providing any grandchildren for me."

Kim had briefly met Bob's daughter and son three years earlier, at the reception to celebrate Bob and Betsy's nuptials. She remembered them vaguely as two polite but reserved teenagers, both only high-school-age then. From what little she'd heard of them since through her mother, she had the impression that Bob traveled to Texas fairly often to see them, though her mother didn't usually accompany him.

Just what, exactly, did Bob get from this marriage? And how much longer would it be until he grew tired of being the one apparently doing all the giving?

Spooning baby cereal into Daryn's eagerly opened mouth, she watched surreptitiously while Bob and Tate worked congenially together to prepare waffles and bacon for the family. They seemed to get along well, despite the nearly two-decade age difference. Watching her stepfather-for-now and husband-for-the-weekend chuckling together gave her an oddly wistful feeling—one she ruthlessly suppressed as she focused on feeding her daughter.

Impeccably dressed, coiffed and made-up, her mother waltzed into the kitchen a short time later. Kim, Tate and Bob were chatting and eating their strawberry-topped waffles while Daryn, still sitting in Kim's lap, pounded happily on the table top with a wooden spoon Bob had given her to play with.

"Good morning, my darlings," Betsy trilled, blowing kisses to all of them.

Even as she shook her head in response to her mother's theatrics, Kim noted that Bob's blue eyes lit up with the beaming smile he directed toward his wife. Whatever Kim might see as lacking in the relationship, it was hard to deny that Bob seemed genuinely in love with her mother, and outwardly, at least, content.

"Good morning, dear," he said, leaping to his feet. "Have a seat, I'll get you some coffee and waffles."

"Thank you, sweetie, but I'll just have coffee this morning," she answered him affectionately. "Have to watch the calories with that big family luncheon ahead, you know. How were your waffles, Kim?"

Glancing down at her almost-empty plate, Kim made an effort not to react defensively. "They were delicious."

"Do you mind if I hold little Daryn for a bit? You can have some more breakfast, if you like—though don't forget there will be lots of food at Grandma Dyess's house later today."

"I'm fine, thanks."

Her smile bright, Betsy held out her hands to the baby. "Come to Grammie, sweetie."

Kim was almost as relieved as her mother probably was that Daryn made the transfer agreeable enough. She wasn't particularly surprised; Daryn enjoyed attention and wasn't usually shy in accepting it.

Daryn made a quick grab for her grandmother's red-framed glasses, but Betsy was able to catch the little hand and plant a cooing kiss on it. Though cynically aware that part of this touching encounter was a performance for Bob and Tate's benefit, Kim wanted to believe she saw a measure of real affection in her mom's smile. She warned herself not to let past slights make her too jaded when it came to her mother, but sometimes that wasn't easy.

While her mother played with the baby, Kim helped Bob clear away the breakfast dishes. They wrapped up a plate of leftover waffles in case Stuart wanted them later, though Bob repeated that Stuart rarely ate breakfast, despite his mother's disapproval.

"I'd better go give Daryn her bath and get her ready for the reunion," Kim said when the kitchen was spotless again.

"Be sure to dress her in something especially adorable, since she'll be meeting her great-grandmother for the first time," Betsy advised, leaving a bright smear of lipstick on the baby's soft cheek before handing her over. "And there's plenty of time for you to get dressed, too, Kim, so don't feel you have to rush."

Kim lifted an eyebrow. "I'm dressed, Mom. This is what I'm wearing today."

"Oh. Really? I thought maybe a skirt?"

"No. This is what I brought to wear."

Her mother gave a mournful little sigh. "Well, I'm sure it's fine, then. Everyone understands a busy young mother has little time for primping."

Daryn bounced in Kim's arms, still waving the wooden spoon and coming very close to bopping Kim in the head with it. "Mamamama," she trilled.

"She said *Mama!*" Her criticisms apparently forgotten, Betsy clapped her hands. "That's the first time I've heard her speak. Has she said it before?"

Smiling at the child, Kim swiped at the lipstick smear with one fingertip as she answered, "A few times, though I'm never quite sure if she's saying my name or just babbling."

"Sounded like *Mama* to me," Bob assured her. "You can tell she's a smart one. Say *Grandpa,* Daryn."

Daryn responded with an unintelligible string of syllables that ended with what sounded very much like a raspberry, making all the adults laugh.

"Okay, so much for that," Bob said good-naturedly.

Betsy reached out to pat Daryn's back, motioning toward Tate with her other hand. "Say *DaDa,* Daryn. It would be lovely if you'd say that today at the reunion. *DaDa?*"

The pleasant moment was ruined. Kim turned

sharply, drawing Daryn out of her mother's reach. "Honestly, Mom," she snapped.

Betsy blinked in oblivious innocence. "What?"

"Just stop, okay? If you want Tate and me to go to this thing today, you'll have to back off."

Looking aggrieved, Betsy began, "But I was only—"

"I'll go get her dressed. Bob, while I'm gone, maybe you can explain to my mother that she's skating on very thin ice this weekend, and she needs to watch her step for the rest of the day."

Without giving anyone a chance to reply, she carried Daryn out of the kitchen. She sensed Tate hesitate a moment, as if unsure what to do, then he followed her out.

Chapter Five

"I must have completely lost my mind to agree to this nutty plan in the first place. What was I thinking, letting a silly bet and a few dares convince me to bring my child into this insanity?"

Fifteen minutes after storming out of the kitchen, Kim was still muttering beneath her breath, even as she efficiently dressed her freshly bathed daughter in a frilly lavender romper.

Looking up from the chair where he'd been checking and answering email on his phone while Kim took care of the baby, Tate said cautiously, "Maybe you'll have such a nice visit with your grandmother that it will all be worth it."

"I'm not sure any visit could be that nice," she grumbled. She closed her eyes momentarily and exhaled gustily. "I'm sorry, Tate. I don't mean to take out my frustration with my mother on you again."

"Hey, that's what I'm here for."

She wrinkled her nose at him, a rueful smile reflected in her eyes. "Not exactly, but thanks, anyway."

She reached for the lavender hair bow that matched Daryn's romper. The bow was attached to a soft, stretchy band that circled the baby's head. Tate figured Daryn's wispy brown hair was still too fine and thin for a barrette-style bow, but she didn't seem to mind wearing the headbands. She did look cute as all get-out in them, he had to admit, even though he didn't usually notice such details with babies.

Looking away from the kid, he studied Kim's face, noting her frown was relaxing as she arranged her daughter's hair into soft curls. "I have to admit I'm curious to meet the rest of the family now."

Kim blinked at Tate in surprise. "Seriously? Why?"

"Just wondering if they're more like you or your mother. Because, frankly, you and your mom couldn't be much more different."

"I'm going to take that as a compliment."

He chuckled. "I can see why you would, but it was merely an observation."

"I'll let you decide for yourself who the rest of the family resembles." Kim hoisted Daryn onto her hip. "And, by the way, I won't be in the least disappointed if you decide you need to escape early. Just give me a sign and we'll be out of there."

Considering the way things had gone thus far this weekend, he figured Kim would be more likely than he to bolt from the reunion. Frankly, he found her family dynamics very interesting. They explained a lot about her. He supposed the same would be true in reverse if she were to observe his family as an objective insider for a weekend.

He was tempted to advise her not to let her mother push her buttons so easily. Just to laugh it all off, as she seemed to have done in the past. But maybe that was easier done from a distance rather than in person—and frankly, it was none of his business, anyway. Probably if he'd been put through the chaos Betsy had inflicted on Kim, he wouldn't be able to shrug it off so easily, either.

Daryn gave her toy monkey a vigorous pump, making the bells inside it chime merrily. She made a face of dismay when the toy flew from her hand, landing on the floor with a clanging thump.

"I've got it," Tate said when Kim automatically started to bend to retrieve it. He leaned over to scoop up the toy and offer it to Daryn. "Here's your Mr. Jingles, kiddo."

Accepting the toy, she gazed at him with such intensity that he couldn't help feeling a little self-conscious. He saw a strong look of her mother in her eyes. Both of them had a way of studying him sometimes that made him wonder if his hair was untidy or if there was a smudge on his nose.

Daryn broke into a sudden wide, slightly damp grin that displayed both her tiny white teeth. He smiled automatically in return. The kid had that in common with her mother, too. Tate couldn't help but respond to their smiles.

Suddenly aware that he was standing very close to Kim, he glanced at her. Their gazes met, and he found himself unable to be the first to look away. Those whiskey eyes were most definitely intoxicating.

He almost winced as that sappy analogy wafted through his thoughts. Wouldn't Evan mock him if he'd heard it?

Daryn waved her toy again; simultaneous jingling and babbling roused Tate from his momentary daze. He dragged his gaze from Kim's and glanced at his watch. "Your family is probably waiting for us to rejoin them. It's almost time to leave for your grandmother's house."

Kim's cheeks looked a bit rosier than usual. Was it a result of the baby's energetic bouncing in her arms or was she actually blushing a little? Intrigued by the latter possibility, he followed her from the room, noting as he did so that her figure looked very nice in the casual summery outfit that had elicited such disapproval from her mother.

Kim and Tate took her car to the reunion, Tate behind the wheel again as he followed Bob and Betsy in their car. Kim twisted her fingers in her lap during the twenty-minute ride, so tightly her knuckles whitened and ached. She wasn't aware of quite how tightly she held them until Tate reached over to briefly pat her clenched fists with his right hand before returning his hand to the steering wheel.

"Relax," he said, glancing away from the road ahead for a moment to smile at her. "It will be fine."

Telling herself she was being foolish, she made a deliberate effort to loosen her muscles. Feeling the cold gold band on her left ring finger did not help her to relax about the upcoming ordeal. "You know, there was a time when I would have had a ball with this."

She was hardly aware she'd mused aloud until Tate asked encouragingly, "With what?"

"This whole charade." She held up her left hand to display the ring. "I'd have seen it as a big joke, a dare I had to win with panache. I was always in on the big practical jokes in high school and college, even while I trained for my career. One of the things that drew me to Chris was that he was always up for a challenge, never really serious about anything. Back then, if anyone had bet me I couldn't pull the wool over my obnoxious family's eyes, I'd have thrown myself into the part with such enthusiasm, I'd have practically convinced myself I was happily married. We're talking Betsy Shaw levels of deception."

Though he kept his attention outwardly centered on his driving, Tate was obviously listening closely. "What happened?"

She glanced over her shoulder. "Daryn happened."

"Ah."

"She might have been the result of my previously reckless behavior, but once I realized she was on her way, I vowed that she wouldn't have to pay for it. I wasn't going to raise her in the confusion and uncertainty my unreliable mother inflicted on us, letting her get attached to people who wouldn't stay in her life, never knowing where we'd be living next."

Turning to face the front of the car again, she added, "I guess that's one reason I've been so grouchy this weekend. I let myself be swept up in a prank again at the urging of my friends and I've regretted it ever since. Daryn doesn't need to get attached to Bob or my brothers or my grandmother or even my mother, considering I can't say for certain when or if I'll see any of them again."

She could have put Tate into that category, as well,

but it wasn't as much of an issue with him, since he was carefully keeping his distance from Daryn. Kim was the only one in danger of becoming too attached to Tate; but at least she was old enough to keep reminding herself how futile that would be.

Mimicking Bob ahead, Tate activated the left turn signal and braked for a red light. "I haven't noticed you being particularly grouchy. I've got to agree that your mom would try anyone's patience. As far as Daryn, she's too young to remember any of this, anyway. But is it really such a bad thing for her to meet new people, even if it's only fleetingly? For that matter, you never really know when you'll see anyone again. You just have to enjoy the time you spend with them when you can."

She shrugged lightly, wondering why she'd even started this conversation. "I guess you're right. It's just a hard lesson to learn as a child."

And one that left lingering scars, she added silently. Scars she never wanted to inflict on her daughter—and never wanted to add to her own barely healed collection.

Parking behind Bob at the curb of an older brick house at which several other cars already filled the driveway and lined the street, Tate killed the engine and turned to face her before releasing his seat belt. "I think we should make a pact today."

"What kind of pact?"

Taking her by surprise, he reached out to trace her bottom lip with one fingertip. "You let out that old Kim—the daring, mischievous one—just for today. Throw yourself into this silly bet as if it were for a million dollars. Keep your mother so confused even she doesn't know any longer what's true and what's fabricated. Have a great time, collect a dozen stories to tell our friends during lunches for the next six months, let Daryn be pampered and coddled all afternoon. Have fun, Kim. Just because you're a mom doesn't mean you can't still let loose and have a good time occasionally—even at a wacky family reunion."

Her mouth tingling from that brief, light contact, she swallowed. "Um—"

"Besides," he reminded her with a smile so roguish and sexy it made her lungs stutter, "we have a side bet, remember? I've got to pay you fifty dollars if you pull this off."

She cleared her throat. "You're going to regret making that bet when I take your fifty."

Looking pleased with her response, he chuckled. "Evan bet me a hundred, remember? I'm still going to come out fifty ahead. Unless, of course, you screw up, and then I've got a hundred from him and fifty from you. I might just treat myself to the Emperor's Platter next Wednesday."

The Emperor's Platter was the most expensive item on the menu of the Chinese restaurant where they met each week, and a running joke among the five friends who all lived on budgets while establishing their careers. Deciding she didn't want Tate reporting back to their friends that she'd been a stick-in-the-mud—or worse, a failure at holding up her end of the plot they had all conceived—Kim raised her chin. "I might just order the same thing—on your fifty."

"Bring it, cupcake," he taunted.

She laughed. "You're on, pretty boy."

They might have sat there teasing—okay, flirting—

for several minutes longer had they not been summoned impatiently by Kim's mother tapping on the hood of the car.

"Are you two coming in?" she called through the glass, her hands filled with one of the dishes she'd brought for lunch—and that Kim suspected Bob had been primarily responsible for preparing.

Kim reached for her door handle. "I'll get the baby. Would you bring the diaper bag, please, honey?"

Laughing again in response to the open challenge in her tone, Tate opened his door. "Yes, dear."

Betsy insisted on preceding Kim and Tate into Grandma Dyess's house, so that she could "announce them," she explained.

"Mom, we don't need to be announced. We're not exactly royalty."

Her mother merely laughed and crowded in front of them at the door. "I just want to let everyone know you're here."

"Emperor's Platter," Tate murmured humorously in Kim's ear.

She gave him a look, but took the hint to let her mother's dramatics pass without further argument.

Keeping Bob at her side, her mother reached out to ring the doorbell. Kim drew a breath, gave her daughter a little hug, then glanced at Tate.

"I should probably apologize in advance," she whispered when he tilted his head toward her.

He chuckled and startled her by brushing a kiss against her cheek. "Not necessary," he murmured.

Daryn reached out with the hand not holding Mr. Jingles and patted Tate's cheek. And it was in that position—his mouth near Kim's cheek, Daryn's hand on his face—that Kim's aunt Treva first saw them when she opened the door. If they had been trying deliberately to pose as a happy little family at that moment, they couldn't have done a better job.

Or maybe that was exactly what Tate had intended.

Her mother beamed at them in approval. "Treva, I'm so glad to finally introduce you to my dear son-in-law, Tate Price, and my sweet little granddaughter, Daryn. Kim, honey, say hello to your aunt," she added as if Kim were still a child.

Feeling Tate give her waist an encouraging squeeze with the arm he'd wrapped loosely around her, Kim forced a smile. "Hello, Aunt Treva. It's nice to see you again."

A near-duplicate of her one-year-older sister, Treva also wore her hair fluffed and curled and bleached. She was a few pounds heavier than Betsy, but dressed in much the same manner—a thin, short-sleeve, animal print summer jacket over a tan scoop neck tank and fashionably cropped pants with sequined flip-flops displaying a bright pink pedicure. Betsy's jacket and capri set was decorated with a field of poppies on a pale yellow background, and her tank top had sparkly studs around the neckline, but other than that, they were almost identical down to the glittering flip-flops and colorful toenails.

Both sisters could have stepped out of a television sitcom set in stereotypical suburbia, Kim thought wryly as she was ushered into the house. It was always interesting to see what personas her mercurial mother and aunt had adopted since she'd last seen them.

"You look very nice, Kim," Treva pronounced, looking her up and down. "I see you've lost most of your pregnancy weight. Good for you, I'm sure you'll get the rest of it off soon."

Hearing Tate make a little sound that sounded like a swallowed groan, Kim chose to ignore her aunt's comment. She had worked hard to regain her healthy pre-pregnancy weight, and she'd succeeded, so the implied criticism didn't bother her.

Unfazed by Kim's lack of reaction, Treva turned to Tate. "So, you're Tate. Betsy called you Trey the very few times she's mentioned you in the past, but she told me on the phone last night that you're dropping your childhood nickname in favor of your real name."

It amazed Kim—not necessarily in a good way—that her mother could always come up with a reasonable explanation for her inconsistencies.

Tate went along again. "That's right. It's very nice to meet you, Mrs.—um?"

"Just call me Treva," she said somewhat gruffly. "I'm not Mrs. anybody at the moment."

Betsy slipped her free hand beneath Bob's elbow and smiled somewhat smugly. "Bob and I will take these dishes into the kitchen. Why don't you take Tate and Kim in to join the others, Treva?"

Judging by the noise level in the house, several entire families were crowded into the midsize rooms. Kim heard adults talking, children shrieking and chattering, a television blaring a baseball game. Just how many had shown up for this gathering?

"Was your whole family able to come today, Aunt Treva?"

Treva nodded in response to Kim's question. "Patty's here with the kids, and Cara Lynn arrived only a few minutes before you did. Come in and say hello. It's been so long since you came to a family gathering that you probably won't even recognize each other."

"I saw them all at the reception for Mom and Bob," Kim reminded her.

"That was three years ago, Kimmie," her mom said over her shoulder as she and Bob moved toward the kitchen. "Bob and I are hardly newlyweds anymore."

"Zing," Tate murmured into Kim's ear.

She laughed softly, settling Daryn more comfortably on her hip while following her aunt toward the noisy family room. At least she could count on Tate to keep her smiling during the next few hours. And they really would have some funny stories to share with their friends at lunch next Wednesday.

Her first impression was that her grandmother's den was filled with children. After a moment, she realized there were only three, all dashing around the room and making enough noise for at least twice the number. Kim identified her cousin Patty's girls, Abby and Harper—who were probably around six and four now. And the tow-haired toddler chasing after them must be her cousin Mike's son, Lucas. Mike's wife, Ashley, had been pregnant at the reception where Kim had last seen her, so that would make Lucas about three.

Seeing the children, Daryn kicked and crowed, eager to play with them, though she couldn't yet join in the running.

Drawing her attention from the children, Kim saw that Treva's daughters, Patty and Cara Lynn, had zeroed in on Tate, eyeing the newcomer assessingly. Patty was divorced from her daughters' father, and Cara Lynn had recently ended a long-time engagement. For some reason, Patty and Cara Lynn had always been competitive with Kim, even though she'd tried to stay out of the contest.

She blamed her aunt and her mother—Treva and Betsy had projected their lifelong rivalry onto their daughters. In Kim's case, it hadn't really worked. Maybe it was because she was the oldest of the three—though only four months older than Patty—or maybe because she had spent her whole life trying not to be like her mother. Whatever the reason, she had never cared who was the most popular or who had the nicest clothes or cutest boyfriends. Her very lack of caring had seemed to annoy her cousins more than if she'd taken the competition seriously.

Despite the undertones, Kim had always gotten along well enough with Patty and Cara Lynn, for the most part. She greeted them with a smile and with air kisses, automatically noting the little changes that had taken place since she'd last seen them. They both cooed over Daryn, and Kim marveled at how much Abby and Harper had grown.

"I wish you'd friend us on the internet so we could at least keep up through pictures of the kids," Patty complained. "It makes it so much easier to stay in touch when we can read each other's status updates."

Kim smiled vaguely, promising to consider opening an account. Thus far, she had deliberately avoided social media, mostly because of her family. She thought again of how easily her mother's lies could have come unraveled if Kim had decided to friend her cousins. Her profile would have revealed her as a single mom, and Betsy's fabrications would have been exposed. Maybe it would have been best if she *had* opened her life to that extent.

While the sisters vied to flirt with Tate, Kim waved to her brothers, who sat on a couch across the room in front of the ball game, then turned to greet the rest of her relatives.

"Nice to see you again, Kim."

She lifted her cheek to receive a light kiss from her mother's older brother. "It's good to see you, too, Uncle Nelson. How have you been?"

"Doing great, thanks." He introduced her to his blonde, fortysomething companion, Sandi, who was obviously besotted with babies, since she immediately asked if she could hold Daryn. Daryn transferred happily enough into the arms of the smiling woman, accepting the admiring attention as her due.

Her uncle, who had been divorced for years, always had a pretty, younger blonde at his side. Kim didn't remember ever seeing him with the same one twice, but they always seemed nice enough. He had good, if predictable, taste in companions.

Drawing Tate away from Patty and Cara Lynn, she led him to her uncle and his two sons, Rusty and Mike, both in their early thirties. Rusty had never married and was reported to be somewhat of a playboy. Mike was the father of the boisterous three-year-old now trying to climb the wooden window blinds.

"Where's Ashley, Mike?" she inquired, glancing around the room. "Is she in the kitchen with Grandma?"

The awkward silence that fell between them gave her a clue to the answer. Mike cleared his throat. "Ashley didn't accompany me this weekend."

So her mother's gossip about the state of Mike's marriage had been true. One never knew with Betsy. Kim regretted that her mother had been correct about this.

She and her uncle and cousins exchanged small talk for a few more minutes, then Kim retrieved Daryn from Sandi. "I'd like to say hello to Grandma now. She's in the kitchen, right?"

"Mom's always in the kitchen," Nelson said. "Mike, you better catch that boy of yours before he pulls those blinds right off the window."

Nodding to Tate in a signal to follow her, Kim turned and carried her daughter from the den. It had been a few years since she'd visited her grandmother's house, but she knew how to find the kitchen. She released a light sigh after stepping out of the den and into the long hallway toward the back of the house. The initial greetings hadn't been as bad as she'd expected, but for just a moment, it was nice not to be on display.

"That was interesting," Tate murmured, keeping his voice low as he walked by her side.

She smiled. "I don't expect you to remember everyone's names."

"Treva's daughters are Patty and Cara Lynn. Patty's kids are Harper and Abby, not necessarily in that birth order. Your uncle Nelson is dating Sandi and is the father of Rusty and Mike, whose son is Lucas."

Pausing, she turned to look at him in surprise.

He chuckled. "I'm good with names."

"No kidding."

"Everyone seems to be getting along well enough."

"So far."

"Your aunt and your mother are the masters of backhanded compliments, aren't they?"

She grimaced. "Definitely. I'm sorry you're being subjected to all this."

"It was my choice, remember?" He caught her forearm to detain her when she would have moved on. "You know, Kim, all big families have tensions and drama. Maybe your family has commitment issues, but others have problems and baggage of their own. I could tell you some stories about some of my maternal relatives that would make your family look like they live in a Norman Rockwell painting."

She nodded. "I hope you don't think I'm being judgmental about my family," she murmured, glancing quickly around to make sure no one could overhear. "I don't really care what they do with their personal lives. I just don't care for all the games they try to play with me. And I guess I'm overly sensitive this time because Mom put me in such a difficult position, having to lie to everyone."

"You haven't actually lied to anyone," he pointed out with a low laugh. "You've introduced me simply as Tate, without once referring to me as your husband. I've been admiring how skillfully you've handled it."

She couldn't help smiling a little in response to his teasing, which was undoubtedly his purpose. "Yes, well, the day is just getting started."

He chuckled. "That's true. There's still hope that I'll be ordering the Emperor's Platter Wednesday—with your fifty."

She tossed her head. "I plan to use your fifty to order the platter and dessert."

Both of them were smiling when they entered the kitchen, which Kim figured could only help their cause, even though her smile was genuine.

From the first glance, it was obvious that the kitchen was the true heart of Grandma Dyess's home. Tate's initial impression was of warm colors and gleaming surfaces, immaculate floors and sparkling windows, functional appliances and retro wallpaper. His other senses were inundated with delicious aromas and the clattering sounds of cookware and cutlery and women talking over each other.

Bob was the only male in the room. He was quietly assembling food and supplies for the upcoming meal while his wife, sister-in-law and mother-in-law barked instructions at him. He even managed to look like he was enjoying himself. Tate had to admire the guy.

Kim's grandmother sat in a chair at the small, round oak table nestled into a breakfast bay. A stainless-steel walker with wheels on the front and yellow tennis balls on the back stood within her reach.

Again, Tate spotted the family resemblances, seeing in the older woman the daughters who looked so much like her. If she'd ever shared their predilection for hair dye, she'd given it up, letting her thin hair go stark white. Judging from experience with his own mother and grandmother, he would bet that Grandma Dyess, as he'd come to think of her, still visited a beauty salon with once-a-week faithfulness. Her hair was crimped and curled and sprayed to a tidy helmet around her narrow, lined face. Large, plastic-framed, peach-toned glasses sparkled at the corners with tiny rhinestones. Her purple dress could have been chosen to make her look regal and imposing, but instead it only emphasized her fragility.

He could see now why a desire to see her grandmother had weakened Kim's resistance to her mother's machinations. Even on the basis of a moment's impression, Tate would have bet that Grandma Dyess wouldn't be around for the next family reunion.

While Betsy looked on approvingly, Kim crossed the room and leaned over to kiss her grandmother's cheek. Tate found himself analyzing Kim's expression, deciding he saw affection, wistfulness and a hint of intimidation there. But maybe he was reading too much.

Grandma Dyess patted Daryn's chubby, bare leg with a gnarled, unsteady hand. "I always think those hairband bows look a little silly, since it's obvious the child doesn't have enough hair for a real bow. Patty always stuck them on her girls, too, and them bald as billiard balls when they were babies. Still, this one's a pretty little thing, isn't she? Looks just like you at her age, Kim."

"I think she has her father's smile," Betsy said quickly, with a broad smile toward Tate that made him inwardly wince. Seriously, did the woman have no sense of self-preservation? Kim was going to strangle her yet.

He stepped forward quickly and cleared his throat, giving Kim a meaningful look.

He heard her take a breath before saying evenly, "Grandma, this is Tate Price. Tate, my grandmother, Wanda Dyess."

He gave her his most winning smile, the one that almost always elicited a positive response from kids and senior citizens. "It's a pleasure to meet you, Mrs. Dyess."

She eyed him somewhat sternly through her glasses. "You might as well call me Grandma," she said somewhat grudgingly, not notably charmed. "Everyone else does. While they're around."

"Oh, Tate's going to be around awhile," Betsy said, giving him a smug pat on the arm as she shot a look at her sister.

Treva frowned. "If you're going to serve that concoction you brought, Betsy, you'd better get it out of the fridge. I don't know about everyone else, but I'm ready for this meal to get started."

"What can I do to help?" Tate looked at Bob as he asked, since Bob seemed to be doing the majority of the work.

"Don't you worry about anything." Betsy patted his arm again. She was beginning to make him feel like a pet poodle. "We'll take care of setting out the food. Go visit with Kim and Mother until we call you to eat."

He glanced toward the table. Kim had taken a seat next to her grandmother, who was studying Daryn with a slight smile. Grandma looked as though she'd have liked to hold the baby, but didn't quite trust her arthritic hands. She contented herself with reaching out occasionally to pat a leg or an arm. Holding her toy monkey snuggled in one arm, Daryn sucked on a finger, leaned back against her mother and studied her great-grandmother curiously, occasionally giving her a damp smile around the little digit.

"Yes, she's a very good baby," Kim was saying as Tate moved to stand behind her chair. "No trouble at all."

Her grandmother nodded. "You're still doing that therapy job?"

"Occupational therapy. Yes, I still love it."

"I've been getting some occupational therapy for my hands lately. For the arthritis. Helps me some."

"I'm glad it helps you. I work with quite a few arthritis patients, myself. I'd be happy to answer any questions while I'm here, if you have any."

"Could be I'll think of some later. So who watches the baby while you're working? Tate?"

"Tate has his own business to run, Grandma. Daryn is enrolled in an excellent day care program. She's very happy there."

"Hmm. Day care centers are full of germs. Hope you're giving her plenty of vitamins."

"She's very healthy."

Kim didn't lack for childcare advice when she was around her family, Tate mused. He wondered if she was aware that her first response toward suggestions from her relatives was defensiveness. He hadn't seen her react that way toward advice from friends, at least not during their months of lunches together. He supposed her complex past relationship with her family had something to do with the difference, but he suspected her own fears and insecurities about being a single mom had become more pronounced this weekend.

Abandoning the armchair psychology, he leaned down to pick up Mr. Jingles when the toy landed on the floor. He was beginning to believe Daryn was dropping the monkey on purpose, just to watch him pick it up. The twinkle in her innocently widened eyes when he returned it to her seemed to confirm his suspicion.

"I'm on to you, kid," he warned her with a smile.

Clutching the toy to her chest, she giggled at Tate. As their gazes met, his smile became a full-blown grin.

Okay, the kid was a cutie. And well aware of it. A guy would have to be careful or he'd find himself wrapped right around her little fingers. A very dangerous position to be in, considering how fragile those tiny fingers really were. It was no wonder Kim had so many qualms; there was so much to worry about when it came to raising a child, from nutrition to safety to education to character building. Terrifying.

Grandma Dyess's still-sharp eyes zeroed in on him. "Betsy just told me you're in the landscaping business, Tate. How's that going?"

"Very well, thank you. My business partner and I are quite pleased with our company's growth during the past year."

"What do you call it?"

"Price-Daugherty Landscape Design. Not the most original name, but at least I got top billing," he said with a self-deprecating chuckle.

She just looked at him. He still hadn't elicited a smile from her. Tough audience, he thought with a swallow.

"How did you meet my granddaughter?"

"My sister introduced us," he replied without hesitation. "Lynette is also an occupational therapist. She and Kim work together."

"You get along well with his sister?"

Kim nodded. "Lynette is one of my best friends."

"Hmm. That's good. At least you see his family often, even if you don't see your own. Not that I blame you entirely for that," the old woman muttered. She cast a somewhat morose look toward her daughters, who were squabbling over whether to serve the salads as a first course or side dishes to the buffet lunch.

All of them watched as Bob tactfully settled the disagreement and began to carry dishes into the dining room. Treva and Betsy followed him with more dishes in hand, though neither overburdened herself.

Grandma Dyess shook her head in resignation. "Those girls have been fighting since the day Treva was born," she informed Tate. "You'd think by now they'd have figured out that neither of them is ever going to win, but don't give them that much credit. Betsy's got Bob trained like one of those little dogs those rich girls carry around in designer bags. Hope he doesn't get fed up with it too soon. He's the best of the bunch of the string of men she's brought to my table."

Tate didn't quite know how to respond to such blunt candor. Fortunately, Mr. Jingles hit the floor again at just that moment, so he was spared the necessity of coming up with a reply. He bent to retrieve the toy again and offered it back to Daryn with a wink. She laughed and gave the chiming toy a vigorous shake.

All in all, the baby was a much easier audience than Grandma Dyess, he thought wryly. They both unnerved him a little, but at least Daryn couldn't talk yet.

Grandma Dyess's long, rather narrow dining room was the largest room in her house. Originally a formal living room/dining room combination, it had been converted to dining alone as the family had expanded, with tables at both ends, each of which held eight adults comfortably, or ten when crowded. Two long buffets pushed against the far wall were covered with salads, casseroles, side dishes, breads and desserts. Kim had offered to bring a dish, but her mother had insisted that she and Bob had prepared more than their share for the family, especially since it would have been difficult for Kim to transport food all the way from Little Rock.

Glancing at the feast being descended on by a horde of hungry relatives, Kim decided that there was, indeed, plenty of food. Standing out of the way with Daryn on her hip and Tate by her side until the first rush settled, she made a quick head count, just for curiosity. Not counting herself, Daryn or Tate, fifteen people had gathered for lunch with Grandma. Some—notably Stuart and Mike—didn't look particularly happy to be there. Her mother and Treva were too busy squabbling and supervising to relax and enjoy themselves; or maybe that was their idea of a good time. Who could tell with them?

Abby and Harper were somewhat undisciplined, dashing around the room and making noise in a way they should have outgrown by now. From her place at the head of the first table, where she waited to be served, Grandma Dyess made the observation that young ladies needed to learn manners at an early age, and then she gave their mother a stern look that had Patty's lip quivering and Treva jumping to the defensive.

"It isn't easy for a single mother to raise two young daughters alone," she argued with Grandma. "The girls are somewhat strong-willed, but Patty does the best she can."

"Needs to try a little harder," Grandma retorted, frowning at Harper, who had just thrown a roll at her sister. "Single or not, it's a mother's job to teach her children how to behave in polite society."

Patty grabbed Harper's shoulder and bustled her out of the room for a lecture, with Harper whining and protesting all the way.

Kim winced a little, hearing echoes of her own previous soapbox comments to Tate about irresponsible parenting. Heavens, was she turning into her grandmother already?

Still, old-fashioned or not, she planned to begin comportment lessons very early with her daughter. She'd have done the same with a son. She noted with a stifled smile that Mike was suddenly hovering over Lucas, frantically whispering directions as he helped the boy fill a plate and carry it to the opposite table from where Grandma Dyess sat.

While Betsy and Treva argued about who would serve the meal to their mother, Bob filled a plate with generous portions and quietly set it in front of his mother-in-law along with a glass of iced tea. "Can I get you anything else, Mother Dyess?"

"No, that's all. Thank you, Bob. Get yourself something and relax awhile. That wife of yours is quite capable of serving herself, you know."

Bob chuckled. "Yes, ma'am, I know."

Grandma Dyess shot a look across the room. "Kim, you and Tate help yourselves and then come sit at this table with me. What are you going to do with the baby while you eat?"

"I'll just hold her. I'm used to eating one-handed."

Nodding, Grandma Dyess efficiently ordered everyone else to the table she chose for them. In addition to Kim and Tate, she seated Betsy and Bob, Treva, Nelson and Sandi at her table. If anyone was unhappy with the assignment, no one had the courage to protest when Grandma Dyess spoke.

Because she was holding the baby, Tate helped Kim fill her plate and carry it to the table along with his own. During the meal, Kim alternated taking bites of her own food with spooning mashed sweet potatoes and bits of banana from the fruit salad into Daryn's mouth. Concentrating on the meal gave her an excuse to avoid some of the scrutiny aimed at her and Tate, who conversed genially with their tablemates while eating and occasionally retrieving Mr. Jingles from the floor.

Though she supposed it was foolish, considering the circumstances, she still found some satisfaction in knowing that neither she nor Tate had outright lied to any of the questions asked of them. After all those weekly lunch conversations, they knew each other well enough to bluff through most of the not-so-subtle inquisition without resorting to outright fabrication.

Her mother was the real problem. For some reason, Betsy wouldn't allow herself to be content with her victory in getting Kim to bring Daryn and Tate to the reunion, thereby backing up Betsy's past lies. Instead, she kept bragging about her daughter and "son-in-law" with stories that grew progressively more fake, despite Kim's efforts to restrain her.

Not to be outdone, Treva continually jumped in with boasts about how much money Patty was making as a nurse practitioner—which was "almost like a doctor, you know"—how much respect Cara Lynn commanded with her newly obtained master's degree in elementary education and how brilliantly both of her granddaughters had performed in first grade and preschool last semester.

Treva made a point of chastising Kim during the meal for not inviting her family to attend her wedding. "I would have enjoyed seeing you walk down the aisle," she said, aggrieved. "And while I doubt that you and Tate could afford a big, fancy celebration, I'm sure your mother could have scraped together a little cash to help you."

"I never wanted a big wedding, Aunt Treva," Kim said, choosing her words carefully. "That has nothing to do with money. My idea of the perfect wedding for myself has always been an intimate ceremony with just me and the man I love. Big weddings are fine for most people, but you know I've always been a bit more private."

"I'd say so," Treva muttered, still looking disgruntled. "Since we hardly ever even see you."

"Did I mention that Tate's writing a book?" Betsy asked rather loudly, drawing the attention back to herself.

Finally, her mother had said something that was true. Kim wasn't sure how Tate felt about his activities being discussed this way in front of a crowd of strangers, but at least he could acknowledge this one without compromising his ethics.

He started to say something, but then Betsy just had to elaborate. "He's already got a deal with a major publisher. I'm sure it will be a bestseller, so that means book tours and television interviews. Isn't that exciting?"

Noting that no one looked particularly excited by yet another boastful update from Betsy, Kim shook her head sternly at her mother in a silent command to stop.

Tossing her head, Betsy looked prepared to continue, but this time Tate interceded. "Actually, my business partner and I are working on a photo-based instruction book for urban vegetable gardening. We don't actually have a publisher yet, though we've had a few promising nibbles."

Betsy pouted a little that Tate had gently shot down her story. "You're just being modest, Tate."

"Now, Betsy, I'm sure everyone knows that you tend to exaggerate a bit," he shot back.

Biting her lower lip to suppress a smile, Kim wondered if her mother recognized the hint of warning in Tate's voice. Tate would allow himself to be pushed only so far—and Betsy was getting very close to the limit.

Several barks of laughter, some quickly stifled, followed Tate's challenge of Betsy's exaggerations. Kim was pretty sure she heard her brothers' voices among that outburst. Betsy's cheeks went pink, though her chin remained high.

Treva, of course, made no effort to hide her gleeful amusement. "*Exaggeration* is a polite term for some of Betsy's outright—"

"Not at the table, Treva," Grandma Dyess cut in firmly, effectively ending the brewing quarrel. Both her daughters subsided into seething looks at each other.

Somewhat inevitably, Betsy took out her annoyance on Kim in a last-ditch attempt to save face. "You're the one who told me about your husband's book deal."

Kim caught Daryn's hand when the baby reached for Kim's fork. "I told you Tate's working on a book, Mom, but I didn't give you any other details."

"Well, yes, but you said—"

"You really don't want to take this any further, Mom." Kim hoped she injected the same amount of subtle warning in her tone that Tate had earlier. If it worked for him, maybe it was something she should try more often in the future.

"But—"

"Who made this delicious vegetable casserole?" Tate asked quickly, nudging Kim's knee with his own beneath the table. "Reminds me of one of the dishes on the Emperor's Platter at my favorite restaurant."

Taking the hint, Kim focused on her daughter again, though she vowed that if her mother continued to push, it was damn the consequences. Kim was getting close to throwing up her hands and blurting out the whole truth behind her visit. Though she was caring less and less about how her mother would react, she was keeping her mouth shut—for now—out of consideration for her grandmother. But she was making no guarantees even to herself that her patience would last the rest of the day.

Chapter Six

When everyone had eaten their fill, Betsy and Treva—and Bob, of course—headed for the kitchen to start clearing away while most of the other men escaped back to the family room and the ball games. Kim and her cousins tried to help with cleanup, but their offers were declined for lack of space in the kitchen.

"Why don't you come watch the game with us, Tate," Julian suggested. "I want to show you a website on my phone that I found last night. It's got all kinds of useful information about classic muscle cars."

Tate nodded. He'd barely had a chance to speak with Kim's brothers since they'd arrived earlier, and while Stuart seemed no more interested in getting to know him than he had last night, Julian, at least, was making a reasonably friendly overture.

Patty and Cara Lynn decided to pour fresh glasses of iced tea and go out in the backyard with Abby, Harper and Lucas. Patty had brought an assortment of outdoor toys to entertain the kids, and she and Cara Lynn had both brought a stack of magazines for themselves. Treva, Betsy and Bob promised to join them out on the patio as soon as the kitchen was set to rights.

"Since you're not doing anything else right now," Grandma said to Kim, "you and I can go talk about my arthritis. My hands have been giving me some trouble lately. Maybe you'll have some tricks my therapist hasn't thought of yet."

Kim agreed without hesitation. Though basically she was being asked to give a free therapy session on her day off, she didn't seem to mind. Tate suspected both Kim and her grandmother were using the therapy as an excuse to interact a bit more during this rare visit.

"I'll watch the baby," Sandi offered eagerly, stepping forward with extended hands. "Maybe she'd like to come into the den and play on the floor with some toys while we watch the game. I'll put out a blanket for her to lie on and I'll sit by her while she plays."

Kim's pause was almost imperceptible before she said, "I'm sure she would like that. She's probably tired of being held."

As if in confirmation, Daryn kicked her legs energetically. Sandi crooned baby-talk gibberish as she carefully cradled Daryn in her arms.

"There are toys in her bag," Kim said, starting to move that way.

Tate placed a hand on her arm. "I'll get them. Go take care of your grandma, Daryn will be fine in the den with us."

He wasn't certain she would find reassurance in knowing he'd be near Daryn, since he'd had so little to do with the child thus far, but she smiled and nodded. "Thanks."

Feeling somewhat obligated now, he kept an eye on Sandi and the baby when they entered the family room. Sandi directed Nelson to spread a blanket on the spotless hardwood floor, then she put Daryn down on her tummy with her toys within reach. Sandi sat cross-legged next to the baby, positioning herself so she could babysit and watch the game. The older children had left a few toys scattered nearby, but Sandi merely pushed those to one side.

Daryn kicked and squirmed and babbled, happy to be liberated for play time. Sandi cooed at her, eliciting giggles that delighted the woman and made everyone else in the room smile. Even Stuart chuckled a little in response to the sound, though Tate noticed that he did not look up from his tablet computer.

"Oh, look at her!" Sandi trilled when Daryn rose wobbly on her hands and knees and rocked back and forth. "Is she crawling already?"

"Not yet," Tate answered from the couch where he sat next to Julian. "She's almost there but hasn't quite put the moves together."

"She'll be up and running before you know it," Nelson advised from the recliner where he'd settled with an after-lunch beer.

"Very likely."

"Hey, Tate—here's that website I was talking about." Julian passed over his smartphone, pointing to the screen. "How's that for a honey of an old GTO?"

"Sweet," Tate agreed, confident now that he could look away from the baby for a while.

For the next fifteen minutes or so, he divided his attention between Julian's car talk, the ball game and occasional glances toward Daryn. Rusty and Mike were deep in low-voiced conversation on the other side of the room. They looked somber, and Tate wondered if they were talking about the state of Mike's troubled marriage. He wondered why so many members of this particular family were unable to maintain long-term relationships. Sure, they had their flaws, but what family didn't? Overall, they seemed decent enough, reasonably cordial despite the underlying frictions even an outsider could sense from the start.

A cell phone played a cutesy ringtone, and Sandi made a quick grab for her purse with an apologetic look to the others in the room. Seeing that Daryn was contently chewing on the ear of a rubber bunny, Tate turned his attention back to Julian, asking another question about the Mustang restoration. He had to concentrate to hear everything Julian said. The room was rather noisy with the ball game, occasional beeps from Stuart's computer, jingles from Daryn's toys, Sandi's chatter into her phone, Nelson's soft snoring in the recliner and unintelligible rumble of conversation from his sons in the far corner. In other words, a typical family gathering.

He hoped Kim was having a good visit with her grandmother. And that Kim and her mother would be able to part after this visit on at least reasonably good terms. Betsy was undeniably difficult, and Tate didn't blame Kim at all for wanting to keep a cautious distance between herself and her mother, but he thought she would regret it if all ties between them were cut. He didn't like to think of Kim being sad and alone.

"So, anyway," Julian rambled on, "I plan to be on the lookout for a—"

"Daryn? Oh, my God!"

Tate leaped off the couch when Sandi screeched and threw her phone aside with a clatter. Nelson woke with a start in the recliner, saying, "What? What is it?"

Daryn lay on her stomach, her hands flailing, her face contorted. Tate felt as though he'd been kicked in the chest when he saw that the baby's lips were turning blue. "She's choking."

Mass pandemonium followed. The men either froze or jumped to their feet. Sandi seemed close to hysteria as she wrung her hands and stared at the baby in horror, paralyzed with fear.

Without stopping to think, Tate snatched the baby up from the floor. He had taken a CPR class a few years earlier, after his dad had suffered a blessedly minor heart scare. Choking procedures had been covered in the class, and he only hoped he remembered it all now.

He checked inside the baby's mouth. He could see something in her throat, but a quick sweep of his finger didn't dislodge it. She made a noise that sounded like muffled gagging, but he could tell she was unable to cough, and he wasn't sure she was getting sufficient air. Making an immediate decision, he leaned her head-down over his arm and gave her a quick, careful blow to the back, right between her little shoulder blades. He had to repeat the procedure before she expelled the object with a sputtering, gasping cough, followed by a loud shriek of fear.

Righting her so he could hug her against his shoulder, Tate patted her back as soothingly as he knew how. She screamed bloody murder in his ear, but he didn't mind, since it took plenty of air to make that much noise.

"It's okay, Daryn," he murmured, rubbing her back in a way he'd seen Kim do. "You're okay now."

Clutching the collar of his shirt with one hand, she burrowed into his throat, her sobs subsiding to whimpers.

Kim appeared in the family room doorway, her eyes sweeping the room until she found Daryn and Tate. She moved toward them immediately. "What happened?"

"She choked." Julian reached down to pick up a pink plastic doll shoe, holding it gingerly between two fingers. "On this. I guess one of the girls left it in here."

"I'm so sorry, Kim. I thought I was watching her so closely." Still wringing her hands, Sandi sniffled. "I thought all the other toys were out of her reach, since she can't crawl yet. My phone rang and I looked away just for a few moments—"

"She isn't actually crawling, but still she can squirm quite a distance." Looking a little pale, Kim took Daryn, who had reached out as soon as she heard her mother's voice. Kim looked her over quickly, seemingly satisfying herself that there was no lasting damage from the scare.

"Tate handled it perfectly," Nelson assured his niece. "Cool as a cucumber. He had her snatched up off the floor and was doing some Heimlich thing almost before the rest of us knew what was going on. The baby will be fine."

The latter assurance seemed to be directed as much toward Sandi as Kim. Nelson wrapped an arm around his companion and led her off to the kitchen, saying a nice, cold glass of tea would help settle her nerves.

Betsy and Treva entered the room, wanting to know what was going on. Having been filled in, Betsy gave an affecting performance as the distraught grandmother, clutching her throat with one hand while fluttering around Kim and the baby, throwing questions at everyone around.

"She's fine, Mother," Kim said for perhaps the fourth time, visibly beginning to lose patience.

Betsy dabbed at her eyes. "I'm so glad. When I think what could have happened…"

She drew a shuddering breath, then said to Kim, "I trust in the future you'll be a bit more careful about leaving this precious child with just any stranger who volunteers to watch her."

Kim gasped in outrage. Grateful that at least Sandi hadn't been in the room to hear the insult, Tate stepped forward quickly. Maybe cutting all ties with Betsy wouldn't be such a tragedy, after all, but now was probably not the best time to do so.

"Why don't you and I take Daryn out for a walk in her stroller?" he suggested to Kim, angling himself between her and her mother. "I think it would calm us all down."

He could almost see a flood of hurt and angry words swirling in her mind, fighting to rush toward her thoughtless mother. And maybe she should release them, eventually. But not now.

She drew a deep breath, then relieved his tension by nodding. "I think that's a good idea."

Betsy brightened. "Maybe I'll come along."

Moving forward to stand beside his wife, Bob took a firm grip on her arm. "I think Kim and Tate would like a little time alone with Daryn, honey. Why don't we go start that dominoes game we talked about earlier and leave the others to see the end of the ball game? Treva and Grandma both want to play, and maybe Patty and Cara Lynn would like to join us."

Tate sent a look of gratitude toward Bob, and then he and Bob led daughter and mother in opposite directions.

It was another beautiful afternoon, a little warmer than the day before, but still comfortable enough for an afternoon stroll. Large trees lined the old sidewalks, providing nice shade, though roots had kicked through the concrete in places, making the sidewalk somewhat uneven. Concentrating on guiding the stroller along the more level paths helped Kim to push the events of the past few minutes out of her mind, though she knew it would all rush back at her later.

"That's a shame."

Trying to focus on the moment, she glanced at Tate, who strolled beside her with his hands tucked casually into his pockets. "What?"

He nodded toward a large, older home across the street. "Those two nice trees in the side yard? Elms. They'll be dead in a few months."

She frowned as she studied the tall, spreading trees. Only then did she notice that the leaves at the very top of the trees looked wilted and yellow.

"Dutch elm disease?" she hazarded, remembering reading something about that devastating fungus.

"More likely a disease called elm yellows. Still kills the tree."

"Is there anything to do to save them?"

"Not at this stage. The only decision now is when to

cut down the tree to avoid damage to the house when they fall."

"That's a shame. They look old."

"Elms grow fairly fast, which is what made them such popular shade trees. Unfortunately, the older varieties are highly susceptible to diseases spread by beetles, or perhaps by pruning with shears that haven't been disinfected after contact with sick trees."

They kept walking, putting Grandma's house behind them. When they approached a particularly uneven section of sidewalk, Tate stepped up to place his hands beside Kim's on the handle, adding his strength to help guide the stroller over the broken concrete. He didn't move away once they'd passed the section, but continued to match his steps to hers at a leisurely, companionable pace. Daryn had already fallen asleep, Mr. Jingles tucked snugly against her.

The aging neighborhood was quiet on this Saturday afternoon, little traffic on the dead-end road. Kim nodded toward a particularly pretty flower bed in front of a white frame house with an inviting wraparound porch. "I love those roses. The pale yellow ones with the darker yellow centers? They're so cheerful looking."

"Sunny Knock Outs," he said at a glance. "Good, hearty choice for people who don't want to put a lot of effort into their gardening. We plant several varieties of Knock Outs. The yellow is a popular one. I'm partial to the heirloom roses, myself, but they do take a lot more work."

"I'd like to try growing some roses someday. When Daryn's a little older and can potter around in the yard with me."

Tate nodded. "You can always ask me for advice for the best varieties."

At their weekly lunch meetings, she added mentally. Starting tomorrow, she and Tate were no more than lunch buddies again, with only funny anecdotes remaining from this weekend—once she'd put enough distance behind her to find the humor.

"How was your therapy session with your grandmother? Did you have a chance to chat?"

"Some. She showed me what she's been doing, and the exercises she has been given are fine. I gave her a few minor pointers, but I wouldn't want to interfere with the regimen her own therapist has recommended for her."

"Any awkward questions? About us, I mean."

"No, not really. She asked about your landscaping business, and I told her about some of the projects you and Evan have taken on lately. It's hard to tell with Grandma sometimes, but she seemed to approve."

"From what little I've seen, she's an interesting woman."

"She's a little intimidating," Kim confessed. "Always has been. I used to be nervous around her when I was younger. Not so much anymore."

"She doesn't hesitate to speak her mind, does she?"

Kim shook her head. "No, not at all. And she makes no secret that she isn't particularly happy with some of the choices her progeny have made in the past few years."

"How do you think she would really react if she knew the truth—about us, and about Daryn, I mean?"

Kim chewed her lower lip thoughtfully for a few moments, then shrugged. "I've wondered that myself.

She'd be furious with Mom, of course—so mad that things could be very awkward between them for a long time. I'd hate to cause that, because Grandma needs Mom and Treva to watch out for her, especially now that she's getting so fragile. Even with the hired companion she has during the days now, she won't be able to live alone much longer and she's going to need her daughters and son to rally around her.

"As for how she'd react to me being an unmarried mother—I don't know," she admitted. "She's old-fashioned about certain things. She's outspoken in her disapproval of all the divorces in the family, but I don't know how she'd feel about me skipping the marriage step altogether."

"You could be underestimating her, you know. She seems quite fond of you, in her own way."

"I guess she is. Like I said, it's hard to tell with Grandma."

The fresh air and the quiet, combined with the congenial conversation, was draining some of the tension from her shoulders, as Tate had certainly hoped when he'd suggested this outing. For the first time since she'd stormed out of the house, she felt like she could take a full breath again. She filled her lungs and then exhaled slowly, releasing a little more of the stress.

"Thank you," she said. "For the walk, but mostly for taking care of Daryn. I would have thanked you sooner for that, but I had to wait until I could do so without falling apart."

"I'm enjoying the walk very much, and as for taking care of Daryn, I simply reacted faster than anyone else. I had a CPR class fairly recently and I guess the training just kicked in. The whole episode was over in only a few seconds, though it seemed longer at the time. Daryn's fine."

She had to check again, making sure her daughter was sleeping peacefully, breathing evenly. "Yes, she is. Thanks to you."

He smiled down at her, his gaze holding hers, his hand covering hers on the stroller handle. "Don't mention it."

She found it hard to make herself look away from him. Even harder to move her hand from beneath his. It felt unnervingly good to be so connected to him, both visually and physically.

Don't do this, Kim.

Tate's mouth quirked into a sudden, rueful grin. "Okay, I have a confession to make."

"Um—?"

"Everyone keeps talking about how cool and calm I was—but truth is, I was scared spitless. When Daryn burst into tears afterward, I damn near joined her."

She knew he wanted her to smile, but she could only swallow hard instead.

Tate glanced down at the sleeping child. "Just reminded me how much responsibility they are. I mean, elm trees and roses I understand. Babies…well, they terrify me."

She told herself her heart didn't actually sink in response to that admission. That would mean she had almost let herself start to believe in this fantasy they were acting out.

"I guess it's time to start heading back," she said regretfully as they reached the roundabout at the end of the residential street. "Grandma said something about wanting to take pictures while everyone is together. After that, we can make our escape."

Tate nodded and helped her turn the stroller while Daryn slept peacefully on. Taking a deep breath, Kim gave a little push to get them started and Tate again matched his steps to hers. She didn't really need his help pushing the stroller, of course—but just for a little while longer, it was nice to have someone there beside her, helping her face the remainder of this fiasco.

It would be time soon to return to the life she truly loved, she reminded herself. Her job, her house—rented, but home, nevertheless—her evenings and weekends with her adored daughter. She couldn't ask for more.

Getting everyone posed for photos was definitely a challenge. Grandma Dyess had very specific ideas about how she wanted to pictures to look, but her orders were more easily barked than executed. There were just so darned many of them, Kim thought with a shake of her head. Fortunately, Grandma had chosen an outdoor setting, giving the kids room to run and play in the yard between poses, though Patty continuously fussed at her girls to please try to stay clean for their pictures.

Grandma Dyess had actually written out a list of the shots she wanted taken. The first was of her surrounded by her three children. That one was easy enough. With only a little jostling and arguing about who should stand where, Betsy, Treva and Nelson gathered around the wrought-iron patio chair from which their mother reigned. It took only about five shots before Grandma was satisfied with what she saw on the screen of Bob's high-quality digital camera.

Next came a pose with her grandchildren. Handing Daryn to her mother, Kim joined her cousins around Grandma Dyess's chair. She noted in wry amusement that there was much less arguing about positioning from this generation than there had been from their parents.

The great-grandchildren were somewhat more of a test. Lucas didn't want to pose and had to be bribed with candy. Grandma Dyess was reluctant to hold Daryn for fear that her arthritic hands would not be up to the task, even though Kim thought Daryn would be fine sitting up in Grandma's lap. It wasn't as if Daryn were an infant who couldn't even hold up her own head. They compromised by perching Daryn on Grandma's knee with six-year-old Abby keeping one hand on Daryn's back for added support. Bob took those photos quickly, before Lucas's patience and Grandma's knee wore out, but everyone proclaimed the shots quite satisfactory.

Individual family photos were next. Only as Treva, her daughters and granddaughters arranged themselves around the chair did Kim realize how awkward this session was truly about to become. She looked at Tate, to find him gazing back at her with similar questions written on his face.

"Um, Mom—" She pulled her mother aside, whispering in her ear. "What are we going to do about Tate?"

Her mother smiled at her serenely. "What do you mean, dear? We'll have him join our family picture, of course."

"But, Mom—"

"Oh, don't be silly, Kim," her mother managed to

snap even in a low murmur that no one else could hear. "What does it matter if Tate stands with us? Now, make your grandmother happy and do what she asks, please."

Kim sighed and moved closer to Tate. "Looks like you'll be posing for photos. Sorry about that."

"I'll stand on the end," he said with a chuckle. "That way I can be edited out if you ever want to erase me."

Suspecting her answering smile looked rather feeble, she turned away to watch Nelson's sons and grandson move toward "the throne," as she had begun to think of Grandma's patio chair.

"Sandi, you should join them," Betsy instructed loudly, even though Nelson had already invited his girlfriend into the pose. "These pictures are a nice record of everyone who joined us for this lovely gathering today, right?"

Though the words were undoubtedly directed straight toward Kim, they seemed to make sense to everyone. Sandi moved to stand beside Nelson, visibly pleased to be included. The poor woman probably took Betsy's words as a signal that she was forgiven for allowing Betsy's grandchild to choke, Kim thought. As for herself, she held no ill will toward the effusively apologetic woman. Babies were notorious for getting their little hands and mouths on things they shouldn't. Perhaps Sandi shouldn't have let herself be distracted from her volunteer babysitting duties, but truth was, it could have happened to anyone.

Inevitably, it was time for Kim's family to gather round the chair. Bob turned the camera over to Rusty so he could take his place with his wife. Stuart grudgingly set aside his computer to amble into position, though Kim doubted he would bother to smile. Holding Daryn on her hip, she stood beside Tate and faced the camera, suspecting her own smile was a bit forced.

The final pose was a group shot of everyone. Bob set the camera on a tripod, activated the timer, then hurriedly returned to his place by his wife. Three times he went through that procedure, just in case any eyes were closed or heads turned away, and because Lucas was sobbing in the first shot and had to be soothed for the next two.

"That's enough pictures for now," Grandma finally announced after reviewing the shots on the camera screen.

Kim fancied the collective sighs of relief from her relatives ruffled the leaves of the bushes in Grandma's backyard.

Grandma reached for her walker and rose slowly from her chair. The walker wobbled a bit on an uneven patio brick. Though she was never in danger of falling, Tate moved to steady her, as he happened to be standing closest to her just then. Kim watched her grandmother give him a curt nod of thanks and then regally allow him to escort her inside. Following behind them, Betsy gave Kim a smug look that made Kim want to snarl in return, though she managed to resist.

To reward everyone for the photo shoot, and to cool them down after standing around in the afternoon heat outside, Betsy and Treva brought out pitchers of iced tea and lemonade, along with the leftover desserts from lunch for late afternoon snacks. Again, it was all set out buffet-style, and everyone milled around the tables, sipping from glasses and nibbling cakes and pies and cookies.

Glancing at her watch, Kim spoke to her grandmother. "Tate and I are going to have to leave soon, Grandma. We still have a long drive ahead."

"You aren't staying for the entire weekend? I thought maybe you'd attend church with us in the morning."

"We'd love to, Grandma, but we really need to get back home. Tate has a big client presentation first thing Monday morning and he needs to prepare for it." Once again, she'd been able to tell the truth. Kim chided herself that she shouldn't be so proud of that fact, considering the big lie she was allowing to be perpetrated about her and Tate.

Her grandmother nodded in resignation. "I want you and Tate to come with me for a few minutes. Bring the baby, too."

Kim and Tate swapped a quick look. Judging by his expression, she wondered if he, too, questioned whether Grandma had somehow seen through their deception.

She swallowed a bit nervously, but nodded. "Of course."

Without saying anything else, Grandma turned toward the hallway that led to the back of the house, her walker thumping against the floor. Kim and Tate followed, Kim carrying Daryn.

"Where are you going, Mother?" Betsy asked, rushing forward when she saw them. "Is there something you need?"

"I need you to stay in here while I talk to my granddaughter," her mother answered flatly. "Try not to get into a fight with your sister for the few minutes while I'm out of the room."

Good luck with that, Kim thought with a slight smile that faded when Grandma led them into her bedroom and ordered Tate to close the door.

Kim wasn't sure she'd ever even been in her grandmother's room. She took a quick glance around, noting the four-poster bed with a hand-crocheted spread, and the nightstand that held a lamp with a beaded shade, a soft leather bible and a photograph of the grandfather who had died when Betsy was still in high school. A double dresser with an attached mirror sat against the opposite wall, an antique silver dresser set with hand mirror and brush centered precisely on the gleaming surface, along with a bottle of rose-scented face cream.

Grandma moved straight to that dresser, where she opened a drawer and drew out a small cardboard box. She turned and looked at Kim. "Give the baby to Tate for a minute."

"Um—"

Tate reached out for the sleepy baby and cradled her against his shoulder as if he did so every day. If he felt any hesitation about taking her, he didn't allow it to show as he nodded slightly toward Kim.

Kim felt her heart beating in her throat when she opened the little box her grandmother pressed into her hands. She had a sick feeling of what she was going to find inside—and she was right.

"I can't take this, Grandma."

"It's the engagement ring your grandfather gave me back in '54. I can't wear it anymore because of my arthritis. I want you to have it."

Kim's hands were shaking as she closed the lid of the box, hiding the pretty little platinum band with its small, but perfect, round diamond. "You said this ring was to go to one of your grandchildren who was a part of a long, stable marriage. That isn't me, Grandma."

"I know you and Tate aren't much more than newlyweds, but I have a good feeling about this one." Grandma nodded firmly as she spoke, as if there was no use arguing with her "feelings."

Kim looked despairingly at Tate. His gaze locked with hers over Daryn's head, he gave a little shrug, effectively leaving the decision about what to do next entirely up to her.

She drew a deep breath. "Grandma, there's something I need to tell you. Maybe you should sit down."

Chapter Seven

Stark silence reigned in Grandma Dyess's bedroom when Kim finished speaking. Kim sat on the bed beside her grandmother, one hand resting gently on Grandma's arm. Tate had settled onto a little boutique chair nearby. At any other time, Kim might have found some humor in the sight of him perched precariously on that delicate little chair, cradling her sleeping baby in his strong, tanned arms.

"I'm so sorry, Grandma," she said when the quiet became too awkward to bear. "I really wasn't trying to pull anything over on you. But I wanted to see you, and, well…"

"And your mother put you in such an untenable position that you didn't know what else to do," Grandma concluded for her, a scowl on her face. "I swear, I don't know where I went wrong raising that girl. She wouldn't recognize common sense if it walked up and bit her in the butt."

Kim heard a faint sound from Tate, but she knew he wouldn't dare chuckle at that moment.

"I know you're probably angry with her—and with me, for that matter—but I hope you can forgive us both."

Her grandmother was still frowning. "Now that I think about it, you haven't really flat-out lied to me, have you?"

"I tried not to. But by omission, I suppose…"

"For more than a year, whenever she has mentioned you, Betsy has referred to your husband and child. Now I will say, she hasn't talked about you much. You know Betsy, always more interested in herself than anyone else, even her children. But all this time, she has led her family to believe that you were married. And then she had the nerve to blackmail you into cooperating."

"It wasn't blackmail, exactly—"

"Coercion, then. If you wanted to see your ailing grandmother, you had to play along with your mother's trickery."

"Well, yes, but—"

Grandma nodded. "I should have taken her behind the woodshed more when she was a child. I blame her father. He spoiled her rotten."

Kim didn't quite know what to say to that.

"So." Grandma looked narrowly at Tate. "Is your name really Tate?"

He did chuckle then. "Yes, ma'am. Tate Price. Not Trey."

"Good. Always thought Trey was a silly nickname."

"Yes, ma'am."

"And you and my granddaughter are—?"

"Friends," he supplied with a smile for Kim. "Very good friends."

"Hmm." She studied him for a few moments later, then glanced at the dozing baby. "Not yours?"

"Daryn is mine," Kim said firmly. "Her father was a decent man, but not interested in having a family. He's no longer in our lives."

It was obvious that her grandmother did not like hearing that. "Don't you be following in your mother's footsteps, Kim. You got tangled up with one man who didn't stick around, but I hope you learned your lesson that time."

"Trust me."

Grandma looked at Tate again. "What about you, young man? How did you get roped into this?"

"I volunteered, actually. Kim mentioned her mother's request and said she wasn't planning to attend. I could tell she wanted to see you, so I suggested I come along to appease her mother."

"Humph. Can't say I approve of what you two did, but I guess I can understand how it came about."

"I'm sorry, Grandma. I know you're angry with Mother—and heaven knows you should be—but, well, I hope you can find a way to forgive her. I mean, she's definitely difficult, but—"

"But she's my daughter," her grandmother filled in with a rueful shake of her head. "And your mother. We can't just cut her out of our lives, no matter how tempting she makes it at times."

"I guess that's true," Kim agreed with a similar resignation in her voice.

Grandma sighed lightly and patted Kim's knee. "I've

understood why you felt the need to distance yourself from the family for a while. Wasn't sure if that fictitious husband of yours had anything to do with it, but mostly I figured you just needed a break from the chaos your mother seems to enjoy surrounding herself with. Last time we all got together was at the reception she pretty much threw for herself and Bob, though she somehow strong-armed Treva into hosting it, along with that husband of hers at the time…what was his name?"

Kim figured her grandmother was fully aware of the name, but she supplied it, anyway. "Greg."

"Right. Couldn't stand that one. Anyway, Treva and Greg were already headed for a split by that time. That reception was filled with tension and back-biting and your mother's melodrama, and I could see even then that you'd had your fill of it. Next I heard, you'd married and had a baby. I hoped you'd finally found the security and stability you lacked when you were growing up."

"Other than the marriage, that's exactly what I have found, Grandma. I love my job, I love being a mother to Daryn, I have a nice home and very good friends. I'm happy."

"That's all I ever wanted for any of my children or grandchildren. I don't know what's gone wrong with the rest. Your grandfather always said I was too critical and had too high expectations, which made the kids rebel and do the opposite of what I said, even when it was to their own detriment. But I did the best I knew how."

"I'm sure you did, Grandma. And they aren't so bad, really. Mom lives in her own fantasy world, but she seems happy now with Bob. The boys and I are all doing well enough, despite the instability of our childhoods. Treva loves being a grandmother to Harper and Abby and her daughters are successful in their careers. Uncle Nelson always seems content, and his boys are fine, even if Mike seems to be going through a rough patch. As Tate has pointed out to me a few times this weekend, all families have their baggage and issues. Ours just tend to air their problems more openly than some."

Grandma glanced at Tate, who was somewhat of a captive audience to their conversation. "I guess that's true."

"I did need a break from the family," Kim admitted. "I had to concentrate on my own life for a while. Daryn was an unexpected development, and I needed to deal with the resulting changes on my own. But I am glad I came this weekend, even though I allowed myself to be persuaded to do so under false pretenses. It's been nice seeing you again, Grandma. I'm sorry I deceived you."

"I forgive you, Kim. Just don't let Betsy manipulate you like that again."

"No, I won't. Anyway, now you see why I can't accept your ring."

"The ring is still yours," her grandmother shocked her by stating flatly. "I want you to take it."

"But I can't! I—"

"It's yours," Grandma repeated, her tone even more determined now. "It was foolish of me to use the ring as an incentive for any of my grandkids to enter into a lasting marriage. Maybe I've been right about the unsuitability of their matches so far, but who am I to judge, really? You're my oldest granddaughter, daughter of my oldest daughter, so it seems only natural for it to be passed down to you.

"Besides which," she added with a shake of her head, "you're the only one in the bunch who'd risk telling the truth rather than just take the ring. You're the one with the courage to walk away from the drama rather than get bogged down in it. And you're the only one who ever sent me thank-you notes when I gave you gifts for Christmas and graduations. Of all my grandchildren, I think you're the most like me—and while you may not think of that as a compliment, it's meant as one."

The rare glimpse of self-deprecating humor made Kim smile, even though her eyes burned with emotion. "What about Patty and Cara Lynn? They could be offended that you've given me the ring."

"You let me handle that." Grandma had returned to her brusque, regal tone now. "It's my ring, I can give it to whoever I want. And let's be honest, it's not exactly the Hope Diamond. It's a pretty little bauble, but you wouldn't be set for life by selling it."

"I wouldn't sell it, anyway. I'll treasure it and save it to give to Daryn someday."

Her grandmother nodded. "Do what you want with it, it's yours now."

Kim swallowed hard, knowing her grandmother would not appreciate an excessive show of emotion. "What are we going to do now? Should we just go out there and tell everyone the truth, and let Mom handle the fallout?"

"Let me think about that awhile. Don't say anything to her, you just carry on the way you have been for now. I'll decide what to do about Betsy. The truth will come out. And I'll make sure she's the one who confesses to the others. But perhaps we won't do it today. Frankly, I don't want this gathering to end on such an unpleasant note."

"Um, Grandma?"

"Don't worry, I'm not going to disown her or ban her from my house. Frankly, I need her—well, I need Bob. That fine man has been very helpful to me during the past few years. I only hope she keeps him around until I'm gone. Maybe she will. It won't be that much longer."

Kim felt a lump develop in her throat. "Don't say that, Grandma."

Her grandmother merely shrugged matter-of-factly. "We're not going to get maudlin, but you and I are the kind to face the truth, Kim. I'm glad you decided to come today."

She pushed herself up to clutch the walker, nodding to Tate as he rose ultracarefully with Daryn. "Despite the circumstances, I'm glad you came, too, young man. Kim is fortunate to have such a good friend."

"I have to admit I've had a great time," Tate confessed with a grin. "It's been—interesting."

Grandma gave a rusty chuckle and winked at Kim. "This one's got a mischievous streak."

"Yes, he does," Kim agreed with a smile that was still a bit shaky.

"Reminds me of your grandfather."

Grandma moved toward the door with a hint of spryness belied by her halting steps. Transferring Daryn to Kim, Tate moved quickly to open the door for the older woman. She nodded her thanks to him, then glanced over her shoulder at her granddaughter as she left the room.

"You'd be foolish not to consider turning this make-believe romance into a real one," she said with characteristic bluntness. "You're no fool, Kim."

Her cheeks warming, Kim stuffed the ring box into her pocket with her free hand and followed her grandmother out of the room without looking at Tate.

Most of the others were preparing for departure when Kim, Tate and Grandma rejoined them. Patty supervised as her girls and Lucas packed away their toys. Stacks of leftovers in covered plastic dishes sat ready to be dispersed. Bags and purses were stacked on a table by the door. No one had yet slipped out, since doing so without saying goodbye to Grandma Dyess was sternly frowned upon, but several were notably impatient to be on their way.

Despite all the earlier squabbling, obligatory hugs and kisses were shared all around.

"It was very nice to finally meet you, Tate," Treva said as Kim and Tate took their leave. "Let us know if your little book ever finds a publisher. I'm sure the garden club would love to have you come for a signing."

"I'll let you know," he replied, a smile in his eyes.

Treva kissed Daryn's cheek, though the sleepy child barely stirred in response to the contact. "Be sure and call if you have any questions about toddlers, Kim. My Patty is quite the expert with that stage now. Of course, both my granddaughters were crawling by nine months, and Harper walked by eleven months."

Kim had always refused to put herself in competition with her cousins, and she certainly wasn't going to do so with her child. "It was nice to see you again, Aunt Treva," she said, ignoring the comments about the girls.

"Maybe you'll come see us again before Daryn starts school."

Even that was a little dig, but Kim answered politely, "I'll certainly try."

Treva nodded. "And Tate, I hope you'll still be around to come with her."

He merely chuckled with a wry shake of his head at Kim.

"Your aunt is so going to love it when your mother's deception is exposed," Tate observed when he was back behind the wheel of Kim's car a few minutes later. "I could almost feel sorry for Betsy."

Seeing that Daryn had settled into her car seat with Mr. Jingles, awake again now despite having missed the long nap she usually took in the afternoons, Kim turned back to Tate. "She brought it on herself. However Grandma decides to handle it, Mom deserves any consequences she gets."

"That's true, but it will still be embarrassing for her."

"Maybe. Or she'll find a way to make it all my fault, somehow. She's pretty good at that."

"She doesn't quite understand you, you know. Maybe she rewrites your life so she can identify with you a bit more easily."

"Maybe. That doesn't make it right," Kim said.

"She definitely lives in her own little universe, doesn't she?"

"Yes, she does. And she allows the rest of us to join her there only if we play by her rules."

Tate shrugged. "My mother has her own little world, too. It's a bit more grounded in reality than Betsy's, but Mom likes to maintain her comfortable illusions, especially when it comes to Lynette and me. Maybe it's a mother thing. Maybe someday you'll do the same with Daryn."

"Not the way my mother does." She was appalled by the very suggestion.

Tate laughed. "No. Not like your mother."

He parked at the curb of her mother's house.

"We won't be staying," she told him. "Mom invited us for dinner, but I told her I just want to get the rest of Daryn's things and head home. We can stop to eat somewhere along the way, if that's okay with you."

Already it was going to be around 9:00 p.m. by the time they got to her house, and that was if they didn't dwell long over dinner. Daryn would sleep in her car seat, but still she needed to be in her bed. Besides which, Kim had taken just about all of her family she could deal with for one weekend.

"Whatever you want to do. I'm not hungry yet, anyway."

With Bob helping Tate load up, it took only a few minutes for everything to be ready to go. Betsy was a bit more subdued than usual as she watched them prepare to leave. Whether because she was truly sorry to see them go, or because Grandma had given her a hint of what was to come, Kim couldn't have said.

Carrying Daryn and trailed by Tate, Kim searched out her brothers. Stuart was already on the couch with his computer again, his expression more distantly sullen than usual. He looked up when Kim stood in front of him.

"I'm leaving now," she said. "I wanted to say goodbye to you first."

He nodded. "Okay. See you."

She frowned, finding his brusque words unsatisfying. Granted, she hardly knew Stuart, since he'd been just a kid when she'd left home, but it would have been nice if they could have treated each other as a little more than strangers.

"Good luck with starting college next week. I'm sure you'll do very well."

"Yeah, thanks, Kim. I, uh, used the money you sent me for graduation for supplies. Thanks again."

He had sent her an awkwardly worded thank-you note at the time. She'd received it with a pang of sadness that they had never had a chance to grow closer. "You're welcome again. See you later, Stuart."

He nodded, giving a little wave to Daryn. "See you, kid."

"Say bye-bye to Uncle Stuart, Daryn."

Stuart blinked, and Kim thought he looked startled to hear himself referred to by that title. Had he not thought of himself in that manner before with Daryn?

Kim stood back to allow Tate to step forward and offer a hand to the teen. "It was nice to meet you, Stuart."

"Yeah. So…I'll see you around. Maybe."

Without giving Tate a real chance to respond, Stuart turned his attention back to his computer, letting his shaggy hair fall over his face to hide his expression.

Torn between regret and annoyance, Kim turned to Julian. "So long, Julian."

He surprised her by brushing a kiss against her cheek. "Tate seems like a decent guy," he said quietly. "I hope things work out for you two."

"Um, Julian, you need to talk to Mom when we leave, okay? And before you do, let me just say ahead of time that I'm sorry."

Her brother looked confused. "Sorry about what?"

"Just talk to Mom." She swallowed hard, wondering if either of her brothers would ever forgive her. Even though they had to know how hard it was to keep from getting pulled into their mother's schemes, she wouldn't blame them for directing some of their inevitable resentment in her direction.

Still looking confused, Julian shook hands with Tate. "Maybe we can talk cars again sometime soon."

"I'd like that," Tate replied with obvious sincerity. "I've enjoyed meeting you, Julian."

"Yeah, you, too." Remembering his niece, Julian somewhat awkwardly tickled Daryn's tummy in farewell.

Betsy and Bob stood beside the car to say their goodbyes. Betsy hugged Daryn and snuggled kisses against her cheek and neck until Kim finally retrieved the baby so she could strap her into her car seat.

Making sure Daryn was secure, and that Mr. Jingles was within her reach, Kim turned then to her mother. "Bye, Mom."

"Goodbye, dear. Call soon?"

"Oh, I figure I'll be talking to you soon." She expected her mother would express her displeasure that Kim had leveled with Grandma Dyess about her relationship with Tate.

Oblivious, Betsy nodded. "Good."

She gave Kim a smacking kiss on the cheek, then turned to throw her arms around Tate. "I'm so glad you could come, dear. I hope you'll be back soon."

"Um—" At a loss for how to respond to that, Tate settled for a wry smile toward Kim and a noncommittal, "Goodbye, Betsy."

Shaking her head in exasperation, Kim turned to take her leave of Bob. Who knew if she would ever see him again? She wouldn't blame him at all if he took to his heels after this.

She held out her hand. "It was very nice to see you again, Bob."

Ignoring the extended hand, he swept her into an affectionate hug. "Thanks so much for coming. It meant a lot to your mother. Next time, we'll make it a little easier for you. I'll see to it."

It was nice of him to say so, but she wasn't making any more bets this weekend. Especially on such a shaky basis.

Tate and Bob shook hands warmly, and then Tate and Kim belted themselves into the car. Kim did not look back over her shoulder as Tate drove away from the house. The weekend was over, and the make-believe along with it. It was time for a return to reality.

Kim was very quiet during the initial half of the trip home. Tate wasn't sure if she was tired or overwhelmed or both, but it bothered him that he sensed undertones of sadness in her mood. When they'd started out this weekend, he'd hoped she would see the adventure as a lark. Fun. He'd realized rather quickly that he'd been unrealistic with that expectation; there was too much going on in Kim's family for her to find a great deal of humor in the situation. But he hadn't wanted her to leave sad.

They chose an inviting-looking family restaurant just over halfway through the drive. Daryn sat in a high chair, so Kim's hands were free to feed her and herself. Because he felt as though he should, Tate offered to help, but Kim politely declined any assistance. She was very much back into independence mode, he noted.

He figured she would make an effort to get things quickly back to usual between them. She started during the meal, chatting about her work and his, about their friends and routines back at home, anything but the family gathering they had just attended. He went along, teasing with her and laughing at Daryn's attempts to help herself to food off their plates.

"I don't blame you, kid," he said to the baby. "I'd rather have steak and grilled veggies than pureed food myself."

He speared a grill-marked cauliflower floret and popped it into his mouth, aware that Daryn watched his every move. "And now you're making me feel guilty," he told her after swallowing.

Kim chuckled. "She'd better stick to the pureed stuff until she has more than two little teeth nubbins."

She spooned another bite of baby food into her daughter's mouth, and Daryn seemed happy enough to accept it, though she still eyed Tate's plate in a way that made him scoot it a bit farther out of her reach.

"Maybe she could have some ice cream for dessert?" he suggested, nodding toward the open dessert bar with the soft-freeze dispenser at the end.

"No, she doesn't need all that sugar."

"Oh. Right." Another one of those things he hadn't considered. It was a very good thing he wasn't responsible for a kid's nutrition, he reminded himself.

Maybe Kim was afraid she'd hurt his feelings by shooting down his suggestion. "I have a little jar of unsweetened applesauce in the bag. She loves that for dessert."

"Sounds like a much healthier option," he assured her with a smile.

"Feel free to have ice cream if you want."

"As tempting as it sounds, I'd better skip it tonight. I've had more than enough sweets today."

"I see applesauce on the dessert bar," she teased.

He chuckled. "Maybe I'll have some of that. What do you think, Daryn? If it's good enough for you, it should be good enough for me, right?"

Daryn babbled at him in response. He thought he probably should have been grossed out by the mouthful of pureed peas revealed by her grin, but she just looked too darned cute.

Kim swiped efficiently with a napkin, encouraging her daughter to swallow. Figuring he'd better let the kid finish her dinner, Tate concentrated on his own.

Kim seemed to have relaxed a little by the time they were on the road again, which pleased him, but he thought he still sensed a little melancholy in the car.

He gave her a few more minutes, then spoke quietly over the softly playing radio. "Want to talk about it?"

"About what?" she asked without looking away from the side window.

"The weekend. Your mother. Whatever you might need to talk about."

She shrugged. "I'm good, thanks."

Keeping his eyes on the road ahead, he said casually, "I'm a good listener, you know. I've heard you vent about other things before, just as you've heard me complain about various annoyances in the past, so if you want to unload..."

She glanced back at her snoozing child, then faced the front again. "Really, I'm okay. But thanks."

"Anytime."

Another three miles passed before Kim spoke again. "It's just so messed up."

He murmured something both unintelligible and encouraging, leaving it entirely up to her how much she wanted to share.

"My grandmother is in terrible health, my brothers don't seem to like me very much, my mother is bug-nuts and my cousins are probably going to hate me when they find out Grandma gave me her ring when I'm not even married."

Out of that spate of words, several things stood out to him, but one phrase in particular made him have to fight an inappropriate smile. "Um—bug-nuts?"

"It was one of the kinder descriptions I could come up with," Kim muttered.

Replaying her other words in his mind, he decided to try to address a couple of her concerns. "As for your grandmother's ring, she has a right to give it to whomever she wants. It made sense that she would pass it down to the daughter of her older daughter. Your aunt and cousins will probably pout some, but honestly, wouldn't one or the other pout no matter who got the ring?"

"Well, yes, but—"

"Let them argue with your grandmother if they're unhappy with her decision."

"They wouldn't dare."

"Exactly. And they know you'd have no more success in doing so."

"I suppose that's true."

He could think of nothing to say to reassure her about her grandmother's health. Instead, he asked, "What makes you think your brothers don't like you?"

Her hand fluttered in her lap. "You saw them. Stuart wouldn't even get up from the couch to say goodbye."

"First, Stuart is a teenager. Teenage boys aren't known for being warm and demonstrative, especially with their older siblings."

She gave a little sigh. "I know. I guess I was just hoping for a little more."

Tate hesitated a moment, trying to decide how to phrase his next words. "I think Stuart wants more, too. And I think he's a little angry with you because it isn't there."

That seemed to catch her attention. She turned her head to look at him then. "You think Stuart is angry with me?"

He nodded. "Maybe a little. Maybe not even entirely consciously. But let's face it, you haven't been home in three years, and only sporadically before that, you've said. Kids take that sort of thing rather personally. Didn't you?"

"I…never thought of it that way," she admitted reluctantly. "I had to get away from home for my own sake, but I never considered that my staying away would hurt Stuart. He's so much younger than I am and he always seemed so self-contained. The kind of kid who entertained himself for the most part and hardly seemed to notice I was around. I figured my being gone just gave him more attention from Mom."

"You're still his big sister. Maybe he won't or can't express his feelings to you, but I'd bet he would like very much to get to know you better."

"I'd like to know him better, too," she murmured wistfully.

Tate kept his voice gentle. "It's not too late, Kim. Heck, I hardly even spoke to Lynette before I turned eighteen, and now she and I are pretty close. Granted, there's not as much of an age gap between us, but I think you and Stuart could still find common ground."

"If he ever speaks to me again after finding out I lied to him about you."

Tate shook his head. "You didn't lie, your mother did. There's your common ground right there. You can sympathize with each other about having a mother who's, er, bug-nuts."

"Maybe. I'll send him an email of explanation and apology once I know Mom's come clean with everyone. Stuart's probably easier to reach through his computer than by phone call."

"Very likely. You can ask him about school, maybe consult him about a computer issue, letting him feel like you need his advice for something. Tell him a few funny stories about his niece. It seemed to catch his attention when you referred to him as Uncle Stuart."

"Yes, I noticed that."

"He kind of liked the idea of being an uncle. Stuart's as hungry for stability as you have been, Kim. I could tell he rather likes Bob, but—"

"But he's afraid to let himself get too attached," Kim cut in knowingly. "It hurts too much to say goodbye to another father figure."

"Something tells me Bob will win him over. He's almost there now."

"I'm not sure that's such a good thing. I'd hate to see Stuart hurt again."

"It's impossible to avoid all hurt and disappointment in life. But you know? I wouldn't be surprised if Bob stays around for a while. Despite all your mother's, um, eccentricities, he seems crazy about her. I think he just likes having a fixer-upper project underway at all times, and your mom gives him plenty of challenge in that respect."

"I like him," Kim admitted with a reluctance Tate fully understood.

"So do I."

A moment later, she asked, "Since you seem to know so much about my brothers, what about Julian? Is he angry with me, too?"

"Oh, Julian's pissed off at everyone right now," he answered lightly. "Starting with his ex-wife and including you and his mother. He's going to be even madder at both of you when he finds out about me, but I think he'll get over it. It's going to take some groveling on your part. Maybe a few tears. But he'll come around. He's not quite ready to cut all ties with the family, any more than you are."

"Groveling and tears, huh?" As he'd hoped, his wry words had roused a faint smile from her.

"Maybe a shipment of homemade brownies. I noticed your brother has a weakness for chocolate."

"I usually make brownies from a boxed mix. But I make a pretty decent chocolate cake from scratch."

"That would probably suffice."

He glanced at her with a sympathetic smile. "But, seriously, Kim, Julian will come around if you explain to him exactly what happened. Don't leave that entirely up to your mom. Who knows what she'd tell him?"

"I'll talk to him. Thanks for the advice."

"Just giving you a guy's perspective. For what it's worth."

"It's worth quite a bit. You've given me a lot to think about."

He shrugged. "I'm hardly a family dynamics expert. But like I said, I know how guys tend to think."

She seemed to be struck by his observation that Julian was angry with everyone. "Julian was so besotted with Mindy. Everyone thought he rushed her into marriage because he didn't want to leave her single while he was off at boot camp and then deployed. Maybe it was inevitable that she cheated on him while he was gone. She just wasn't really ready to get married from the start."

"Makes sense. But he'll recover. He's still young."

He thought about asking if Kim still had feelings for Daryn's father, but something held him back. A disconcerting little voice deep inside him hinted that his reluctance could be because wasn't sure he really wanted to hear her answer.

Kim sat back in her seat and looked out the side window again, listening to the music. While she was rather quiet for the remainder of the ride to her house, Tate believed she was more thoughtful now than sad. He hoped he'd managed to cheer her at least a little.

A soft chime from the backseat made him glance in the rearview mirror. Daryn was still groggy, but had shifted in the seat, and her toy monkey had fallen to the floor. Kim reached back to retrieve it and replace it in her daughter's arms, then patted Daryn's arm lovingly before turning back around.

Tate frowned at the road ahead. That Chris guy who'd walked away from Kim and their daughter had to be an idiot. While Tate might not be looking for a ready-made family of his own, Kim and Daryn made a pretty irresistible pair. If Chris had a lick of sense, he'd have done whatever it took to keep them in his life.

Kim carried the baby into her house, and Tate followed with a couple of bags. She unlocked the door and led him inside, then turned to him in the living room. "I need to give Daryn a bottle and put her to bed now. I'll bring the rest of the things in from the car later."

"Go take care of your daughter. I'll unload the car."

"It's late. I'm sure you're ready to get home."

He gave her a look and spoke with a laugh. "Kim. It's nine o'clock. Only to the mother of a nine-month-old is that considered late on a Saturday night."

She smiled wryly. "I guess you're right. Thank you."

He nodded and took a couple of steps closer to look at Daryn, who was awake, but drowsily resting her head against Kim's shoulder. "Good night, kid. It's been fun."

Kim glanced down to see Daryn give Tate a sweet, sleepy smile. And then the child offered Tate her beloved Mr. Jingles.

Tate looked as startled by the gesture as Kim felt. He smiled crookedly, then tucked the toy back into Daryn's arms. "Thanks, Daryn, but I think you need this guy more than I do. You sleep well, you hear?"

Daryn giggled. Swallowing hard, Kim turned somewhat quickly and carried her daughter off to the nursery, where she changed her diaper and dressed her in a soft little sleeper. Daryn was too sleepy to drink more than half her bottle, but she'd had plenty. Kim kissed her and tucked her and Mr. Jingles into the crib.

Only then did she look toward the door, wiping her slightly damp palms down the legs of her pants. She'd heard the front door open and close a few times while she was putting Daryn to bed, but she wasn't sure if Tate was still in there. Would he have driven away without saying goodbye? She hadn't heard his truck.

Leaving the nursery, she realized she was still wearing the band Lynette had lent her. She twisted at it as she entered the living room. Her finger had swollen a little during the warm, active day and the ring seemed tighter now than it had when she'd put it on. She thought she might have to resort to soaping her finger to get the band to slide off.

Seeing her difficulty, Tate stepped forward when she entered the room. "Here, let me help you with that."

Before she could argue, he had her left hand in both of his, his head bent next to hers. He tugged lightly at the ring, which didn't budge. "Wow, that's tight."

She swallowed and tried to speak casually, as if she weren't aware of how very closely he stood to her. "Yes. I think my hand swelled a little during the car ride."

His eyes met hers. "I don't want to hurt you."

She moistened her lips automatically. "Um—don't worry, I won't let you do that."

They were still talking about the ring, right?

"Good. So maybe if I just do this quickly…"

Expecting a tug on her ring finger, she was shocked when he covered her mouth with his instead.

Chapter Eight

Kim was so startled she simply froze for a moment, unable to either respond or draw back from the wholly unexpected kiss. Even as she told herself she should put a stop to this and quickly, she found herself melting into him.

How could this happen every time he kissed her? Shouldn't the effects have lessened at least a little after the first time or two? Should it be getting harder every time to remind herself why kissing Tate Price was not a good idea?

One kiss, she promised herself.

Okay, two.

By the time they finally surfaced for oxygen, she'd lost count.

Somehow she'd ended up wrapped around him like a vine on a fencepost. She didn't immediately disentangle herself, but frowned sternly at him with her face still inches from his. "This is a really bad idea."

As closely as she was pressed against him, she could tell exactly how aroused he was by their kisses, though he nodded in agreement with her words. "You're right. Very bad idea."

He brushed his lips across her forehead and she shivered a little. "We have to stop," she said with a soft moan.

He drew back. "Okay."

She looked at him somberly, then found herself kissing him again. This time she couldn't have said who started it. Nor who unfastened the first button, or dragged first at a shirt hem.

"Still a bad idea," she muttered even as she half dragged him toward her bedroom.

He planted kisses on her ear, her lips, her chin. "I know."

"And it doesn't change a thing between us." She kicked off her shoes.

"No," he agreed, making her shudder with a well-placed stroke.

"Starting Monday, everything goes back to usual."

"Okay. Sure."

"We're just…scratching an itch."

"A little more than that," he corrected, rolling with her on the bed.

"Nothing serious," she insisted, arching her neck when he pressed his lips to the pounding pulse in her throat. "Just this once."

"Probably for the best," he agreed, stringing a line of kisses down to the center of her chest.

Her breasts tightened in eager anticipation. It was

growing increasingly difficult to even think clearly, much less form halfway intelligible words. "And none of our…"

She squirmed, moaned softly, then tried to complete her sentence. "None of our friends need to know about this. Your sister—"

"This is none of her business."

"No, but—oh, Tate…"

Raising his head, he looked at her in the deeply shadowed bedroom. His hair was tumbled around his face, and she could see his eyes glittering almost feverishly in the dim light. "Kim. I can leave now and we'll put this behind us. Or I can stay. Your call."

She reminded herself that she liked being in charge. That she didn't want other people making decisions for her. That she wasn't the type to appreciate being swept off her feet by a handsome prince who would take care of all potential consequences for her. It might have been easier, though, if she could have just left it all up to Tate.

Because she wasn't that dependent type, she drew a deep breath and reached for the drawer in the nightstand. The box she kept stashed there had not been needed in a long while, but she would take no more careless chances in that respect.

"Stay," she said, setting the box within easy reach. "Just this once."

His lips only a breath from hers, he smiled. "What did I tell you about the next time we shared a bed?"

She tangled her hands in his hair. "Just shut up and kiss me, Price."

He chuckled. "Yes, dear."

* * *

Kim lay on her back against her pillows, staring blindly at the bedroom ceiling and wondering if her breathing would ever return to a slow, steady pace. She'd already given up on her heart rate returning to normal. But she didn't want to think about her heart at that moment.

She distracted herself by glancing sideways. Her eyes had long since adjusted to the dim light seeping through the curtains, so she could see Tate clearly enough as he lay beside her, his own breathing still ragged in the otherwise quiet room.

She held the top sheet loosely over her breasts, but Tate had tossed it aside. For consideration of her budget during these hot summer months, she kept the central air-conditioning set just cool enough to be comfortable. The fine sheet of sweat glistening on Tate's chest was an indication of how energetic they had been. She could feel a thin film of dampness on her own skin.

She wasn't sure how she should be feeling just then. She wouldn't say she regretted her decision, exactly. She didn't believe in living with regrets. She did, however, try not to make the same mistakes more than once. Giving in to her attraction to Tate could be filed under the mistake category.

Which did not mean that the attraction had passed. Just lying there looking at him made her pulse jump again. At this rate, her vital signs would never return to normal.

He turned his head to smile at her. "Would it be uncool of me to say *Wow?*"

She couldn't help but smile. "Yes."

"Oh. Then consider it unsaid. I'm trying to be cool here."

Rolling onto her side, she curled her right arm beneath her head, resting her cheek on her hand. "I think that's a lost cause."

Turning to face her, he chuckled. "You don't think I'm cool?"

"I think you're a very nice guy."

She wasn't sure why that compliment made him wince. "Ouch."

"Nice guy is an insult?"

"Nice guy is a pal. A dude who's steady and reliable and as exciting as boiled oatmeal."

She was laughing before he finished his descriptive litany. How could he make her laugh even now, after just turning her world on end?

"You are not boiled oatmeal. But you are still a nice guy. I think you knew my ego and my disposition took a beating this weekend, and you made me feel much better. Thank you for that."

Tate sighed lightly. "If you're actually thanking me for making love with you, then save your breath. There was nothing altruistic about it. I've been attracted to you since the day Lynette introduced us, and spending this time with you just made that even clearer to me.

"I know you aren't looking for anything serious," he added quickly, before she could speak. "And you know I haven't been, either, at this point in my life. But I wasn't able to resist acting quite selfishly on that attraction just this once."

He seemed to have chosen just the right words to put her even more at ease. He'd somehow managed to soothe her bruised ego even further with his compliments, yet reassure her at the same time that he expected nothing more from her than this.

She met his gaze frankly. “I don’t want things to be awkward between us now. I know better than to say we should just forget this ever happened—I doubt that either of us will completely forget—but I hope we can still be comfortable during our lunch gatherings.”

“I see no reason why we can’t. If we managed to convince your entire family we’re married, I don’t see why we can’t act as though nothing at all has changed between us in front of our friends and my sister.”

Though he was teasing, she nodded thoughtfully. “I suppose you’re right.”

“Haven’t you figured out by now that I’m always right?”

Lightly, she punched his arm. “You’re always full of hot air, you mean.”

Catching her hand, he brushed a kiss across her knuckles. “You wound me with your callous words.”

She laughed, feeling as though he’d just made her point.

He was grinning when he pressed his lips to hers. Their smiles soon faded into another long, deep kiss.

Kim learned somewhat to her dismay that her reactions to Tate’s kisses had not lessened in the least. Nor had her hunger for him abated, even as sated as she had felt only minutes earlier.

After kissing her until she was a limp puddle on the sheet, Tate caught her earlobe lightly between his teeth before murmuring into her ear. “When you said just this one time, you meant this one night, right?”

“Yes,” she assured him, knowing he knew she lied.

Wrapping her arms around him, she drew him to her. "That's exactly what I meant."

Settling on top of her, he spoke against her lips again. "Let's not waste it, then."

Tate did not want to leave. He felt as though heavy weights were attached to his ankles, making his feet drag when he moved toward the door of Kim's house. There was nothing he'd have liked more than to climb back into bed with her, to make love with her at least once more before the sun rose, and then to wake in her arms to start all over again at dawn.

But that couldn't happen even if Kim wasn't pretty much rushing him out the door, he reminded himself. When morning came, Daryn would expect her mother's undivided attention, and she would have it. Single moms didn't have a lot of free time for flirting and playing.

Looking at Kim, he sighed rather wistfully. She appeared so young and carefree with her hair tousled around her relaxed face, her slender body wrapped in a thin red robe, her bare feet revealing whimsically pink toenails. He couldn't help having a few fleeting fantasies about how it might have been between them had circumstances been different. But they weren't, and Kim's priorities understandably did not include him.

"So," he said, "I guess I'll see you at lunch Wednesday?"

She nodded. "As far as I know."

He hesitated before reaching for the doorknob. "About those silly bets…"

Her mouth quirked into a half smile, half grimace.

"I owe you fifty dollars. I'm the one who spilled the beans to Grandma, after all."

"Actually, the bet was that you would unintentionally give us away," he reminded her. "Had you not chosen to be honest, no one would have suspected a thing. So I think I'm the one who lost the bet."

"I'm not taking your money."

"And I'm not taking yours. It was pretty much a joke, anyway. So let's just call it a draw, shall we?"

She shrugged. "If that's what you want to do."

"I do. As for the bet with Evan—I'm going to pay him the hundred."

Kim's eyes widened in surprise. "Why would you do that? You won the bet, no question. As you said, no one expressed doubts about us. Grandma even gave me her ring, which Lynette said was the ultimate test."

"Right." He ran a hand through his still-mussed hair. "The thing is, it just doesn't feel right turning that sweet gesture into a funny story, you know? I mean, there are plenty of other things to joke about with your family, but your grandmother giving you her ring isn't one of them."

She bit her lower lip, considering his words.

Because he didn't like thinking of tooth marks marring that soft, perfect lip, he reached out to smooth her mouth with one fingertip. "Don't worry about it, Evan won't take the money, anyway. Like I said, the bets were just jokes."

She nodded.

Standing so close to her just made him want to kiss her again. Because he knew where that would lead, he forced himself to take a step back. "You'd better get some rest. Daryn will be up at six."

The words were aimed as much to himself as to her, a reminder of the reason he was leaving when he wanted so badly to stay.

"Yes. Good night, Tate."

Keeping his hands to himself, he brushed a quick kiss over her lips. Just one last taste, he promised himself. "Good night, Kim."

He reached for the doorknob, then paused to look over his shoulder. "You know, maybe we could…I don't know, have pizza or see a movie or something sometime. I mean, you can get a babysitter for a few hours, can't you? Even moms get to have a little time to themselves sometimes, right?"

She was shaking her head before he even finished speaking. "I don't like leaving Daryn with a sitter when I already have to leave her at day care while I work. Any free time I have now belongs to her."

It wasn't his place to argue, of course, but that didn't sound entirely healthy to him. Then again, maybe he was letting himself be influenced by his own selfish interests. "Maybe we could have pizza and a movie here sometime. You know, after she goes to bed."

What was he doing? Hadn't they agreed this was a one-time thing? Not quite as casual as "scratching an itch," as Kim had described it, but not the start of anything more, either. Still, what would it hurt to get together occasionally for a pizza or something? He had a sneaking suspicion of what that "something" entailed, at least in his vague imaginings.

Kim turned him down yet again. "That's not a good idea. I wouldn't be opposed to having the lunch gang over for pizza or something some evening, but as far as you and I are concerned, it's better for everyone involved if we just end it now."

Better for herself and for Daryn, she might as well have said. And okay, maybe better for him, too, but he would have liked to make that decision for himself.

"Yeah, okay. It was just a thought, but I'm sure you know best." He opened the door. "Good night, Kim. See you around."

"Tate?"

He hesitated, half in, half out the door. He didn't look at her, not wanting her to see that his feelings were foolishly hurt by her rejection.

Maybe she sensed it, anyway. "I just want you to know that if it weren't for Daryn—well, I wouldn't be sending you away tonight. And I wouldn't have said no to a pizza or a movie with you. It isn't that I don't want to spend more time with you. It's that I just can't."

He nodded and closed the door behind him on the way out, only partially appeased.

He was being ridiculous to be so annoyed, he told himself as he climbed into his truck and closed the door harder than he should have, considering the late hour. Technically, he agreed with Kim. She wasn't in a position to have a fling, even had she been interested, and he wasn't looking for more right now. Yet no matter how often he reminded himself of those facts, it still irked him that she'd shot him down when he had tentatively suggested they spend more time together.

Must be a male pride thing, he told himself as he drove away from her house. Though his ego had certainly gotten a boost from her earlier in the evening, all she'd had to do was decline his suggestions to deflate it again. He hadn't realized his feelings were quite so delicate when it came to Kim.

He reached out to flip the turn signal level and a glint of gold on his hand reflected a passing streetlight, catching his attention. He realized he still wore his grandfather's wedding band. The ring had felt odd at first, since he rarely wore jewelry other than a serviceable watch. Sometime during the past thirty-six hours or so, he'd grown accustomed to it being there.

He'd forgotten to leave the usual lamp burning in his apartment, so the rooms were dark when he unlocked the door and let himself in. He didn't bother with lights when he crossed the living room into his bedroom; enough illumination filtered in through the blinds for him to find his way easily through the familiar path. Dropping his bags on the floor of the bedroom, he crossed to the dresser where he kept the box for his grandfather's ring in a drawer with a few other miscellaneous, mostly sentimental treasures.

For several long moments, he studied the ring on his hand. And then he removed it, stuffed it into its box and closed the drawer with a snap that echoed through the quiet room.

When Kim's phone rang the next afternoon, her heart beat a bit too quickly as she answered it. She glanced at the ID screen and told herself she was relieved to see Lynette's number. It wasn't that she was expecting anyone else to call, she assured herself quickly. Lynette was simply the least problematic of the list of potential callers just then.

"Hi, Lynn."

"My place. Five o'clock. I'm making veggie lasagna.

Don't say you can't come, I've already started cooking and you know how I hate to cook. Em and I want to hear all the juicy details."

"But I—"

"Five o'clock," her friend repeated. "Emma's bringing dessert. You pick up a loaf of French bread. We'll smear butter and garlic on it and pop it in the oven here. Tell Daryn to bring her own bottle."

Kim smiled ruefully. She knew when she'd be wasting her breath to argue. Besides, she supposed she'd just as soon spend some time laughing with Lynette and Emma than sitting in her living room trying not to think about Tate. She needed to return the wedding band, anyway. "All right. I'll be there."

"Of course. See you."

Lynette disconnected without further ado, leaving Kim laughing. "Looks like we have plans for this evening," she told Daryn, who sat on the floor with her favorite toys gathered around her.

"Mamamama."

"Why, yes, I will have to be careful about what I say," Kim mused aloud. "Lynette might pretend to be a bit of a ditz at times, but she sees a lot more than she lets on."

Daryn blew a raspberry, then giggled at her own wit.

Kim wondered if Lynette had already talked to her brother. She wondered what Tate had said if they'd spoken. She wondered if he was thinking of her at that moment the way she was thinking of him.

And then she wondered in irritation if she was losing her mind.

"Let's go into the kitchen, sweetie," she said, scooping her daughter from the floor. "You can sit in your high chair and eat puffed snacks while I pack something for your dinner tonight."

Daryn seemed perfectly happy with that plan.

After a quick stop at her favorite bakery for a loaf of good bread, she made the short drive to Lynette's apartment complex. With the ease of experience, she threw the strap of the diaper bag over her shoulder, balanced Daryn on her hip and tucked the big loaf of bread beneath the other arm. She closed the car door with her free hip and locked it with the remote fob before heading toward Lynette's door.

Her friend's apartment opened to the outside on the top floor of the three-story building. There was no elevator, so Kim climbed the two flights of metal stairs leading up to the top landing. Lynette's was the last door down.

Kim paused at the end of the landing to admire the scenery. The immaculately landscaped complex grounds ended at a raised, grassy levy, beyond which lay the south bank of the swiftly flowing Arkansas River. Tall rock bluffs rose on the other side of the river; to the east lay downtown Little Rock. To the west lay the 4,226-foot long pedestrian and biking structure known as the "Big Dam Bridge" over the Murray Lock and Dam. Before she'd had Daryn, Kim had biked across that bridge many times, enjoying the view from ninety feet above the river surface. She had little time for biking these days, though she hoped to buy a bike seat for Daryn next spring and get back out on the trails.

Holding the bread beneath her arm, she tapped on Lynette's door, expecting Lynette or Emma to open it.

She did not expect to see Tate on the other side of the door.

He smiled easily at her, though his eyes focused on her face with more than usual intensity. "Hi, Kim. Come on in."

Had Lynette deliberately forgotten to mention that her brother would be here this evening? And if so, why?

"Hi, Tate."

Seeing the familiar face, Daryn grinned and shook Mr. Jingles at him.

"Hey, Daryn. How's it going, kiddo?"

She babbled a response, making Tate chuckle. "Yeah, okay. Whatever you say."

Lynette rushed forward to take the bread and greet Kim with a hug and Daryn with a smacking kiss. "I can't wait to hear your stories," she teased Kim. "Tate wouldn't tell us a thing. He said since it's your family, you're the one who gets to decide which stories get told."

Emma reached out her hands to Daryn, who dove willingly into the welcoming arms, always amenable to extra attention. Kim set the diaper bag on the floor at the end of the couch, greeting Evan, who had risen when she'd entered.

"Tate won't even tell me whether I won the bet," Evan complained. "He keeps saying it's a draw, so no money will be changing hands. That doesn't even make sense."

"He just doesn't want to take your money," Kim said without looking at Tate. Smiling brightly, she added, "He won the bet, fair and square. No one in my family had any reason to doubt that he was exactly who my mother said he was."

Lynette hooted victoriously. "I told you he could do it," she bragged to Evan and Emma. "Tate's a great actor."

"I didn't have to do a thing," Tate corrected her, looking uncharacteristically uncomfortable. "No one even questioned it. We simply visited Kim's family for a few hours, then headed back home. Piece of cake. Hardly worth a hundred-dollar payoff."

"Okay, fine. Lunch is on me Wednesday," Evan said. "For everyone."

"You're on," Lynette said quickly, as if to accept before he could change his mind.

Evan laughed. "Deal."

Lynette headed toward the kitchen. "Okay, I'm putting this bread in to brown and then you two can tell us everything while we eat."

Kim glanced toward Tate, then looked away quickly. They wouldn't be telling everything, of course. Which didn't mean she wouldn't be thinking of those things while they shared their carefully edited version of their adventure. She was sure Tate would be thinking of those things, too, which would make her even more self-conscious when she met his eyes.

She had hoped for a few days' break from him, a chance to pack away her memories of their lovemaking along with some of her other treasured moments, to regain her equilibrium around him so she could think of him again as nothing more than a very good friend. Today her feelings were still too raw, those memories still too close to the surface. She wasn't sure Wednesday would be far enough away for her to get her emotions entirely under control, but at least she'd have had a few extra days to work on it.

She called on all the acting skills she had barely needed at the family reunion to get through dinner with her friends without revealing her inner turmoil. Apparently she succeeded well enough. Laughter reigned around the table. Sitting in a high chair borrowed from Lynette's next door neighbor—an older woman who frequently babysat her small grandchildren—Daryn contributed to the general frivolity with happy crows and bangs of the wooden spoon Lynette had found for her.

"I don't know why I buy toys for her," Kim observed after one particularly enthusiastic episode of tray-top drumming. "All she needs to make her happy is a wooden spoon."

"Well, that and this monkey," Tate added, scooping the toy from the floor yet again and handing it back to Daryn with a wink that made her crow and kick.

"You and the kid seem to be getting along well enough," Evan observed.

"You could say we have an understanding. She throws the monkey, I retrieve it for her, she laughs and then we both go back to what we were doing."

So far all the anecdotes they had shared had been humorous ones, but Kim thought Tate deserved credit for his act of heroism yesterday. As for herself, she would always be grateful to him. "It's a little more than that. Tate saved Daryn's life yesterday."

"What?" Emma gasped.

"Are you kidding?" Evan asked doubtfully, looking from Kim to Tate and back again.

"Tell," Lynette demanded.

Kim gave a succinct recounting of Tate's quick-thinking rescue of the choking baby. All three of the others were staring at him in open-mouthed admiration when she finished.

"It wasn't quite as dramatic as all that," he muttered, a touch of pink on his cheeks that Kim found endearing—to her exasperation.

"My uncle said her lips were turning blue," she insisted. "If Tate hadn't been there, I don't know what would have happened."

"And you said you aren't any good with babies," Lynette chided her brother, her eyes glowing with pride for him.

He shrugged. "I'd have reacted the same way if Kim had choked. I was taught that the procedure for choking is very similar with adults and babies, you just have to be a little more careful with babies. Of course, all of you trained in first aid and CPR, so you know that."

"I had CPR training back in college, but I'm not sure I'd have kept my head enough to remember it," Evan admitted, warily eyeing the now-healthy baby. "I might have been one of those standing on the sidelines panicking."

"I've got to admit I just reacted without thinking. After it was over, I went straight to the nearest bathroom and threw cold water on my face," Tate confessed. "It's not something I ever want to have to do again."

Kim looked at him with a frown, wondering if it were true about the cold water. He certainly sounded sincere.

"So you won't be volunteering to babysit anytime soon?" Evan teased him.

Tate laughed and held up both hands toward Daryn in a sigh of surrender. "Being wholly responsible for that little angel would scare the stuffing out of me."

Kim focused very hard on her nearly finished meal. She kept being reminded of why it was just as well she hadn't woven any romantic fantasies around her night with Tate.

"So, your aunt wasn't as tough an audience as you expected?" Emma asked after a moment, apparently wanting more funny stories about the reunion.

Tate chuckled. "Considering the first words I heard her say to Kim was that if she worked hard, she could lose all that leftover prcgnancy weight…"

Both Emma and Lynette gasped in outrage.

"Oh, no, she didn't!" Lynette said dramatically.

"Oh, yes, she did." Kim's smile was rueful.

Emma scowled. "Why, that old biddy. She's completely wrong, of course. You're in excellent shape, Kim."

"I'll say," Evan agreed with a teasing leer that was a nice little boost for her ego.

Tate cleared his throat rather loudly. "Treva isn't really an old biddy. She's not even fifty yet. But she certainly can be catty."

"It sounds like it was a very interesting weekend," Emma decided.

"*Interesting* is a good word for it," Kim agreed in a murmur.

"Do you think you'll go back and see them again?" Emma asked.

Kim hesitated a moment, then shrugged. "I guess I'll wait and see how everyone reacts to Mother's confession about Tate and me."

"You really think she's going to 'fess up?"

Kim nodded in response to Evan's question. "Just before I left, Grandma told me that she's giving her a choice of doing it herself or risking being humiliated by having Grandma break the news at the worst possible opportunity. Like in front of the church or garden club. As it is, she's giving her a chance to present herself in the best light by telling everyone she was simply embarrassed to admit that I had a child out of wedlock, so she made up a husband for me."

"That's the *best* light?" Lynette scoffed.

"I guess so. Anyway, Grandma said she was going to tell everyone I gave in to my mother's pleas and brought a good friend with me to the reunion, but she's going to point out that I never once introduced Tate as my husband. That way, maybe they won't lump me in with Mother's lies."

Lynette propped her elbow on the table and rested her chin in her hand. "You said you confessed to your grandmother because you felt bad about deceiving her. I guess the subject of her ring never came up?"

Kim and Tate shared a look across the table.

"Kim's grandmother is in very poor health," Tate said carefully. "I doubt that Kim wants to talk about her possessions right now."

"Oh, of course." Lynette looked at Kim guiltily. "Sorry, Kim, I wasn't thinking."

Daryn saved her from having to respond by tossing a handful of puffed baby treats into the air with a squeal that sounded much like, "Whee!"

Everyone laughed, which pleased Daryn so much that she performed a bit more while Kim and Tate scooped up puffed treats from the floor.

Kim didn't linger long after dinner. "I need to get Daryn back on to her usual schedule," she explained to her hostess. "I'll see you at work tomorrow, okay?"

"Of course."

"Oh, I almost forgot." She dug into an outer pocket of the diaper bag for the carefully wrapped wedding band. "Here you go. Thanks, Lynette."

"You're welcome. I enjoyed watching my brother squirm." Lynette glanced across the room to where Tate and Evan were absorbed in conversation about business. "So, Kim…you and Tate—you got along well this weekend?"

"Oh, no. Don't even think about it," Kim warned her friend with a fierce frown.

Lynette blinked at her innocently. "What do you mean?"

"Do not try to fix me up with Tate," Kim warned, making sure he couldn't hear from across the room. "I mean it."

"Geez, Kim, it was just a question. Sure seemed to push one of your buttons, though, huh?"

"Just don't, okay, Lynn? You'd only be causing tension in our lunches. None of us want that."

"Well, no," Lynette admitted. "You're just so darned cute together."

"So are you and Evan. Should I start pushing you at each other?"

"Evan and me? That's crazy. Besides, I think Emma's more his type if he were particularly interested in any of us—which he isn't."

"Hey, Kim, you need any help getting out to the car?" Tate called from across the room.

"No, I've got it, thanks," she replied lightly. "I'll see you guys Wednesday."

Tate turned back to Evan, returning to whatever serious discussion they'd been engaged in before.

Nodding to Lynette to reinforce her earlier point, Kim shifted Daryn on her hip, threw the diaper bag over her other shoulder and moved to the door with her car keys in hand. She was making it clear that she needed no assistance in this or any other area of her life. She was getting along just fine on her own.

Starting right now, it was time to get back to the perfectly comfortable way things had been prior to this bizarre weekend.

She drove straight home, muttering her displeasure with Lynette beneath her breath. They'd all been so careful to avoid any potential drama during these past months of pleasant, undemanding lunches. She didn't want Lynette rocking that boat with any ill-advised attempts at matchmaking.

Come to think of it, Lynette had been one of the driving forces behind that trip to Springfield. She'd pushed and prodded and challenged until it had all somehow seemed almost logical. Kim had thought at the time that Lynette saw it all as a lark, but had there been an ulterior motive behind her seemingly innocuous manipulations?

She really hoped not. It was bad enough that there would always be a slight undertone of tension between Kim and Tate now, even after they put this weekend long behind them. She'd hate to think any wedge would form between herself and Lynette. Lynette and Emma had become her closest friends, and she wanted nothing to change in that respect, even if the guys eventually grew tired of the weekly lunches and drifted away—a possibility that made her rather sad to even consider, despite her best efforts not to let herself get that attached to the ritual.

She did not recognize the older model used car parked at her curb when she pulled into her driveway. But she immediately identified the young man sitting on the edge of her low porch. Moving slowly in shock, she climbed from behind the wheel of the car and stared at his glum, wary face.

"Stuart? What on earth are you doing here?"

Chapter Nine

Stuart stood when Kim spoke to him, his hair falling into his face, his hands shoved deep into the pockets of his baggy jeans. "Hey, Kim."

"You didn't—wait, let me get the baby out of the car and then you can come inside and tell me why you're here."

Her head was spinning as she opened the back door and unstrapped her daughter from the car seat. This weekend just kept getting stranger. Carrying the baby and the diaper bag, she walked past her brother to unlock the front door. "How did you even find me? Did you drive here by yourself?"

"Your address was in Mom's book," he muttered, following her inside. "I used the map app on my phone to find your house. Wasn't that hard."

"And Mom said it was okay for you to make that four-hour drive by yourself?" She turned to frown at him doubtfully while Daryn studied him curiously from her arms.

"I didn't ask her. I've moved out."

A dull ache was beginning to throb in her temples. She bent to set Daryn on her play blanket on the floor, then turned to her brother with her hands on her hips. "What do you mean, you've moved out? I thought you were planning to live at home while you attend college."

Stuart drew a deep breath, then blurted in a tone that was both wary and defiant, "I'm not going to college."

Kim's hands fell limply to her sides in shock. "You're—what? But—"

He pushed a hand through his brown hair, leaving it tangled around his miserable-looking young face.

"It was all Mom's idea for me to live at home and go to classes, not mine. But I've left home, and I'm not going back. I went to Julian's place, but he threw a fit and told me I had to go back home and start school like everyone expects me to, so I came here. I mean, you left because you couldn't deal with all the crap anymore, right? So you can understand why I'm doing the same thing."

It was probably the most he'd said to her…well, ever. His expression held a mixture of appeal and defiance. She had no idea what to say to him.

She pushed a hand through her hair. "Okay, wait. We should sit down, talk about this rationally. Have you had anything to eat?"

"I had a hamburger a couple of hours ago." Looking at her with a touch of shyness now, he added, "I'm still kind of hungry, though."

She nodded. "I have some lunch meat and cheese. Why don't you sit down and I'll make you a sandwich."

"Okay, thanks. I'll uh, I'll watch the baby while you're in the kitchen. I *am* her uncle," he added defensively when she hesitated.

She softened. "Yes, you are. Okay, I'll just be a minute. Call if you need me."

"I won't take my eyes off her," he promised, obviously remembering the scare at their grandmother's house.

Kim hurried into the kitchen to prepare food for him, thinking that doing so would give her a chance to wrap her head about her brother's announcements. He must have had a falling-out with her mother or Bob or both. She was stunned that he'd come to her, but maybe he'd felt as though he had nowhere else to go. Was he really using her as a role model for leaving home? Didn't he remember that she had left to go to college, not to avoid doing so?

Both her hands were full a few minutes later when she heard her doorbell ring. "Oh my gosh, now what?" she asked of no one in particular.

"Got it," Stuart called from the other room.

"Um—"

But she heard the door open before she could rush in to see for herself who was ringing the bell. Setting the sandwich plate on the table, she moved quickly toward the living room. Her steps faltered when she saw who had just entered.

Could this day get any more difficult?

Tate gave her a quizzical look. "I wasn't expecting to see your brother here."

"Neither was I," she assured him. "Stuart was just about to explain to me why he's here. Why are *you?*"

Maybe she'd spoken a bit too bluntly for courtesy, but she was reaching the end of her tether.

Tate didn't seem to take offense. He held up a baby bottle. "You left this in Lynette's fridge. She asked me to bring it by to you on my way home."

Lynette could very well have dumped the milk, rinsed the bottle and returned it to her tomorrow at work. Apparently it was going to take another stern talk before Lynette gave up completely on pushing Kim and Tate together.

"You didn't have to do that, but thank you. Stuart, your sandwich is on the table."

Rather than immediately moving in that direction, Stuart looked from Tate to her. "I heard the truth about you guys. Finally. I was pretty mad at you both at first, but then I realized that Mom's the one who's been lying to me all this time. She just dragged you into it."

"I was going to tell you, Stuart," she assured him guiltily. "I mean, I didn't know myself that she'd made up a husband for me until recently, and then I let her talk me into—but I can't blame her, really. I should have said no. I just..."

"You wanted to see Grandma again before she dies," he said quietly, his prominent Adam's apple bobbing with a hard swallow. He didn't look angry, she decided. Just tired, and a little sad. "Mom told me that was why you did it. She tried to make herself sound all noble for giving you a way to come to the reunion without being embarrassed by your circumstances, but I told her she was full of bull. She just wanted you not to expose the truth about her."

Kim studied his face. "That's why you left? Because you found out the truth about Tate and me?"

"Final straw," he said with a shrug. "I'm just fed up with being jerked around by her. Dragged from place to place. Never knowing what's real or what's a figment of her self-centered imagination. Trying to be who she wants me to be. It's no wonder you and Julian both got out of there as soon as you were eighteen. She ran you both off, and I was stuck there by myself. But now I'm eighteen, and it's my turn to leave."

Every word he said struck her like a blow. She'd had no idea her younger brother had been so unhappy. So lonely. Had she really been so wrapped up in herself that she hadn't even considered she'd left him in the same circumstances she had been so impatient to escape? Of course, when she'd left Julian had still been at home. She'd always assumed the boys had a closer bond with each other than they did with her.

"What are you going to do now?" she asked in bewilderment. "Do you even know?"

"First, I'm going to eat that sandwich." He moved toward the kitchen. "You want something, Tate?"

Tate gave Kim a look of rueful amusement as he replied, "You go ahead."

He turned fully to her when Stuart was out of the room. "Making himself at home, isn't he?"

"Can you believe this? He just packed his car and drove four hours to find me after having not seen me in three years."

"I told you he wanted a relationship with you," Tate reminded her in a low voice. "He's decided to blame your mother for driving you away. It makes it easier for him, I guess."

"I don't know what to say to him." It galled her to have to ask Tate for help again, but she didn't have a clue what to do with Stuart. Tate was the one who seemed to have insight into a teenage boy's mind. "Should I try to defend Mother's actions and send him back home? Should I offer him a place to stay until he decides for himself what he wants to do? I hate to think he'd be missing the first week of college."

"You need to talk to him. Find out exactly what happened to make him leave home. Find out what he wants. Then you can offer advice."

She drew a deep breath and looked at him in appeal. "Will you stay for a little while?"

"I think he wants to talk to his sister," Tate said gently. "I don't want to intrude."

"No, stay, Tate," Stuart said, coming back into the room with the more-than-half-eaten sandwich in hand just in time to overhear. "I wouldn't mind a dude's opinion."

Kim lifted her eyebrows. "You've already almost finished that sandwich?"

"I was hungry. So, could we, like, sit down or something? You, too, Tate."

Tate watched as Stuart dropped onto the couch. "You remember I'm not really family, right, Stu?"

Stuart smiled a little, but shook his head as he swallowed the last of the sandwich. "I know. But you and Kim are friends, right?"

Tate sent a smile toward Kim that made her toes curl. "Yes. Good friends."

Oblivious to the undertones, Stuart continued to focus on his own problems. "So you can give me some pointers. You own a business, right? Do you have any jobs available? I'm going to need a paycheck. Place to live, that sort of thing."

Settling into a chair, Tate nodded gravely. "I could put you to work. The only jobs I have available for someone your age and with your lack of experience would be minimum wage, manual labor. Digging, hauling supplies, cleaning up the sites, that sort of thing. Entry-level. You wouldn't be able to afford much rent, so you'll either have to find a roommate or settle for a dump."

Stuart looked a bit daunted, but he swallowed. "Okay. Fine. I can do that."

"Now, if you'd get your degree, either in mathematics or computers, I could maybe offer you a job that's more interesting and rewarding."

Stuart scowled. "You're not going to start lecturing me about going back home to school, are you?"

"You really don't want to go to college?" Kim asked tentatively. "I mean, I know college isn't for everyone, but you've always been such a good student. Mom sent me copies of your report cards and your academic awards, and you did so well in everything. I know you were an honor graduate. I have a photo of you accepting your diploma on my computer. I'd have been there to see you graduate in person, but Daryn was still so little then, and harder for me to travel with on my own."

He looked taken aback. "You've kept up with my schoolwork?"

"Of course, Stuart. Just because I needed to put some distance between myself and Mom didn't mean I'd lost all interest in your welfare. I always asked about you when I called, even if that wasn't very often."

"Mom didn't tell me that."

"Yes, well, she's not very reliable when it comes to communications. I should have made more of an effort to reach out to you myself. I'm afraid I've been in the habit of thinking of you as a kid who wouldn't really be interested in hearing from me. Then I found out I was expecting Daryn and I became absorbed with the changes in my own life. I'm sorry I didn't try harder with you."

"It's okay," he muttered. "Like you said, I was a just a kid when you left. I thought of you as a lot older than me. An adult, you know? I was on the ranch then, and I liked it well enough there, but then Julian left and then Mom moved me to Springfield, and then she married Bob."

After which, Betsy had changed her whole persona again. And no one had thought to provide a cake for Stuart's fifteenth birthday.

Flooded with guilt, she said, "Bob seems like a very nice guy. You like him, don't you?"

Stuart shrugged. "Sure. But, you know—"

Yes, she knew. He'd liked Stan, too. She doubted that he'd heard a word from his former stepfather since Betsy had walked away. That was the usual pattern in their life.

"Your sister and I think Bob could stay around awhile," Tate offered, having been quietly listening to that point.

"Yeah, maybe. He and Mom seem pretty happy together. They don't fight as much as Mom and Stan used to—actually, Mom and Bob don't fight at all. He just gives her these sort of sad looks and she starts apologizing for whatever it was she did, and then they seem happy again. They had one of those not-fights about you, by the way, Kim."

"About me?"

Stuart nodded, flipping his hair out of his eyes with the movement. "I don't think Bob knew Mom had been lying to Grandma and Aunt Treva. I guess she told him before you got there. As much as she lies to everyone else, she's usually honest with Bob—as honest as she is with herself, anyway. Anyway, I heard her and Bob talking last night and he was telling her it was her own fault she was embarrassed by the truth coming out, and that he wished she hadn't put everyone, especially you, in such a difficult situation, but then when she started crying he told her it would all work out. So I asked what was going on and that's when Mom told me she'd been lying to me about you and Tate."

A spark of remembered hurt and anger glinted in Stuart's eyes. "That's when I told her I was fed up. You and Julian got out while you were still reasonably sane and I've got to do the same thing."

"I understand, Stuart—obviously I do. But Julian and I had plans when we left. I had a full scholarship to college, which included room and board. Julian went into the service. You—well, you don't even have a place to live, though of course you're welcome to stay here until you decide what you want to do."

He nodded glumly. "I have a scholarship, but it doesn't cover room and board."

"Then let's consider this." Tate leaned forward a little, resting his forearms on his knees, a thoughtful expression on his face. "What if you could still go to college and move out of your mother's home? You could prepare for your own future without completely severing ties with your mother. That's what your sister and brother did, right?"

Stuart sighed. "But Mom doesn't have money for

room and board, and Bob's already got two kids of his own in school."

"I'll help you," Kim told him. "I don't have a lot, but I make enough to put some money away each month. I can contribute toward your room and board. Julian will probably kick in a little, too. And you can work part-time to make spending money. I did while I was in school. It's doable, as long as you're careful about your time management."

His eyes wide, Stuart shook his head. "I can't let you do that. You need your money for you and the baby."

"You can get a student loan for expenses," Tate suggested. "It could be too late for this semester, but you can let your sister and brother help until you get everything approved. Going into debt for an education is never ideal, but with your scholarship and part-time work, you shouldn't have to dip in too deeply."

He shifted in the chair, adding a bit hesitantly, "And if you need a little extra to tide you over this first semester, I can probably arrange that. Evan and I have talked about starting a scholarship fund in memory of a friend of ours who died in a motorcycle accident a few years ago. He was a high school teacher, wanted to teach on a college level eventually. I see no reason why you couldn't be the first recipient of the Jason Sanchez Memorial Scholarship. It wouldn't be a full ride or anything, but it would probably pay for your books and a few extra supplies."

Though Kim was touched by the gesture—and fully believed his backstory about his friend—she was still a little uncomfortable with his offer of help. She regretted that Tate was once again getting drawn into her family issues, both because it embarrassed her that her family had so many issues and because she was doing her best to rebuild the boundaries between herself and Tate.

"You'd really do that?" Stuart asked, stunned.

"I'd have to discuss it with my business partner, of course. And I imagine he would want to see your transcript and either interview you or have you write a letter assuring us you would take your education seriously so we'd know we weren't throwing away our money—but, yes. I would definitely recommend you to him, if you can tell me now that you understand the importance of preparing yourself for your future."

Stuart sprang to his feet and began to pace in front of the couch in agitation, carefully avoiding the baby's play blanket. "I can't live with Mom again. Even if it means putting off school for a while or something, I can't move back in there. Maybe I can get along with her like you and Julian do, Kim—you know, just talk on the phone occasionally and see her at holidays and stuff. But if I try to live with her again, I just know it's going to lead to a blow-up that's going to be permanent."

Kim nodded and tried to speak reassuringly, motioning for her brother to take his seat again. "You'll need to talk to the school, find out if it's too late to get a dorm room. There are usually some last-minute cancellations, so you should be able to get housing. It's going to be easier for you to take care of things from there than here. I'll call Julian and ask if you can stay with him for a few days. I'm sure the reason he turned you away yesterday was because you told him you weren't going to school. He didn't want to be responsible for enabling that impulsive decision."

At least, she hoped that was the only reason. Surely

Julian would help once he heard all the details. As Stuart had pointed out, Julian knew quite well how it felt to need to get away from their mother's chronic chaos.

"In the meantime, you should call Mom," she added. "Despite everything, you know she does care about you. About all of us, I guess, in her own strange way. She's probably worried sick. Or if you can't talk to her just yet, call Bob and let him know you're safe and that you're developing a sensible plan for your future."

"I'll call Bob," Stuart agreed only a little grudgingly.

"Good. I'll call Julian."

"And I'll get out of your hair," Tate said, standing.

Seeing at a glance that Daryn had fallen asleep on her blanket, Kim stood, too. "I'll walk you out. Keep an eye on the baby while you call Bob, will you, Stuart? I'll just be a minute."

Stuart nodded and pulled his phone out of his pocket. "I'll watch her."

"You're sure Daryn's okay in there with him?" Tate fretted as Kim closed the front door behind them, leaving them standing on her tiny porch.

"She's sound asleep. This busy weekend has worn her out. I'll probably have to wake her to get her ready for bed. She'll be fine for a couple of minutes."

He nodded. "So, finding your brother here was a big surprise, huh?"

Though it wasn't at all cool out, she crossed her arms tightly over her chest, reliving the shock of seeing Stuart on her doorstep. "You could say that again. And about that...as generous as it was of you to offer, you don't have to give Stuart money for school. Julian and I will help him figure out some sort of plan."

"I'm sure you will. That's what brothers and sisters do, right?"

"Supposedly," she agreed wryly.

"The thing is, Evan and I really have discussed setting up a scholarship fund in memory of our friend. I'll have to tell you about him sometime, he was a great guy. Still miss him like crazy. Anyway, we were going to do it for this semester, and then we got busy and kept putting it off. I think he'll be pleased that I've found a worthy first recipient among our group of friends."

Before she could argue any further, he rested a hand on her shoulder. "As I told Stuart, it won't be a lot, but maybe it'll help out. If it keeps him from dropping out of college before he even begins, Evan and I will both consider it money well spent. Jason would have felt the same way."

It would have felt both rude and ungrateful to continue to resist, especially when the gesture seemed to be a genuine tribute to Tate's late friend. Still she couldn't help feeling a little awkward about it.

"I'll leave it all up to you and Evan and Stuart, then," she said. "I'll give Stuart your email address, and he can send you his transcript and whatever other paperwork you need, but other than that, I'll stay out of it." All of the lunch friends had shared email addresses and phone numbers in case they needed to make contact.

"That will work. So, do you have a place for him to sleep tonight?"

She shrugged. "He'll have to make do with the couch."

"I'm sure that will work for him. Most teen boys can sleep anywhere."

Pushing a hand wearily through her hair, Kim sighed. "It's been a crazy couple of days."

"I know. But I think your decision to attend the reunion has accomplished some good things, don't you? You had a chance to visit with your grandmother, and to reconnect with your brothers. Maybe Bob will step up and help your mother see that her behavior is hurting the family. Maybe once Stuart is out on his own, Bob and Betsy can focus on strengthening their relationship, which already seems pretty good, considering."

"Until Bob gets as fed up with her as everyone else eventually does," Kim muttered.

"Has it ever occurred to you that your mother has a lot of insecurities herself? She lost her father young, her mother was admittedly distant and critical, her early marriages didn't work out. Maybe Betsy learned to push people away before they could hurt her. To create a world she wanted to live in because the real world was too difficult for her to handle."

After taking a moment to consider his surprising analysis, Kim moistened her lips. "You're being rather generous to her. But, if there is some truth in what you say, she has been very selfish about her choices in dealing with her problems and disappointments."

"I guess you never know how people will choose to cope with adversity," Tate said quietly.

She spoke more brusquely. "Anyway, thank you again for all you've done this weekend. I promise I won't ask for anything more of you. Oh, and thanks for returning Daryn's bottle, even though it wasn't necessary for Lynette to ask you to. She could have just given it back to mc tomorrow."

Tate cleared his throat. "Yeah, that's what she said when she found it in the fridge. I sort of volunteered to drop it by. Since it was on my way and all."

"My house is a good five miles out of your way from Lynette's apartment to yours," she said with a shake of her head.

"Maybe I just wanted to see you one more time this evening."

Something about his tone made a little ripple of panic run through her. "We talked about this, Tate. About last night being an aberration. About getting back to the way things were between us before we ever left for Springfield. We agreed that was best."

He looked at the hand he had resting on her shoulder, and his fingers flexed a little. "I'm just not entirely sure it's possible."

The ripple of panic gushed into a flood. "Please don't do this, Tate."

He lifted his eyes back to hers. "I know you've got a lot to deal with right now, so I won't push you. But I'm not sure I can pretend nothing has changed. I can act a role for other people, Kim, but not with you."

She bit her lip before saying in little more than a whisper, "I don't want to lose your friendship."

"You'll never lose that."

She wished she could count on that, but sadly, she knew better.

Reading her expression, he sighed. "Stop lumping me in with all those other guys, Kim. If you're going to shoot me down, do it because of my own shortcomings, not for someone else's."

"It has nothing to do with shortcomings. You're a very special man, Tate, and if I had no other obligations, I would... But I have to put Daryn first," she said firmly. "You of all people should understand why I refuse to risk disrupting her life."

Tate scowled. "So you're never going to date again? You don't think your daughter would expect her mother to have needs of her own?"

"All I need for myself is to be a good mother and a good therapist."

Tate's low snort held both skepticism and annoyance. "Very noble. And very full of hot air."

She gasped in outrage. "I was being entirely honest."

"Not even with yourself," he contradicted. "You want and need a hell of a lot more than that in your life. You're just afraid to go for it. With good reason, maybe, but it's still based on fear, not logic."

She looked away from him, keenly aware that they stood on her porch with cars passing on the street and her brother and daughter waiting in the house behind her. "This isn't the time or place for this conversation."

"No." He looked vaguely regretful. "I should have waited. Like I said, I can't seem to be anything but completely up-front with you. Before this weekend, I was able to mask my feelings for you—maybe even from myself—but now I can't imagine never being with you again as more than lunch pals. I can't fathom seeing you for an hour once a week across a restaurant table, not seeing you or hearing from you in between. Never spending time alone with you again, touching you, kissing you."

His voice had deepened as he finished, and Kim shivered a little in response to the sexy rumble. It would be so easy to take the short step that separated them, to wrap herself around him and lose herself in him again. Everything he said resonated within her—but it had not escaped her attention that not once during that impassioned speech had he mentioned her daughter.

She swallowed hard. "Just give it time, Tate. Once we've put this weekend completely behind us, you'll be relieved that I, at least, didn't get carried away with it all. You know you don't really want to get involved with a single mother. You said to Evan only a couple of hours ago that being solely responsible for Daryn would scare the stuffing out of you.

"Well, the thing is, Daryn and I come as a package. If I were looking for a relationship with anyone—which I'm not—it would be someone who isn't afraid of long-term commitment and parenthood. Since I'm not sure anyone like that even exists anymore, I'm going to stick with my policy, despite what happened last night."

"I know Daryn complicates things, but—"

She took a step back from him, her chin rising. "My daughter is not a complication."

"Poor choice of words," he said, raising a hand in a gesture of apology. "I didn't mean it quite that way."

"I have to get back inside and put her to bed. Good night, Tate. Maybe I'll see you at lunch Wednesday."

Barely giving him time to begin a response, she whirled and stepped through the door, closing it behind her with a snap. Or was that the sound of her heart breaking, when she had done everything she knew how to protect it from that?

Looking as though he'd hardly moved a muscle, Stuart was still on the couch, his eyes focused on the baby.

"She's still asleep," he reported unnecessarily.

"Thank you for watching her. Did you reach Bob?"

"Yeah. I told him I'm here with you. He said he was glad I'm safe. He wants me to come to the house tomorrow afternoon and talk with him and Mom, but I said I'd have to think about it. I told him I'm moving out, and he said he'd go with me to the school housing office if I want him to. He even said he'd help out with some expenses, even though I know he's got his own kids to take care of."

Kim was relieved that Bob seemed to be supporting Stuart's decision. Even if it was just because Bob was ready for his stepson to move out of the house, at least he seemed willing to help. "I think this will work out fine for you, Stuart. I know you'll do well in school. You won't regret going."

"I don't mind so much going to school," he admitted. "I just didn't want to live at home any longer."

She smiled a little. "Yes, I think you've made that clear."

He cleared his throat, and she thought he looked a little abashed. She hadn't meant to embarrass him with her teasing. She supposed he just didn't know her well enough to read her clearly yet. It was long past time to remedy that situation.

"I'm going to put Daryn to bed," she said, moving toward the baby. "After that, you and I can have some herbal tea or something and talk for a while before bedtime. You'll be sleeping on the couch, I'm afraid."

"I don't mind the couch. I'll go out and get my bag while you take care of her."

"All right. I have to be at work by seven-thirty tomorrow morning, so Daryn and I get up pretty early."

"That's okay. I'll probably head back to Springfield

in the morning. If Julian won't let me bunk with him for a few days, maybe I can stay at Grandma's house."

"We'll call Julian together after I put the baby to bed."

Stuart nodded and moved toward the door, then paused. "I like herbal tea okay—but do you have anything else to eat? Like some cookies or something?"

She smothered a smile, looking at her brother's stick-thin frame and thinking he must burn calories like a furnace. "I'm sure I can come up with something."

"Okay. Thanks, sis," he said just a little too casually, then darted out the door.

Feeling a hard lump in her throat, Kim carefully scooped up her daughter and headed toward the nursery. Her emotions had been through the wringer during the past three days. The only way she could deal with it all at the moment was to focus on the tasks at hand.

She couldn't think about Tate just then. Not without falling apart. And that would be of no help to any of the people who were depending on her.

Tate was disappointed, but not terrible surprised, to see an empty chair at the restaurant table when he and Evan entered on the last Wednesday in August.

"Where's Kim this week?" he asked casually of Emma and Lynette, who'd arrived a few minutes before them.

"She said she had some errands to run today," Emma explained. "And she wanted to stop by the day care center. She said Daryn was acting a little draggy this morning and she wants to make sure she's not coming down with something."

Tate hoped the baby wasn't really getting sick, but

he couldn't help wondering if Kim had simply been looking for excuses to avoid him. Last Wednesday, he'd been told she had an appointment for a haircut. She hadn't mentioned having that appointment when they'd parted from the others Sunday evening, so he had figured she'd made it specifically to avoid seeing him again so soon. Now she had skipped out on a second gathering.

He had neither seen nor heard from her since they'd parted so tersely outside her house, though he must have reached for his phone half a dozen times to call her. He had resisted only because he'd told himself he needed to give her time to come to terms with what he'd said to her. Pushing her would only drive her farther away.

Would she be back next week, thinking enough time had passed by then for him to get the message that nothing more was going to happen between them? If she knew he'd spent the past week and a half lying awake at night missing her and replaying in his mind every minute they had spent together, would she realize that a couple of weeks wasn't nearly long enough to make him forget?

When had he actually fallen in love with her? Had it been sometime during their "weekend marriage" or even before that? Had the main reason he'd been willing to subject himself to that challenge in the first place been that he'd wanted an excuse to spend more time with Kim, outside this restaurant?

Hell, yes.

It turned out he was an even better actor than he'd realized. He'd managed to fool himself for several months that he hadn't fallen head over heels in love with a pretty, prickly single mother. He'd even convinced himself that he hadn't asked anyone else out almost since the first time he'd met Kim because he was just too busy and preoccupied with his business.

No wonder he'd rushed her into the bedroom the minute he'd had a private moment with her. Of course, Kim had been doing some rushing herself, which had been a serious boost to his self-esteem, even though she had pretty much shattered it since.

So where did that leave him now? Aching, brooding, perplexed, sleep-deprived. Missing her like crazy—as a lover and as a friend. Wondering what it would take to win her back as either or even better, both. Asking himself repeatedly if he was really ready to take on the responsibility of her child, and fully, nervously aware that was an intrinsic part of the bargain, if he could somehow convince Kim to give them a chance.

"Um, Tate? Were you going to order, like, sometime today?"

Evan's quizzical question brought Tate out of his thoughts abruptly. "Um, yeah. Kung pao chicken," he said to the server waiting with her pen poised patiently over the order pad.

"Something on your mind, Tate?" His sister eyed him speculatively.

"No, just hungry. So, how are things at work this week?" he asked, deliberately changing the subject. He directed the question toward Emma, hoping she'd take the question as a conversational cue.

"Hectic." As he'd hoped, she launched into a discussion of things that had happened at work since the last time they had seen each other. Tate made a show of paying attention, though he couldn't stop glancing at that empty space at the table. He was aware that his sister watched him a bit more closely than usual during the meal, but he avoided her eyes studiously.

He stayed busy at work during the next few days as the Labor Day weekend approached. There was a lot to be done prior to the three-day weekend and as the end of summer approached. A good month of warm days lay ahead, but winter would arrive inevitably and that required advance planning in the landscape business. The time passed in a blur of meetings and paperwork and scheduling, problems to handle, decisions to make. He was so busy he hardly had time to think of Kim at all—probably no more than a dozen times an hour, he thought wearily Friday afternoon, squeezing the taut muscles at the back of his neck with one hand.

Checking email on his phone, he smiled faintly when he saw a note from Stuart O'Hara. The message was brief, merely reporting that Stuart liked his roommate and had done well in his first week of classes and was still grateful for the scholarship. Tate had invited Stuart to stay in touch, and the young man was taking that offer seriously, as though to reassure Tate and Evan that they had chosen a worthy recipient for their first scholarship.

Jason really would be proud, Tate thought with the familiar wistfulness that always accompanied thoughts of his late friend. He was sure Kim was proud of her brother. He hoped they were growing closer, even if they did still live in separate states.

So, his thoughts had come back around to Kim. For the thirteenth time that hour.

His phone rang in his hand just as he was preparing to put it away. Glancing at the screen, he saw his sister's number displayed above the time. He lifted the phone to his ear. "Lynn? I thought you and Emma were supposed to be on your way to your friend's lake house for the long weekend."

"I'm on my way now to pick up Emma. I just wanted to ask you to check on Kim, will you? I'll feel a lot better going off for a holiday if I know she's okay."

Tate frowned, going onto full alert. "What's wrong with Kim? Why wouldn't she be okay?"

"She's sick. She started feeling bad at work yesterday and today she couldn't even make it in. It's the first time since I've known her that she's missed a day of work. And since she doesn't have any family nearby, and Emma and I are going to be out of town for a few days, I just want to know there's someone here to check on her. I mean, I know she has other friends, but you know how stubborn she is. She would never ask for help. So maybe you could just go by and see if she needs anything?"

"Kim's sick? What about the baby?"

"The baby wasn't feeling well yesterday. Kim had to leave her with a neighbor who watches her when the day care center is closed or any other time Kim needs a babysitter."

"Have you called Kim?"

"Of course. A couple of times. She assured me she was feeling better, but she sounded terrible. I offered to skip the lake house trip this weekend and help her out, but she wouldn't even consider it."

"I'll check on her."

"Thanks, Tate."

Tate wasn't sure how grateful Kim would be. She'd made it clear enough that she wanted him to stay out of her personal life from now on. But he'd promised Lynette, and now that he knew about it, he needed to reassure himself that Kim and Daryn were okay. And he didn't want to simply call and ask; he needed to see them both for himself.

Chapter Ten

He should have called. Standing at Kim's front door an hour after Lynette's call, one finger poised over the doorbell button, Tate hesitated before announcing his presence. Should he turn around, drive away and call to ask if she needed or wanted him to visit? That would probably be the courteously correct procedure. Yet he knew what would happen if he did call. She would assure him she was fine, as she had Lynette, and then she would stubbornly struggle to deal with her problems on her own, as she always did.

Oh, she'd probably ask for help if it were important for Daryn, but she would request nothing for herself. She had learned not to depend on anyone else to be there for her even if she reached out.

So, knowing she would politely decline if he called to offer help, and knowing he wouldn't be comfortable until he determined for himself that she was okay, and knowing the worst that could happen would be that she would turn him away—maybe with a firm request that he stay away afterward—he pushed the doorbell button.

It took so long for Kim to respond that he was beginning to think she wasn't going to do so. But then he heard movement and heard Daryn crying, the sound growing louder as she neared the other side of the door. A curtain flicked, which probably meant that Kim had checked the identity of her caller. Did he only imagine hearing her groan when she saw him?

After a very brief pause, the door opened. Tate was shocked at the sight that met his eyes.

Kim was visibly ill. Pale, hollow-eyed, her hair disarrayed, her lips nearly colorless. Barefoot, wearing a wrinkled T-shirt and shorts, she stood somewhat unsteadily with the crying baby on her hip. Daryn wore a one-piece sleeper and while she, too, was more disheveled than usual, she looked more cranky than sick, at least to Tate's inexperienced assessment.

"Hi, Tate," Kim said, her voice hoarse. "I would ask you in, but I've got a little cold. I wouldn't want you to get sick, too."

"I think it's more than a little cold. And I'm not here for a friendly visit, Kim. I'm here to help."

She sighed. "Did Lynette call you?"

"Yes. She said you were ill, but I don't think she knew how bad it really is or she'd have been here herself. Have you seen a doctor?"

"Yes. I'm to rest and drink fluids. I'll be fine, Tate, I have three days to recover before I have to be back at work."

Her throat must have been extremely painful; each word sounded as though it were forced through broken glass. Daryn wailed again, and Kim winced, a sign that her head was pounding in addition to her sore throat.

"Is anyone staying with you?" he asked, though he suspected he already knew the answer.

"I don't need anyone, I'll be— What are you doing?"

Without waiting for an invitation, Tate moved past her into the house. Kim whirled to glare at him, but the sudden movement must have made the room spin around her. She rocked on her feet.

Tate reached out quickly to relieve her of the disgruntled baby.

"Go lie down before you fall down," he ordered her gruffly. Had it not been for Daryn, he would have been tempted to lift Kim off her feet and carry her to bed—but only to tuck her in tenderly and let her rest. "I'll take care of Daryn while you get some sleep."

"No, really, Tate, it would be better if you—"

Somewhat awkwardly patting Daryn's back as he rocked her against him, Tate spoke in a quiet voice intended to soothe the baby and convince the mother. "Unless you want to have me escorted out, you aren't getting rid of me that easily, Kim. There is no way I'm leaving you this sick and with no one here to help you. Now, go get some rest and when you feel better, you can berate me all you want and then throw me out on my ear."

She looked torn between anger and temptation. He supposed it would have been too much to expect gratitude, considering the way he'd barged in on her. "You don't know what to do with Daryn."

"I think I can figure it out." Daryn had already stopped crying, subsiding to little sniffles as she rested her head on Tate's shoulder. "If not, I'll come get you. Now, go."

Kim's eyes looked suspiciously damp now. It was a measure of just how sick she was that she finally nodded and locked the front door. "Okay, fine. You'll probably get sick, too, and then you'll be sorry. And it will serve you right."

"Yes, it will. Has Daryn eaten?"

Running a trembling hand over her hair, Kim nodded. "I just fed her a little. She wasn't very hungry. I was going to give her a bottle."

"I can do that. Is the bottle in the fridge?"

"I had just taken it out and set it on the counter when you rang the bell."

"Okay. Go to bed. Sleep. Don't worry about Daryn."

She turned toward the bedroom, then looked over her shoulder. "I forgot to check her diaper."

"Go to bed, Kim."

Her steps dragged as she left the room.

Tate looked down at the tear-streaked child in his arms. Okay, now what? He had so confidently assured Kim she had nothing at all to worry about, but she must have been near delirium to have let him talk her into leaving him with her daughter. He didn't have the faintest idea what he was doing.

Daryn gazed up at him with wide, curious eyes. Probably wondering what he was going to do next. Good question.

"So…bottle, huh? Or, uh, guess we should check the diaper first."

She blinked, then gave him a faint smile of acknowledgment before turning somber again.

"Okay, we can do this," he assured her. "Let's go change that diaper."

He carried the baby quietly into the hallway, shaking his head when he saw that Kim's bedroom door was open. Probably so she could monitor every little sound coming from the other room. Peeking inside, he saw that she lay on the bed still wearing her T-shirt and shorts, as though she had intended to lie down for only a few minutes. She was sound asleep. Deciding she would be warm enough without coverings, he pulled the door almost closed so as not to disturb her when he passed by to Daryn's room.

The nursery was both cheery and functional. The walls were yellow, the furnishings a dark honey wood, the bedding soft yellows and greens. Framed prints of nursery rhyme characters decorated the walls and an inviting rocker with a footrest sat in the corner facing the door. Toys were arranged neatly on shelves, and a changing table was stocked with diapers and wipes. Even a novice like himself could find everything easily in here, thanks to Kim's efficient organization.

Somehow he managed to get a clean diaper on the baby. He vaguely remembered putting a diaper on a doll in a high school class that included "life skills" lessons, one of which had been diapering a child. As he recalled, they had also tested the heat of bathwater with their elbows and of heated bottles by sprinkling milk on their wrists, but he had no intention of giving Daryn a bath and he remembered that she liked her milk cold, so neither of those skills would be called upon.

"We can do this, kiddo," he assured her, refastening her sleeper and lifting her back into his arms. "Piece of cake."

She made a fretting sound that perhaps expressed doubt, but he didn't let her skepticism daunt his determined optimism. "Let's go get that bottle."

It was an interesting night, to say the least. Daryn was fussier than he'd ever seen her and wouldn't let him put her down even when she finished her bottle. He sat for hours with her and Mr. Jingles snuggled in his lap while he watched baseball and news programming on TV.

He dealt with two particularly nasty diapers that he could only assume were worse than usual because she'd been ill. And somehow he handled them without being sick himself. He even managed to wrestle the kid into a clean sleeper, which seemed to have a couple dozen tiny little snaps that were not made for a man's clumsy fingers.

Every so often he tiptoed into the hallway to peek in and check on Kim. She didn't stir. Some part of her, at least, must have trusted him with the baby, he thought in satisfaction as he pulled the door to again. Could she really have slept so soundly if she hadn't, no matter how sick she was?

Growing hungry once his appetite recovered from the unpleasantness of the second dirty diaper, he rummaged in the fridge and found the makings for a sandwich. Assembling it with one hand while holding the baby in the other arm proved to be a challenge, but he managed. He swallowed the sandwich in a few bites while Daryn watched him with an intensity that was both amusing and a little disconcerting.

He talked to the child in a low voice during the evening, a running commentary of what he was doing or what was going on in the ball game. He didn't expect her to understand a word he was saying, but it seemed natural to speak to her when she was awake. At least the monologue seemed to entertain her enough that she didn't cry, though she whimpered occasionally until he rocked her or jostled her or—at one desperate moment—sang softly to her. That seemed to surprise her more than impress her, but at least her fussing subsided before growing into shrieks that would have disturbed her mother.

Daryn finally fell asleep, so deeply that Tate was able to carefully lay her in her crib without waking her. He remembered that Kim had laid the baby on her back in the travel crib, so he did the same now. He set Mr. Jingles nearby, then hesitated there, uneasy about walking away. He rested a hand lightly against her flushed cheek. Did she feel a bit too warm?

Maybe he'd just sit in the rocker for a few minutes, until he was sure she was resting comfortably. He'd slip out in a little while to check on Kim, then crash on the couch until Daryn woke up at her usual early hour. He imagined Kim would feel better in the morning, after a good night's rest, and she'd probably throw him out then. But as soon as he was sure she was fully recovered, they were going to have to talk.

Every muscle in her body ached. Kim stretched slowly on the bed, trying to work out kinks that seemed to have set in permanently. She was still wearing her T-shirt and shorts—even her bra—none of which were particularly comfortable for sleeping. Her hair was a tangled mess around her face and her mouth felt as though it were filled with sand. She rolled to the side of the bed, groaned when the movement resulted in even more discomfort, and staggered to the bathroom.

A few minutes later, she returned to the bedroom, still feeling terrible but somewhat more presentable. Peering blearily at the bedside clock, she was shocked to see that it was almost 5:00 a.m. Had she really just slept for ten solid hours?

Daryn! She jerked open the door she knew she had left fully open the night before and hurried toward the nursery, only to stop short in the doorway. She could see at a glance that Daryn was still sleeping peacefully, but it was the man sprawled in the rocker who held her attention.

Tate had kicked off his shoes and propped his feet on the footstool. He was sound asleep, his head resting against the back cushion of the padded chair, his arms lying loosely in his lap. He wore his usual work clothes of khakis and a polo shirt—maroon, this time—and there was a tiny hole in the toe of one of his khaki-colored socks. Maybe her illness weakened her to the point of finding that rather adorable.

He couldn't possibly be comfortable. He was going to be as sore as she was when he awoke. Should she rouse him now? He seemed to be sleeping so soundly.

She swallowed, and her inflamed throat protested angrily. Lifting a hand to her throat, she bit her lip for a moment in indecision, looked at her daughter again, then turned away. Maybe she'd go back to bed and let everyone sleep undisturbed for a little while longer.

Dressed more comfortably in yoga pants and a clean, looser T-shirt, she slipped beneath the top sheet on her bed and rested her aching head on the pillow. She really should contemplate the fact that Tate had spent the night babysitting. Or she should try to decide what to say to him when he woke. Instead, she closed her eyes and let her mind go blank—not a difficult task considering how lousy she felt.

The next time she opened her eyes, another two hours had passed. She groaned.

Her head still hurt, her throat was still sore, and her muscles still hated her, but she thought maybe she felt just a little better. Maybe she would survive this bug, after all.

She needed to check on Daryn again. And she needed to face Tate, though she still had no clue what she was going to say to him. She wasn't even sure how she felt about him being there. Annoyed? Grateful? Embarrassed? All of the above?

The nursery was empty now. She headed for the front of the house, stunned that she had slept so soundly again that she hadn't heard Daryn wake up. Daryn should have had her breakfast an hour ago. Maybe Tate had given her a bottle to hold her over.

She stood in the living room doorway, taking in the scene there. Daryn sat on her play blanket on the floor, her prop pillow behind her to keep her from toppling backward as she played with the toys strewn in front of her. She wore a lavender romper and one of her stretchy headbands with a lavender bow. The bow was tipped a little far over one ear and her hair was combed rather oddly, but it was obvious that Tate had made an effort to dress her nicely.

It was so darned annoying that he kept being so sweet.

Speaking of Tate, he sat cross-legged on the floor in front of Daryn, making the baby gurgle by dancing Mr.

Jingles across the blanket. Along with the impromptu puppeteering, he sang a little song about monkeys dancing in the jungle…not a song she recognized. Apparently, he was making it up as he went along. Whatever its source, the song delighted Daryn—and it was causing a similar reaction in Kim, despite her resistance.

She cleared her throat, which she immediately regretted. "Good morning."

Daryn squealed and kicked, almost tipping over despite the pillow. She caught herself at the last minute. Tate put down the monkey, looking a little sheepish as he climbed to his feet. "Good morning. How do you feel?"

"Better."

He eyed her closely, then stepped forward to rest a hand against her forehead. "You're still too warm. I'd say you still have a low-grade fever."

She drew back a little, not quite trusting herself to be touched by him without melting into a puddle. "Since when did you get a medical degree?"

"Doesn't take a medical degree to see that your cheeks are red, your eyes glassy and you're swaying on your feet. Sit down, I'll get you something to drink. You don't want to dehydrate. Water or juice?"

The litany of ways that she looked ill wasn't particularly flattering, but she told herself that didn't matter. "You don't have to stay. I'll be fine now that I've had some rest."

"I'll just hang around for a little while longer. I haven't had breakfast yet. You wouldn't send me out hungry, would you?"

That was an excuse, of course, but she sighed and

conceded, "Of course you're welcome to have breakfast before you go."

After all, the least she could do in repayment for his selflessness last night was to feed him. "I could make some eggs or pancakes."

He grinned. "Um—thanks, but no thanks, Germ Lady. You sit down. I'll cook."

Pouting a little, she sank to the couch. "So I'm a germ lady with a red face and glassy eyes. Lovely."

"Yes," he said with a smile that made her toes curl. "You are lovely."

She gulped and said hastily, "Fine. You can make breakfast. I guess I don't have to tell you to make yourself at home."

"I guess I have. By the way, I helped myself to a new toothbrush I found in your guest bath." Handing Mr. Jingles to Daryn, he sauntered into the kitchen.

What was wrong with her? Even his ambling looked sexy.

"Mamamama."

Directing her attention quickly back to her daughter, she moved to pick her up and snuggle her. "I'm sorry I neglected you last night, sweetie. But it looks as though you were well cared for."

Daryn grinned and patted her cheek with a hand still damp from being in her mouth. Kim didn't care about that. She was still feeling guilty about crashing the way she had. She wanted to believe she'd have been fine taking care of her daughter during the night even if Tate hadn't shown up out of the blue to take over, but she knew she had needed the sleep.

A short while later, Tate called her to the kitchen. "Breakfast is ready."

Carrying Daryn with her, Kim joined him. "Oatmeal?"

He nodded, setting two steaming bowls on the table. "I thought you'd appreciate something soft and easy to swallow. Sounds as though your throat is still pretty sore."

"It is," she conceded. "And this smells delicious."

"I added a little brown sugar and cinnamon. My mom always made this for me when I was sick."

She put Daryn in the high chair and handed her a wooden spoon to play with. "Actually, my mom did, too. She made oatmeal a lot on the ranch. It was Stan's favorite breakfast. He liked it with raisins and walnuts sprinkled on top."

Adding a glass of orange juice at each place, Tate asked lightly, "You said you liked Stan?"

"He was okay. A total mismatch for Mom, obviously. He didn't have the patience for her shenanigans, as he called them. Has Daryn eaten?"

Following the change of subject willingly enough, Tate nodded. "I fed her a jar of that baby cereal I found in the pantry and a sippy cup of milk. I assumed that would be suitable."

She blinked a few times as she sank into her seat. "Yes, that was fine. I have to admit I'm impressed that you managed to take care of everything while I was out of commission."

He settled into his own seat and reached for his spoon. "Impressed or stunned?"

She smiled wryly. "Both. You're the one who said you know nothing about taking care of babies."

"I don't," he confessed. "But I'm a quick study. I watched you take care of her and just imitated what I saw. It helps that she's an easygoing type of kid. Some would have pitched a fit at being cared for by an awkward greenhorn, but Daryn just went with it, for the most part."

"Well, it's not like you're a stranger to her. She knows you."

Tate winked at Daryn. "Yeah. I'm the monkey wrangler, right, Daryn?"

Daryn beat a slow tattoo on the high chair tray with her spoon. Kim was reassured that her daughter, at least, was feeling better this morning, even if the child wasn't quite back to her usual upbeat self.

She let a spoonful of warm oatmeal slide down her raw throat, followed it with a sip of juice, then looked again at Tate. "You slept in the rocking chair."

When he lifted his eyebrows in question, she explained, "I got up before dawn to check on Daryn and I saw you there. I didn't know whether to wake you."

"I meant to crash on the couch, but every time I woke to make sure Daryn was okay I fell asleep in the chair again," he admitted.

"You couldn't have been comfortable."

He shrugged. "I've slept in less comfortable places."

Kim's appetite faded before she finished the bowl of oatmeal. She took another couple of bites because he had gone to the trouble of preparing it for her, but then set down her spoon, unable to swallow any more.

"I made coffee earlier. Should still be hot. Want a cup?"

She shook her head. "No, thank you."

"How about some herbal tea? I saw several kinds in the cupboard. That would probably feel good on your throat."

"I'll have some later. Seriously, Tate, you can leave anytime. I'm sure you'd like to go home and change. You probably have other plans for today. Daryn and I will be fine."

"Yeah, okay," he said, a bit vaguely. "But first I'll clean up the kitchen. Don't want to leave you with dirty dishes when you aren't feeling well."

"That isn't necessary."

He merely gave her a look and started gathering dishes.

Knowing when to concede, she took Daryn out of the high chair and carried her back into the living room. She would deal with Tate after she took something for her aching head, she promised herself.

Leaving Daryn on her tummy on the play blanket, Kim ducked into the bathroom to swallow two over-the-counter pain relievers with a handful of water from the tap. She rubbed her temples as she returned to the living room.

"Head still hurting?"

Seeing Tate on the couch, she dropped her hands. "That was some fast cleaning."

He shrugged. "I clean as I go. All I had to do was rinse the bowls and stick them in the dishwasher."

"I see. Then you can—"

"You didn't answer. Do you still have a headache?"

"Yes, but I'll be fine—"

He patted the couch beside him. "Sit. Unless you want to go lie down again? The monkette and I will be fine in here."

"The monkette?"

He chuckled. "Yeah, I called her that a few times last

night and it always made her laugh. Not that I think she really understood me or anything, but something about the word struck her as funny. Right, monkette?"

Daryn giggled.

"See?"

Kim looked from Tate to Daryn and back again. She wasn't sure how she felt about him giving her daughter a cutesy nickname, making himself indispensable when they were sick, acting as though she could count on him to be there next time she needed him.

"Really, Tate. You should go."

"Why?"

"Why? Well…because you should."

"That's not much of an answer, Kim. And sit down, you're looking wobbly again."

"I am not wobbly." She pushed a hand through her hair, then had to take a quick sidestep when her head spun with the movement. "Not much, anyway," she muttered.

He stood, put a hand on her shoulder and guided her to the couch. "I know you can handle anything life throws at you without asking for a thing, and I admire you enormously for your courage and self-sufficiency, but every once in a while it's okay to let someone give you a hand, you know? I have nothing better to do today than to keep an eye on Daryn while you get over this bug. I even have a change of clothes in the car."

She frowned. Did that mean he made a habit of staying over at random places?

Perhaps he read her thoughts on her face as he took a seat beside her. "I keep a pair of jeans, a T-shirt and some running shoes in the trunk in case someone suggests a game of pickup basketball or touch football after work. I don't make a practice of spending the night out. You're actually the only woman I've shared a bed with since we met that day in the Chinese restaurant. Five months and three weeks ago, not that I'm counting. I'm not sure if I've just lost some cool points by admitting that, but I thought you should know."

It was a good thing she was already sitting down, because her knees might have buckled then. Surely he wasn't saying that she was the reason he hadn't been with another woman in all that time? "You—uh—"

"It's strange, I know," he continued conversationally, though his eyes were focused intently on her face. "All those months I kept telling myself I couldn't ask you out because of your daughter, and because of your friendship with Lynette—but the minute an opportunity arose for me to spend time with you and Daryn, I jumped on it with both feet. Even though it was a pretty damned crazy idea."

She couldn't smile in response to the description, even though he spoke teasingly. Unless she was mistaken—and she wasn't—Tate was making a declaration here. And the spinning in her head had little to do now with whatever germ had been skipping around in her bloodstream.

"Tate, we agreed. We're friends, nothing more. I told you there can't be anything more for me. Because of Daryn."

"Nice excuse. But I don't buy it anymore."

She frowned. "I don't—"

"Let's leave Daryn out of this for a minute. If you didn't have her—if it was just you and me—would you be sending me away?"

"I… That isn't relevant. I can't pretend my daughter doesn't exist."

"I'm not asking you to. I'm asking if she wasn't in the picture, would you be interested in me?"

"I think you know the answer to that," she said, the memory of their night together deepening her voice.

He nodded in satisfaction. "You care about me."

It wasn't a question.

"I…could," she admitted grudgingly. "If things were different."

"You know what I think, Kim?" His voice was as gentle as his hands when he took both of hers in his. "I think you're hiding behind Daryn to protect yourself."

Her eyes narrowed. "You're wrong about that. I can take care of myself. I can deal with disappointment and loss. I don't want Daryn to have to learn how so early."

"You're so sure there's going to be disappointment and loss," he said solemnly.

"Because there always is," she whispered.

His fingers tightened around hers. "I'm not those men from your past, Kim. I'm not your father or your stepfathers or Daryn's father. I come from a long line of men who create families and then stay with them for a lifetime. My grandparents have been married fifty-four years. My parents will celebrate their thirty-fourth anniversary in November. I had an uncle who divorced his wife once, but they remarried two years later and stayed together until he died. We stick, thick or thin."

His mouth tilted into a little smile. "When my dad had the talk with me—the one about always using protection?—he told me a real man doesn't have kids he isn't willing to raise. He told me not to make commitments if I wasn't prepared to do whatever it took to fulfill them. He told me if I couldn't offer everything I have—my heart, my loyalty, my entire future—then I shouldn't be making any offers at all. I took those words to heart. I've had girlfriends, but they knew from the start that I wouldn't be pressured into saying anything I didn't mean or making promises I couldn't keep. I've never told any woman I loved her. Until now."

Her hands jumped in his. "You—"

"I love you," he supplied when her voice faded. "I have for months. And I plan to stick around for however long it takes to convince you that you can count on me not to take off when the going gets rough."

"Tate, I—"

"You're sick. You're feverish. I'm unshaven and grubby from a night in a rocking chair. I didn't exactly choose the most romantic moment to spring this on you, did I?" he asked ruefully. "But maybe that helps make my point? Even after the night I just spent, I'm in no hurry to leave. And even when you're sick and feverish and trying your best to chase me away, I want you so badly my teeth hurt."

Her pulse rate jumped. "I can't—"

"You aren't ready. I understand. I just thought you should know how I feel. You keep saying you don't want Daryn hurt, that you don't want to be hurt yourself, but I'm telling you that if I leave now, it wouldn't be because I don't want to stay, but because you would be sending me away."

She found herself wanting so badly to believe him that she ached with it, an ache she didn't even try to blame on her illness. Tate was in love with her? Or thought he was. But there was no way he could guarantee it would last a lifetime, despite his family history.

As for herself—she loved him so much her heart felt close to bursting with it. Like him, she had never allowed herself to truly fall in love before, not even with Daryn's father. But Tate's hesitation had been more noble than hers; he had worried about hurting someone else, while she had feared being hurt yet again. She'd said she was shielding Daryn from heartache—and that was true. But was Tate right that she had used her defense of her daughter as an excuse to protect herself, as well?

"Take all the time you need to decide whether you want to give us a chance. I promise I won't rush you. If you want me to stay away from Daryn until you feel you can trust me, I'll do it, though I have to admit I'll miss her," Tate added with a glance at the quietly playing baby. "It took me a while to wrap my head around the enormity of the responsibility, but I know now it's a challenge I'm ready to take on. I'm willing to make the same lifelong commitment to Daryn that I am to you. I can't imagine ever regretting that decision.

"I just hope you won't shut me out entirely while you decide how you feel about me," he finished quietly. "I've missed you every day since we parted last. The Wednesday lunches weren't the same without you. Nothing is the same without you."

Kim raised her hands to rub her temples in slow circles. She wanted nothing more than to burrow into Tate's arms and tell him she loved him, too. For the first time since childhood, she was tempted to entrust her heart to someone. But was she really prepared to entrust her daughter?

"I do need time to think," she said, her voice raspy again. "I can't deal with this right now."

He looked penitent. "I know. I'm sorry about my lousy timing. Why don't you go lie down again? I'll take care of everything in here."

She made one last attempt to reassert her independence. "You don't have to stay. It's almost time for me to put Daryn down for her morning nap. I'll rest while she does."

"I can take care of that. And while she naps, I can take a quick shower and do some busywork on my computer. You need to give yourself time to fully recover, for Daryn's sake and for your own."

Maybe she could have continued to resist had her head not been threatening to explode. Fighting back the tears she refused to release, she nodded and stood. She hesitated another moment, looking at her daughter, but Daryn was preoccupied with a yellow plastic car and seemed content.

Tate rose, and through her fog of pain his expression appeared apologetic. "If I'm making things worse for you, just say so, Kim. I'll leave. I can call someone else to come help you out, if you want me to. I wanted to help, but maybe I've overstepped my bounds."

She drew a shaky breath. "I just need to lie down again for a few minutes. Daryn is happy with you here, so if you could stay a bit longer..."

He nodded. "Of course. Is there anything I can get for you?"

"No. Thanks, but I just need a little time for the headache meds to kick in. Wake me if you need help with Daryn, please."

"I will, but I'm sure we'll be fine." He reached out to touch her flushed face. "Go rest, Kim. We'll talk again later."

She definitely needed rest before facing the next talk with him. Turning on one heel, she headed for the bedroom and the blissful oblivion of sleep.

Her dreams were chaotic, flashes of images and voices, memories and fantasies. People who had drifted in and out of her life, others she had deliberately pushed away. Her mother and brothers. Her grandmother. Coworkers and clients. Friends and enemies. Chris. Daryn. Tate.

The house was very quiet when she woke. Daryn must still be napping. Before glancing at the clock, she lay on her back staring up at the ceiling and trying to assess how she felt.

Better, she decided tentatively, feeling no pain shooting through her temples now. She swallowed experimentally, and her throat, while dry, seemed less inflamed. Even her joints ached less than before. Sleep really did have healing powers.

The last two days seemed almost like a dream themselves now that she was thinking a little more clearly. Had Tate really said he loved her?

She chewed her chapped lower lip, replaying everything he had said, every word of which suddenly stood out clearly amid the hazy other memories. He had professed his love for her. And his intention to be the one man who stayed, unlike the ones who had walked away.

Every cell of her longed to believe him. She had missed him so much during the past week and a half, even while she had so carefully avoided him. She'd had a glimpse of what her life would be like without Tate in it at all, and it had made her so sad. And that was before he'd offered her a chance at a serious relationship with him. If she took that chance, if she acknowledged her own love for him—to him and to herself—would she be opening herself up for yet another heartbreak?

Even worse, would she be setting Daryn up for bitter disappointment? Daryn was already growing attached to Tate, despite Kim's efforts to protect her. To be fair, Tate seemed to be growing fond of Daryn, too. Of course, who wouldn't? Not that she was at all objective. Still—could she trust that his affection for the baby would survive the daily challenges of family life? The day-to-day routines and grinds and difficulties of raising a child?

He'd had a taste of those difficulties during the past few hours, and she had to admit he'd handled it all beautifully. He'd even told her he loved her after a night that had to have been harrowing for him. But long-term?

Not in her experience.

Sighing lightly, she glanced at the clock, expecting to find that she'd slept for an hour or so. She gasped audibly when she saw that four hours had passed since she'd fallen onto the bed.

Four hours?

Climbing from the bed, she moved straight to the bathroom. Since Tate hadn't disturbed her, she trusted he had everything under control, at least long enough for her to clean up. She was in and out of the shower in five minutes. Ten minutes later, her hair was blown mostly dry, her teeth were brushed and she was dressed in a pink T-shirt and black athletic pants with a narrow pink stripe down the side. Donning black slippers, she decided she looked more controlled and composed and less helpless and sickly than before. Better able to make critical decisions that could affect the rest of her life—and her daughter's.

With her head held high and her confidence in place, at least outwardly, she walked toward the living room.

Dressed now in a dark green polo and jeans, looking as though he, too, had showered since they'd last parted, Tate sat on the couch, bouncing Daryn and Mr. Jingles on his knees. Daryn gurgled happily, still wearing the lavender romper, her headband bow arranged a bit more tidily now than it had been before. She looked clean, healthy, content and secure with this man who had saved her life, and had promised to be there for her for the rest of his own. Her little heart was open to love. Would it really be in Daryn's best interest to teach her to spend her life hiding behind preemptive, self-protective emotional barriers?

Kim understood that she wasn't like her mother. She would never subject Daryn to the chaos Betsy habitually created around her. Wasn't it time for her to acknowledge that Tate wasn't like her father, or any of the other men Betsy had been drawn to? As he'd said himself, Tate deserved to be judged on his own merits, not punished for the shortcomings of others.

As if sensing her standing there, he looked around, smiling in approval when he saw her. "I hope you're feeling as much better as you look."

"I love you, Tate."

His legs stopped moving abruptly, so that Daryn bobbled a bit on his knees. Tate righted her instantly, gathering her into his arms as he rose slowly from the couch. "Sorry, monkette, your mom just knocked me for a loop. Um, Kim—am I coming down with your fever, or did you just say—?"

"I said I love you," she repeated a bit more clearly this time. "And it scares the stuffing out of me."

"I can understand that." His voice was just a little unsteady, as if shaken by emotions he was holding barely in check. "I'm a little nervous about all this myself. But every fiber of my being tells me it's right. In fact..."

His eyes glinted with a return of the infectious humor that was so much a part of the man she had fallen in love with over Chinese food. "I'd be willing to wager on it. I'll bet you that I'll be around to walk Daryn up the aisle in, say, twenty-five years or so. Assuming we let her date by then, of course."

Nerves merged with hope, both mixed with almost overwhelming love. She moistened her lips and tried to match his light tone. "What are you willing to bet? Another hundred bucks?"

"I'm willing to bet everything I have," he answered simply, his eyes burning with sincerity. "I'm betting my heart."

Taking all her courage metaphorically in both hands, Kim moved into a group hug with Tate and Daryn, smiling up at him mistily. "I'll take that bet."

While Daryn patted their faces enthusiastically, she and Tate sealed the wager with a kiss.

Epilogue

Guided by the dim glow of a nightlight, Kim made her way back to her bed in the middle of that night. Dropping her lightweight summer robe to the floor, she lifted the sheet and slipped beneath, where she was gathered immediately into Tate's bare arms.

"Is she okay?" he asked, his voice husky.

"She's fine. Just making noises in her sleep again, I guess."

"She makes some funny ones," he agreed with a chuckle. "Startled me a couple of times last night when I was snoozing in the chair."

"I worry a little that you've only seen the best side of her," she fretted, resting her head on Tate's chest, just above his steadily beating heart. "I mean, she's a very good baby, but she can be a pill sometimes."

He laughed softly. "The best side of her? Did I mention the two toxic-level diapers I changed last night? Or that I learned the hard way not to bounce her up and down immediately after giving her some milk? Or that she tuned up for a scream-fest every time I dared to lay her down for a minute last night? I had to time my bathroom breaks with her naps, which wasn't always ideal, by the way."

"No, you, um, didn't mention any of that." She was amazed yet again by what he had encountered with such admirable equanimity last night.

"But then this morning when she woke up and gave me one of those slobbery little two-toothed grins? Well, my heart melted."

"I react exactly the same way to that smile every morning," she admitted.

Tate shifted onto his side and leaned over her, brushing her hair away from her face as he looked down at her. "I know it's going to take some time for you to really trust that I'm in this for the long haul. I'm thinking you should look at the evidence. I've survived a weekend with your mother and her sister, a grilling by your grandmother, a test of on-the-spot resourcefulness by your younger brother, and a night with a sick, cranky baby and her sick, cranky mother—and I'm still here. Still oddly looking forward to whatever else you might throw at me."

She shook her head in bemusement. "Maybe I just can't imagine why you would want to continually subject yourself to my crazy life."

"Because I love you," he answered without hesitation. "And I love Daryn. I love us together as a family. Maybe someday an even bigger family."

She swallowed hard at the thought of having a child with Tate. She'd convinced herself she would never have another child, and she'd thought she was okay with that. Now she realized she liked the idea very much.

"Too soon?"

"Maybe a little," she agreed with a shaky laugh.

He brushed his lips across hers. "We have plenty of time to discuss kids. I guess we should focus on getting married first. To make your mother happy, of course."

"Married," she repeated rather blankly.

He chuckled. "Married. I don't want to be your husband for a weekend, Kim. I want to be your husband for a lifetime. Any thoughts about that?"

"I think…Grandma gave her ring to the right granddaughter, after all," she said shakily.

His smile flashed in the darkness. "Is that a yes?"

"It's a yes. We'll take our time, do it right, make very sure of every decision we make, but—"

"I was thinking we could get married soon. I'd be good with Monday—but if you need a little more time, that's cool, too. I know you can't take any time off right now, but we can plan a vacation next summer, maybe."

"Um—Monday?" The word came out in a near-squeak.

He nodded. "There's no waiting period for a marriage license in this state, so that's not an issue. You don't really want a big, formal affair, do you? The wedding you described to your aunt, just us and an officiate—and Daryn, of course—well, that sounded perfect to me."

"To me, too," she agreed. "But, um, Monday?"

He chuckled. "Okay, maybe next month. Whenever you're ready. Take time to think about it." His hands had begun to roam, making it difficult for her to think about anything coherently.

Monday, she thought, arching reflexively when he lowered his mouth to her breasts. *The day after tomorrow.* She was definitely going to think about that. Later.

Much later, she decided when his legs wrapped around hers.

She would bet Tate would find a way to talk her into it.

* * * * *

THE ANNIVERSARY PARTY

Dear Reader,

I am a big believer in celebrating milestones, and for Special Edition, this is a big one! Thirty years… it hardly seems possible, and yet April 1982 was indeed, yep, thirty years ago! When I walked into the Harlequin offices (only *twenty* years ago, but still), the first books I worked on were Special Edition. I loved the line instantly—for its breadth and its depth, and for its fabulous array of authors, some of whom I've been privileged to work with for twenty years, and some of whom are newer, but no less treasured, friends.

When it came time to plan our thirtieth anniversary celebration, we wanted to give our readers something from the heart—not to mention something from our very beloved April 2012 lineup. So many thanks to RaeAnne Thayne, Christine Rimmer, Susan Crosby, Christyne Butler, Gina Wilkins and Cindy Kirk for their contributions to *The Anniversary Party.* The Morgans, Diana and Frank, are celebrating their thirtieth anniversary along with us. Like us, they've had a great thirty years, and they're looking forward to many more. Like us, though there may be some obstacles along the way, they're getting their happily ever after.

Which is what we wish you, Dear Reader. Thanks for coming along for the first thirty years of Special Edition—we hope you'll be with us for many more!

We hope you enjoy *The Anniversary Party.*

Here's to the next thirty!

All the best,

Gail Chasan
Senior Editor, Special Edition

Chapter One

by RaeAnne Thayne

With the basket of crusty bread sticks she had baked that afternoon in one arm and a mixed salad—*insalata mista,* as the Italians would say—in the other, Melissa Morgan walked into her sister's house and her jaw dropped.

"Oh, my word, Ab! This looks incredible! When did you start decorating? A month ago?"

Predictably, Abby looked a little wild-eyed. Her sister was one of those type A personalities who always sought perfection, whether that was excelling in her college studies, where she'd emerged with a summa cum laude, or decorating for their parents' surprise thirtieth anniversary celebration.

Abby didn't answer for a moment. She was busy arranging a plant in the basket of a rusty bicycle resting against one wall so the greenery spilled over the top, almost to the front tire. Melissa had no idea how she'd managed it but somehow Abby had hung wooden lattice from her ceiling to form a faux pergola over her dining table. Grapevines, fairy lights and more greenery had been woven through the lattice and, at various intervals, candles hung in colored jars like something out of a Tuscan vineyard.

Adorning the walls were framed posters of Venice and the beautiful and calming Lake Como.

"It feels like a month," Abby finally answered, "but actually, I only started last week. Greg helped me hang the lattice. I couldn't have done it without him."

The affection in her sister's voice caused a funny little twinge inside Melissa. Abby and her husband had one of those perfect relationships. They clearly adored each other, no matter what.

She wished she could say the same thing about Josh. After a year of dating, shouldn't she have a little more confidence in their relationship? If someone had asked her a month ago if she thought her boyfriend loved her, she would have been able to answer with complete assurance in the affirmative, but for the past few weeks something had changed. He'd been acting so oddly—dodging phone calls, canceling plans, avoiding her questions.

He seemed to be slipping away more every day. As melodramatic as it sounded, she didn't know how she would survive if he decided to break things off.

Breathe, she reminded herself. She didn't want to ruin the anniversary dinner by worrying about Josh. For now, she really needed to focus on her wonderful parents and how very much they deserved this celebration she and Abby had been planning for a long time.

"You and Greg have really outdone yourself. I love all the little details. The old wine bottles, the flowers. Just beautiful. I know Mom and Dad will be thrilled with your hard work." She paused. "I can only see one little problem."

Abby looked vaguely panicked. "What? What's missing?"

Melissa shook her head ruefully. "Nothing. That's the problem. I was supposed to be helping you. That's why I'm here early, right? Have you left anything for me to do?"

"Are you kidding? I've still got a million things to do. The chicken cacciatore is just about ready to go into the oven. Why don't you help me set the table?"

"Sure," she said, following her sister into the kitchen.

"You talked to Louise, right?" Abby asked.

"Yes. She had everything ready when I stopped at her office on my way over here. I've got a huge gift basket in the car. You should see it. She really went all out. Biscotti, gourmet cappuccino mix, even a bottle of prosecco."

"What about the tickets and the itinerary?" Abby had that panicked look again.

"Relax, Abs. It's all there. She's been amazing. I think she just might be as scarily organized as you are."

Abby made a face. "Did you have a chance to go over the details?"

"She printed everything out and included a copy for us, as well as Mom and Dad. In addition to the plane tickets and the hotel information and the other goodies, she sent over pamphlets, maps, even an Italian-English dictionary and a couple of guidebooks."

"Perfect! They're going to be so surprised."

"Surprised and happy, I hope," Melissa answered, loading her arms with the deep red chargers and honey-gold plates her sister indicated, which perfectly matched the theme for the evening.

"How could they be anything else? They finally have the chance to enjoy the perfect honeymoon they missed out on the first time." Abby smiled, looking more than a little starry-eyed. Despite being married for several years, her sister was a true romantic.

"This has to be better than the original," she said. "The bar was set pretty low thirty years ago, judging by all the stories they've told us over the years. Missed trains, lousy hotels, disappearing luggage."

"Don't forget the pickpocket that stole their cash and passports."

Melissa had to smile. Though their parents' stories always made their honeymoon thirty years ago sound dismal, Frank and Diane always laughed when they shared them, as if they had viewed the whole thing as a huge adventure.

She wanted that. She wanted to share that kind of joy and laughter and tears with Josh. The adventure that was life.

Her smile faded, replaced by that ache of sadness that always seemed so close these days. *Oh, Josh.* She reached into the silverware drawer, avoiding her sister's gaze.

"Okay. What's wrong?" Abby asked anyway.

She forced a smile. "Nothing. I'm just a little tired, that's all."

"Late night with Josh?" her sister teased.

Before she could stop them, tears welled up and

spilled over. She blinked them back but not before her sharp-eyed sister caught them.

"What did I say?" Abby asked with a stunned look.

"Nothing. I just…I didn't have a late night with Josh. Not last night, not last week, not for the last two weeks. He's avoiding my calls and canceled our last two dates. Even when we're together, it's like he's not there. I know he's busy at work but…I think he's planning to break up with me."

Abby's jaw sagged and Melissa saw shock and something else, something furtive, shift across Abby's expression.

"That can't be true. It just…can't be."

She wanted to believe that, too. "I'm sorry. I shouldn't have said anything. Forget it. You've worked so hard to make this night perfect and I don't want to ruin it."

Abby shook her head. "You need to put that wacky idea out of your head right now. Josh is crazy about you. It's clear to anybody who has ever seen the two of you together for five seconds. He couldn't possibly be thinking of breaking things off."

"I'm sure you're right," she lied. Too much evidence pointed otherwise. Worst of all was the casual kiss good-night the past few times she'd seen him, instead of one of their deep, emotional, soul-sharing kisses that made her toes curl.

"I'm serious, Missy. Trust me on this. I'm absolutely positive he's not planning to break up with you. Not Josh. He loves you. In fact…"

She stopped, biting her lip, and furiously turned back to the chicken.

"In fact what?"

Abby's features were evasive. "In fact, would he be out right now with Greg buying the wine and champagne for tonight if he didn't want to have anything to do with the Morgan family?"

Out of the corner of her gaze, Melissa saw that amazingly decorated dining room again, the magical setting her sister had worked so hard to create for their parents who loved each other dearly. She refused to ruin this night for Abby and the rest of her family. For now, she would focus on the celebration and forget the tiny cracks in her heart.

She pasted on a smile and grabbed the napkins, with their rings formed out of entwined grapevine hearts. "You're right. I'm being silly. I'm sure everything will be just fine. Anyway, tonight is for Mom and Dad. That's the important thing."

Abby gave her a searching look and Melissa couldn't help thinking that even with the worry lines on her forehead, Abby seemed to glow tonight.

"It is about them, isn't it?" Abby murmured. Though Melissa's arms were full, her sister reached around the plates and cutlery to give her a hug. "Trust me, baby sister. Everything will be just fine."

Melissa dearly wanted to believe her and as she returned to the dining room, she did her very best to ignore the ache of fear that something infinitely dear was slipping away.

"Hello? Are you still in there?"

His friend Greg's words jerked Josh out of his daze and he glanced up. "Yeah. Sorry. Did you say something?"

"Only about three times. I've been asking your opinion about the champagne and all I'm getting in return is a blank stare. You're a million miles away, man, which is not really helping out much here."

This just might be the most important day of his life. Who could blame a guy if he couldn't seem to string two thoughts together?

"Sorry. I've got a lot of things on my mind."

"And champagne is obviously not one of those things."

He made a face. "It rarely is. I'm afraid I'm more of a Sam Adams kind of guy."

"I hear you. Why do you think I asked you to come along and help me pick out the wine and champagne for tonight?"

He had wondered that himself. "Because my car has a bigger trunk?"

Greg laughed, which eased Josh's nerves a little. He had to admit, he had liked the guy since he met him a year ago when he first started dating Melissa. Josh was married to Melissa's sister, Abby, and if things worked out the way he hoped, they would be brothers-in-law in the not-so-distant future.

"It's only the six of us for dinner," Greg reminded him. "I'm not exactly buying cases here. So what do you think?"

He turned back to the racks of bottles. "No idea. Which one is more expensive?"

Greg picked one up with a fancy label that certainly looked pricey.

"Excellent choice." The snooty clerk who had mostly been ignoring them since they walked in finally deigned to approach them.

"You think so?" Greg asked. "We're celebrating a big occasion."

"You won't be disappointed, I assure you. What else can I help you find?"

Sometime later—and with considerably lightened wallets—the two of them carried two magnums of champagne and two bottles of wine out to Josh's car.

"I, uh, need to make one last quick stop," he said after pulling into traffic. "Do you mind waiting?"

"No problem. The party doesn't start for another two hours. We've got plenty of time."

When Josh pulled up in front of an assuming storefront a few moments later, Greg looked at the sign above the door then back at him with eyebrows raised. "Wow. Seriously? Tonight? I thought Abby was jumping the gun when she said she suspected you were close to proposing. She's always right, that beautiful wife of mine. Don't tell her I said that."

Josh shifted, uncomfortably aware his fingers were shaking a little as he undid his seatbelt. "I bought the ring two weeks ago. When the jeweler told me it would be ready today, I figured that was a sign."

"You're a brave man to pick a ring out without her."

Panic clutched at his gut again, but he took a deep breath and pushed it away. He wanted to make his proposal perfect. Part of that, to his mind, was the element of surprise.

"I found a bridal magazine at Melissa's apartment kind of hidden under a stack of books and she had the page folded down on this ring. I snapped a quick picture with my phone and took that in to the jeweler."

"Nice." Greg's admiring look settled his stomach a little.

"I figure, if she doesn't like it, we can always reset the stone, right?"

"So when are you going to pop the question?"

"I haven't figured that out yet. I thought maybe when I take her home after the party tonight, we might drive up to that overlook above town."

"That could work."

"What about you? How did you propose to Abby?"

"Nothing very original, I'm afraid. I took her to dinner at La Maison Marie. She loves that place. Personally, I think you're only paying for overpriced sauce, but what can you do? Anyway, after dinner, she kept acting like she was expecting something. I *did* take her along to shop for rings a few weeks earlier but hadn't said anything to her since. She seemed kind of disappointed when the dessert came and no big proposal. So we were walking around on the grounds after dinner and we walked past this waterfall and pond she liked. I pretended I tripped over something and did a stupid little magician sleight of hand and pulled out the ring box."

"Did you do the whole drop-to-your-knee thing?"

"Yeah. It seemed important to Abby. Women remember that kind of thing."

"I hope I don't forget that part."

"Don't sweat it. When the moment comes, whatever you do will be right for the two of you, I promise."

"I hope so."

The depth of his love for Melissa still took him by surprise. He loved her with everything inside him and wanted to give her all the hearts and flowers and romance she could ever want.

"It will be," Greg said. "Anyway, look at how lousy

Frank and Diane's marriage started out. Their honeymoon sounded like a nightmare but thirty years later they can still laugh about it."

That was what he wanted with Melissa. Thirty years—and more—of laughter and joy and love.

He just had to get through the proposal first.

Chapter Two
by Christine Rimmer

"Frank. The light is yellow. Frank!" Diana Morgan stomped the passenger-side floor of the Buick. Hard. If only she had the brakes on her side.

Frank Morgan pulled to a smooth stop as the light went red. "There," he said, in that calm, deep, untroubled voice she'd always loved. "We're stopped. No need to wear a hole in the floor."

Diana glanced over at her husband of thirty years. She loved him so much. There were a whole lot of things to worry about in life, but Frank's love was the one thing Diana never doubted. He belonged to her, absolutely, as she belonged to him, and he'd given her two beautiful, perfect daughters. Abby and Melissa were all grown up now.

The years went by way too fast.

Diana sent her husband another glance. Thirty years

together. Amazing. She still loved just looking at him. He was the handsomest man she'd ever met, even at fifty-seven. Nature had been kind to him. He had all his hair and it was only lightly speckled with gray. She smoothed her own shoulder-length bob. No gray there, either. Her hair was still the same auburn shade it had been when she married him. Only in her case, nature didn't have a thing to do with it.

A man only grew more distinguished over the years. A woman had to work at it.

The light turned green. Frank hit the gas.

Too hard, Diana thought. But she didn't say a word. She only straightened her teal-blue silk blouse, recrossed her legs and tried not to make impatient, worried noises. Frank was a wonderful man. But he drove too fast.

Abby and her husband, Greg, were having them over for dinner tonight. They were on their way there now—to Abby's house. Diana was looking forward to the evening. But she was also dreading it. Something was going on with Abby. A mother knows these things.

And something was bothering Melissa, too. Diana's younger daughter was still single. She'd been going out with Josh Wright for a year now. It was a serious relationship.

But was there something wrong between Josh and Melissa? Diana had a sense about these things, a sort of radar for emotional disturbances, especially when it came to her daughters. Right now, tonight, Diana had a suspicion that something wasn't right—both between Melissa and Josh *and* between Abby and Greg.

"Remember Venice?" Frank gave her a fond glance.

She smiled at him—and then stiffened. "Frank. Eyes on the road."

"All right, all right." He patiently faced front again. "Remember that wonderful old hotel on the Grand Canal?"

She made a humphing sound. "It was like the rest of our honeymoon. Nothing went right."

"I loved every moment of it," he said softly.

She reminded him, "You know what happened at that hotel in Venice, how they managed to lose our luggage somewhere between the front desk and our room. How hard can it be, to get the suitcases to the right room? And it smelled a bit moldy in the bathroom, didn't you think?"

"All I remember is you, Diana. Naked in the morning light." He said it softly. Intimately.

She shivered a little, drew in a shaky breath and confessed, "Oh, yes. That. I remember that, too." It was one of the best things about a good marriage. The shared memories. Frank had seen her naked in Venice when they were both young. Together, they had heard Abby's first laugh, watched Melissa as she learned to walk, staggering and falling, but then gamely picking herself right back up and trying again. Together, they had made it through all those years that drew them closer, through the rough times as well as the happy ones....

A good marriage.

Until very recently, she'd been so sure that Abby and Greg were happy. But were they? Really? And what about Melissa and Josh?

Oh, Lord. Being a mother was the hardest job in the world. They grew up. But they stayed in your heart.

And when they were suffering, you ached right along with them.

"All right," Frank said suddenly in an exasperated tone. "You'd better just tell me, Diana. You'd better just say it, whatever it is."

Diana sighed. Deeply. "Oh, Frank…"

"Come on," he coaxed, pulling to another stop at yet another stoplight—at the very last possible second. She didn't even stomp the floor that time, she was that upset. "Tell me," he insisted.

Tears pooled in her eyes and clogged her throat. She sniffed them back. "I wasn't going to do it. I wasn't going to interfere. I wasn't even going to say a word…"

He flipped open the armrest and whipped out a tissue. "Dry your eyes."

"Oh, Frank…" She took the tissue and dabbed at her lower lid. If she wasn't careful, her makeup would be a total mess.

"Now," Frank said, reaching across to pat her knee. "Tell me about it. Whatever it is, you know you'll feel better once we've talked it over."

The light changed. "Go," she said on a sob.

He drove on. "I'm waiting."

She sniffed again. "I think something's wrong between Abby and Greg. And not only that, there's something going on with Melissa, too. I think Melissa's got…a secret, you know? A secret that is worrying her terribly."

"Why do you think something's going on between Abby and Greg?"

"I sensed it. You know how sensitive I am— Oh, God. Do you think Abby and Greg are breaking up? Do you think he might be seeing someone else?"

"Whoa. Diana. Slow down."

"Well, I am *worried.* I am *so* worried. And Melissa. She is suffering. I can hear it in her voice when I talk to her."

"But you haven't told me *why* you think there might be something wrong—with Melissa, or between Abby and Greg. Did Abby say something to you?"

"Of course not. She wants to protect me."

"What about Melissa?"

"What do you *mean,* what about Melissa?"

"Well, did you *ask* her if something is bothering her?"

Another sob caught in Diana's throat. She swallowed it. "I couldn't. I didn't want to butt in."

Frank eased the car to the shoulder and stopped. "Diana," he said. That was all. Just her name.

It was more than enough. "Don't you look at me like that, Frank Morgan."

"Diana, I hate to say this—"

"Then don't. Just don't. And why are we stopped? We'll be late. Even with family, you know I always like to be on time."

"Diana…"

She waved her soggy tissue at him. "Drive, Frank. Just drive."

He leaned closer across the console. "Sweetheart…"

She sagged in her seat. "Oh, fine. What?"

"You know what you're doing, don't you?" He said it gently. But still. She knew exactly what he was getting at and she didn't like it one bit.

She sighed and dropped the wadded tissue in the little wastepaper bag she always carried in the car. "Well, I know you're bound to tell me, now don't I?"

He took her hand, kissed the back of it.

"Don't try to butter me up," she muttered.

"You're jumping to conclusions again," he said tenderly.

"Am not."

"Yes, you are. You've got nothin'. Zip. Admit it. No solid reason why you think Melissa has a secret or why you think Abby and Greg are suddenly on the rocks."

"I don't need a solid reason. I can *feel* it." She laid her hand over her heart. "Here."

"You know it's very possible that what's really going on is a surprise anniversary party for us, don't you?"

Diana smoothed her hair. "What? You mean tonight?"

"That's right. Tonight."

"Oh, I suppose. It could be." She pictured their dear faces. She loved them so much. "They are the sweetest girls, aren't they?"

"The best. I'm the luckiest dad in the world—not to mention the happiest husband."

Diana leaned toward him and kissed him. "You *are* a very special man." She sank back against her seat—and remembered how worried she was. "But Frank, if this *is* a party, it's still not *it*."

"It?" He looked bewildered. Men could be so thickheaded sometimes.

Patiently, she reminded him, "The awful, secret things that are going on with our daughters."

He bent in close, kissed her cheek and then brushed his lips across her own. "We are going to dinner at our daughter's house," he whispered. "We are going to have a wonderful time. You are not going to snoop around trying to find out if something's wrong with Abby. You're not going to worry about Melissa."

"I hate you, Frank."

"No, you don't. You love me *almost* as much as I love you."

She wrinkled her nose at him. "More. I love you more."

He kissed her again. "Promise you won't snoop and you'll stop jumping to conclusions?"

"And if I don't, what? We'll sit here on the side of the road all night?"

"Promise."

"Fine. All right. I promise."

He touched her cheek, a lovely, cherishing touch. "Can we go to Abby's now?"

"I'm not the one who stopped the car."

He only looked at her reproachfully.

She couldn't hold out against him. She never could. "Oh, all right. I've promised, already, okay? Now, let's go."

With a wry smile, he retreated back behind the wheel and eased the car forward into the flow of traffic again.

Abby opened the door. "Surprise!" Abby, Greg, Melissa and Josh all shouted at once. They all started clapping.

Greg announced, "Happy Anniversary!" The rest of them chimed in with "Congratulations!" and "Thirty years!" and "Wahoo!"

Frank was laughing. "Well, what do you know?"

Diana said nothing. One look in her older daughter's big brown eyes and she knew for certain that she wasn't just imagining things. Something was going on in Abby's life. Something important.

They all filed into the dining room, where the walls were decorated with posters of the Grand Canal and the Tuscan countryside, of the Coliseum and the small, beautiful town of Bellagio on Lake Como. The table was set with Abby's best china and tall candles gave a golden glow.

Greg said, "We thought, you know, an Italian theme—in honor of your honeymoon."

"It's lovely," said Diana, going through the motions, hugging first Greg and then Josh.

"Thank you," said Frank as he clapped his son-in-law on the back and shook hands with Josh.

Melissa came close. "Mom." She put on a smile. But her eyes were as shadowed as Abby's. "Happy thirtieth anniversary."

Diana grabbed her and hugged her. No doubt about it. Melissa looked miserable, too.

Yes, Diana had promised Frank that she would mind her own business.

But, well, sometimes a woman just couldn't keep that kind of promise. Sometimes a woman had to find a way to get to the bottom of a bad situation for the sake of the ones she loved most of all.

By the end of the evening, no matter what, Diana would find out the secrets her daughters were keeping from her.

Frank leaned close. "Don't even think about it."

She gave him her sweetest smile. "Happy anniversary, darling."

Chapter Three
by Susan Crosby

Abby Morgan DeSena and her husband, Greg, had hosted quite a few dinner parties during their three years of marriage, but none as special as this one—a celebration of Abby's parents' thirtieth wedding anniversary. Abby and her younger sister, Melissa, had spent weeks planning the Italian-themed party as a sweet reminder for their parents of their honeymoon, and now that the main meal was over, Abby could say, well, so far, so good.

For someone who planned everything down to the last detail, that was high praise. They were on schedule. First, antipasti and wine in the living room, then chicken cacciatore, crusty bread sticks and green salad in the dining room.

But for all that the timetable had been met and the food praised and devoured, an air of tension hovered over the six people at the table, especially between Melissa and her boyfriend, Josh, who were both acting out of character.

"We had chicken cacciatore our first night in Bellagio, remember, Diana?" Abby's father said to her mother as everyone sat back, sated. "And lemon sorbet in prosecco."

"The waiter knocked my glass into my lap," Diana reminded him.

"Your napkin caught most of it, and he fixed you another one. He even took it off the tab. On our newlywed budget, it made a difference." He brought his wife's hand to his lips, his eyes twinkling. "And it was delicious, wasn't it? Tart and sweet and bubbly."

Diana blushed, making Abby wonder if the memory involved more than food. It was inspiring seeing her parents so openly in love after thirty years.

Under the table, Abby felt her hand being squeezed and looked at her own beloved husband. Greg winked, as if reading her mind.

"Well, we don't have sorbet and prosecco," Abby said, standing and stacking dinner plates. "But we certainly have dessert. Please sit down, Mom. You're our guest. Melissa and I will take care of everything."

It didn't take long to clear the table.

"Mom and Dad loved the dinner, didn't they?" Melissa asked as they entered Abby's contemporary kitchen.

"They seemed to," Abby answered, although unsure whether she believed her own words. Had her parents noticed the same tension Abby had? Her mother's gaze had flitted from Melissa to Josh to Abby to Greg all evening, as if searching for clues. It'd made Abby more nervous with every passing minute, and on a night she'd been looking forward to, a night of sweet surprises.

"How about you? Did you enjoy the meal?" Abby asked Melissa, setting dishes in the sink, then started the coffeemaker brewing. "You hardly touched your food."

She shrugged. "I guess I snacked on too many bread sticks before dinner."

Abby took out a raspberry tiramisu from the refrigerator while studying her sister, noting how stiffly Melissa held herself, how shaky her hands were as she rinsed the dinner plates. She seemed fragile. It wasn't a word Abby usually applied to her sister. The conversation they'd had earlier in the evening obviously hadn't set Melissa's mind at ease, but Abby didn't know what else to say to her tightly wrung sister. Only time—and Josh—could relieve Melissa's anxiety.

Abby set the fancy dessert on the counter next to six etched-crystal parfait glasses.

Melissa approached, drying her hands, then picked up one of the glasses. "Grandma gave these to you, didn't she?"

"Mmm-hmm. Three years ago as a wedding present. I know it's a cliché, but it seems like yesterday." Abby smiled at her sister, remembering the wedding, revisiting her wonderful marriage. She couldn't ask for a better husband, friend and partner than Greg. "Grandma plans to give you the other six glasses at your wedding. When we both have big family dinners, we can share them. It'll be our tradition."

Melissa's face paled. Her eyes welled. Horrified, Abby dropped the spoon and reached for her.

"I—I'll grab the gift basket from your office," Melissa said, taking a couple steps back then rushing out.

Frustrated, Abby pressed her face into her hands. If she were the screaming type, she would've screamed. If she were a throw-the-pots-around type, she would've done that, too, as noisily as possible. It would've felt *good.*

"I thought Melissa was in here with you," said a male voice from behind her.

Abby spun around and glared at Josh Wright, the source of Melissa's problems—and subsequently Abby's—as he peeked into the kitchen. He could be the solution, too, if only he'd act instead of sitting on his hands.

"She's getting the anniversary gift from my office," Abby said through gritted teeth, digging deep for the composure she'd inherited from her father.

Josh came all the way into the room. He looked as strained as Melissa. "Need some help?" he asked, shoving his hands into his pockets instead of going in search of Melissa.

"Coward." Abby began dishing up six portions of tiramisu.

"Guilty," Josh said, coming up beside her. "Give me a job. I can't sit still."

"You can pour the decaf into that carafe next to the coffeemaker."

Full of nervous energy, his hands shaking as much as Melissa's had earlier, he got right to the task, fumbling at every step, slopping coffee onto the counter.

"Relax, would you, Josh?" Abby said, exasperated. "You're making everyone jumpy, but especially Melissa. My sister is her mother's daughter, you know.

They both have a flair for the dramatic, but this time Melissa is honestly thrown by your behavior. She's on the edge, and it's not of her own making."

"But it'll all come out okay in the end?"

The way he turned the sentence into a question had Abby staring at him. He and her kid sister were a study in contrasts, Melissa with her black hair and green eyes, Josh all blond and blue-eyed. They'd been dating for a year, were head over heels in love with each other, seeming to validate the theory that opposites attract. It was rare that they weren't touching or staring into each other's eyes, communicating silently.

Tonight was different, however, and Abby knew why. She just didn't know if they would all survive the suspense.

"Whether or not it all turns out okay in the end depends on how long you take to pop the question," Abby said, dropping her voice to a whisper.

"You know I'm planning the perfect proposal," he whispered back. "Your husband gave me advice, but if you'd like to add yours, I'm listening."

She couldn't tell him that Melissa thought he was about to break up with her—that was hers to say. But Abby could offer some perspective.

"Here's my advice, Josh, and it has nothing to do with how to set a romantic scene that she'll remember the rest of her life. My advice is simple—do it sooner rather than later." She spoke in a normal tone again, figuring even if someone came into the room, they wouldn't suspect what she and Josh were talking about. "When Greg and I were in college, I misunderstood something he said. Instead of asking him to clarify it,

I stewed. And stewed some more. I blew it all out of proportion."

She dug deep into memories she'd long ago put aside. "Here's what happens to a couple at times like that. He asks what's wrong, and she says it's nothing. He asks again. She *insists* it's nothing. A gulf widens that can't be crossed because there's no longer a bridge between them, one you used to travel easily. It doesn't even matter how much love you share. Once trust is gone, once the ability to talk to each other openly and freely goes away, the relationship begins to unravel. Sometimes it takes weeks, sometimes months, even years, but it happens and there's no fixing it."

"But you fixed it."

They almost hadn't, Abby remembered. They came so close to breaking up. "At times like that, it can go either way. Even strong partners struggle sometimes in a marriage."

"How do you get through those times?"

"You put on a smile for everyone, then you try to work it out alone together so that no one else gets involved."

"Don't you talk to your mom? She's had a long, successful marriage. She'd give good advice, wouldn't she?"

Abby smiled as she pictured her sweet, sometimes overwrought mother. "Mom's the last one I'd ask for advice," she said.

"I'm going to see what's taking so long," Diana said to her husband, laying her napkin on the table.

"Diana." Implied in his tone of voice were the words he didn't speak aloud—*Don't borrow trouble.*

"I'm sure they'll be right out," Greg said, standing, suddenly looking frantic. Her cool, calm son-in-law never panicked.

It upped her determination to see what was wrong. Because something definitely was.

"I'm going." Diana headed toward the kitchen. She could hear Abby speaking quietly.

"I adore my mother, but she makes mountains out of molehills. Greg and I are a team. We keep our problems to ourselves. And you know she would take my side, as any parent would, and that isn't fair to Greg. She might hold on to her partiality long after I've forgotten the argument. So you see, Josh, sometimes the best way to handle personal problems is to keep other people in the dark. Got it?"

"Clear as a bell."

Diana slapped a hand over her mouth and slid a few feet along the wall outside the kitchen before she let out an audible gasp. Her first born *was* keeping her in the dark about something, just as Diana had suspected. And Frank had pooh-poohed the whole thing.

Men just didn't get it. It wasn't called women's intuition for nothing—and she wasn't just a woman but a mother. Mothers saw every emotion on their children's faces, knew every body movement.

She'd *known* something was wrong with Abby. Now it'd been verified, not by rumor but by the person in question, no less. Abby and Greg were on the verge of separating. Her daughter had hidden their problems, not seeking advice from the one who loved her most in the world. Diana could've helped, too, she was sure of it.

Keep other people in the dark. The words stung. She wasn't "other people." She was Abby's mother.

And what about Melissa? What was her problem—because she definitely had one, something big, too. Had she confided in Abby?

Diana moved out of range, not wanting to hear more distressing words, not on the anniversary of the most wonderful day of her life. But she had to tell Frank what she'd learned, had to share the awful news with her own partner so that she could make it through the rest of the evening.

At least she could count on Frank to understand.

She hoped.

Chapter Four

by Christyne Butler

Don't think, don't feel.

Just keep breathing and you'll get through this night unscathed.

Unscathed, but with a broken heart.

Melissa squared her shoulders, brushed the wetness from her cheeks and heaved a shuddering breath that shook her all the way to her toes.

There. Don't you feel calmer?

No, she didn't, but that wasn't anyone's fault but her own.

She'd fallen in love with Josh on their very first date and after tonight, she'd probably never see him again.

The past two weeks had been crazy at her job. Trying to make it through what had been ten hours without her usual caffeine fix, having decided that two cups of coffee and three diet sodas a day weren't the best thing for her, had taken its toll. She'd been moody and pissy and okay, she was big to admit it, a bit dramatic.

Hey, she was her mother's daughter.

But none of that explained why the man of her dreams was going to break her heart.

Another deep breath did little to help, but it would have to do. Between helping her sister plan tonight's party and Josh's strange behavior, Melissa knew she was holding herself together with the thinnest of threads.

The scent of fresh coffee drifted through the house and Melissa groaned. Oh, how she ached for a hot cup, swimming in cream and lots of sugar.

Pushing the thought from her head, she picked up the gift basket that held everything her parents would need for a perfect second honeymoon in Italy. There was a small alcove right next to the dining room, a perfect place to stash it until just the right moment.

Turning, she headed for the door of her sister's office when the matching antique photo frames on a nearby bookshelf caught her eye.

The one on the right, taken just a few short years ago, was of Abby and Greg standing at the altar just after being presented to their friends and family as Mr. and Mrs. Gregory DeSena. Despite the elaborate setting, and the huge bridal party standing other either side of them, Melissa right there next to her sister, Abby and Greg only had eyes for each other. In fact, the photographer had captured the picture just as Greg had gently wiped a tear from her sister's cheek.

The other photograph, a bit more formal in monochrome colors of black and white, showed her mother and father on their wedding day. Her mother looked so young, so beautiful, so thin. Daddy was as handsome as ever in his tuxedo, his arm around his bride, his hand easily spanning her waist. The bridal bouquet was larger and over-the-top, typical for the early '80s, but her mother's dress…

Melissa squeezed tighter to the basket, the cellophane crinkling loudly in the silent room.

Abby had planned her wedding with the precision of an army general, right down to her chiffon, A-line silhouette gown with just enough crystal bling along the shoulder straps to give a special sparkle. Their mother looked the opposite, but just as beautiful wearing her own mother's gown, a vintage 1960 beauty of satin, lace and tulle with a circular skirt that cried out for layers of crinoline, a square-neck bodice and sleeves that hugged her arms.

A dress that Melissa had always seen herself wearing one day.

The day she married Josh.

Of course, she'd change into something short and sexy and perfect for dancing the night away after the ceremony, but—

"Oh, what does it matter!" Melissa said aloud. "It's not going to happen! It's never going to happen. Josh doesn't want to date you anymore, much less even think about getting down on one knee."

She exited the room and hurried down the long hall, tucking the basket just out of sight. They would have dessert, present the gift and then she would find a way to get Josh to take her home as soon as possible.

For the last time.

This was all Greg's fault.

As heartbreaking as it was, because she and Frank

had always loved Greg, Diana knew deep in her heart that the man they'd welcomed in their home, into their hearts, was on the verge of walking out on their daughter.

How could Greg do this to Abby?

They were perfect together, complemented each other so well because they were so alike. Levelheaded, organized to a fault, methodical even.

Diana paused and grabbed hold of the stairway landing.

Could that be it?

Could Abby and Greg be too much alike? Had her son-in-law found someone else? Someone cute and bubbly who hung on his every word like it was gold?

Abby had mentioned a coworker of Greg's they'd run into one night while out to dinner. She'd said he'd been reluctant to introduce them, which seemed strange as the woman had literally gushed at how much she enjoyed working with Abby's husband when she'd stopped by their table.

The need to get to Frank, to squeeze his hand and have him comfort her, rolled over Diana. She needed him to tell her that everything would be all right, that she'd been right all along, and promise her they'd fight tooth and nail for their daughter so she didn't lose this beautiful home.

"Mom?"

Diana looked up and found Melissa standing there.

"Are you okay?" Melissa asked. "You look a little pale."

"I'm fine."

"You've got a death grip on the railing."

Diana immediately released her hold. "I just got a bit light-headed for a moment."

Concern filled her daughter's beautiful eyes. She motioned to the steps that led to the second floor. "Here, let's sit."

"But your sister is—"

"Perfectly capable of pulling dessert together all on her own," Melissa took her arm and the two of them sat. "Disgustingly capable, as we both know."

Diana sat, basically because she had no choice, taking the time to really look at her daughter. She'd been crying. Her baby suffered the same fate as she did when tears came—puffy eyes. And while Melissa had been acting strange during dinner, this was the first true evidence Diana had that something was terribly wrong.

"Darling, you seem a bit…off this evening." Diana kept her tone light after a few minutes of silence passed. "How is everything with you? You didn't eat very much tonight."

Melissa stared at her clenched hands. "Everything is just fine, mother. It's been a long week and I'm very tired."

"Yes, you said you've been working long hours. That's probably cut into your free time with Josh."

"Y-yes, it has, but I don't think that's going to be a problem much longer."

"What does that mean?"

Melissa rose, one hand pressed against her stomach. "It's nothing. You were right. We should get back into the dining room. You know how Abby gets when things go off schedule."

Yes, she did know. Oh, the divorce was going to

upset Abby's tidy world, but that didn't mean that Diana wouldn't be there for her other daughter, as well. She still had no idea what was bothering her youngest, but she would find out before this evening was through.

And she would make things right.

For both her girls.

She'd easily found the time to attend Abby's debates, girl scout meetings and band concerts and never missed a dance recital, theatre production or football game while Melissa was on the cheerleading squad. Her daughters might be grown, but they still needed their mother.

Now more than ever.

Diana stood, as well. "Yes, let's go back and join everyone."

They walked into the room and Diana's gaze locked with Frank's. Her husband watched her every step as she moved around the table to retake her seat next to him. Thirty years of marriage honed his deduction skills to a razor-sharp point, and she knew that he knew she'd found out something.

"Okay, let's get this celebration going." Greg spoke from where he stood at the buffet filling tall fluted glasses with sparkling liquid, having already popped open the bottle. "Josh, why don't you hand out the champagne to everyone?"

Frank leaned in close. "What's wrong?"

Diana batted her eyes, determined not to cry as his gentle and caring tone was sure to bring on the waterworks. "Not now, darling."

"So you were worried for nothing?"

"Of course not. I was right all along—" She cut off

her words when Abby came in with a tray of desserts in her hands. "Dear, can I help with those?"

"No, you stay seated, Mom. It'll only take me a moment to hand these out."

True to her words, the etched-crystal parfait dishes were soon at everyone's place setting and, immediately after, Josh placed a glass in front of Frank and Diana.

Diana watched as he then went back to get two more for Greg and Abby and one last trip for the final two glasses.

"Here you go, sweetheart." He moved in behind Melissa and reached past her shoulder to place a glass in front of her.

"No, thank you." Her baby girl's voice was strained.

"You don't want any champagne?" Josh was clearly confused. "You love the stuff. We practically finished off a magnum ourselves last New Year's Eve."

Melissa shook her head, her dark locks flying over her shoulder. "I'm sure. I'll just h-have—" She paused, pressing her fingertips to her mouth for a quick moment. "I'd prefer a cup of coffee. Decaf, please."

Oh, everything made sense now!

The tears, the exhaustion, the hand held protectively over her still flat belly, the refusal of alcohol. Her motherly intrusion might have been late in picking up on Melissa's distress, but the realization over what her baby was facing hit Diana like a thunderbolt coming from the sky.

Her heart didn't know whether to break for the certain pain Abby was facing over the end of her marriage or rejoice with the news that she was finally going to be a grandmother!

Her baby was having a baby!

Chapter Five

by Gina Wilkins

During the year he and Melissa Morgan had been together, Josh Wright thought he'd come to know her family fairly well, but there were still times when he felt like an outsider who couldn't quite catch on to the family rhythms. Tonight was one of those occasions.

The undercurrents of tension at the elegantly set dinner table were obvious enough, even to him.

Melissa had been acting oddly all evening. Abby and Greg kept exchanging significant looks, as though messages passed between them that no one else could hear. Even Melissa and Abby's mom, Diana, typically the life of any dinner party, was unnaturally subdued and introspective tonight. Only the family patriarch, Frank, seemed as steady and unruffled as ever, characteristically enjoying the time with his family without getting drawn in to their occasional, usually Diana-generated melodramas.

Josh didn't have a clue what was going on with any of them. Shouldn't he understand them better by now, considering he wanted so badly to be truly one of them soon?

He dipped his spoon into the dessert dish in front of him, scooping up a bite of fresh raspberries, an orange-liqueur flavored mascarpone cheese mixture and ladyfingers spread with what tasted like raspberry jam. "Abby, this dessert is amazing."

She smiled across the table at him. "Thank you. Mom and Dad had tiramisu the first night of their honeymoon, so I tried to recreate that nice memory."

"Ours wasn't flavored with orange and raspberry," Diana seemed compelled to point out. "We had a more traditional espresso-based tiramisu."

Abby's smile turned just a bit wry. "I found this recipe online and thought it sounded good. I wasn't trying to exactly reproduce what you had before, Mom."

"I think this one is even better," Frank interjected hastily, after swallowing a big bite of his dessert. "Who'd have thought thirty years later we'd be eating tiramisu made by our own little girl, eh, Diana?"

Everyone smiled—except Melissa, who was playing with her dessert without her usual enthusiasm for sweets. It bothered Josh that Melissa seemed to become more withdrawn and somber as the evening progressed. Though she had made a noticeable effort to participate in the dining table conversation, her eyes were darkened to almost jade and the few smiles she'd managed looked forced. As well as he knew her, as much as he loved her, he sensed when she was stressed or unhappy.

For some reason, she seemed both tonight, and that was twisting him into knots.

Maybe Abby had been right when she'd warned him that his nervous anticipation was affecting Melissa, though he thought he'd done a better job of hiding it from her. Apparently, she knew him a bit too well, also.

Encouraged by the response to his compliment of the dessert, he thought he would try again to keep the conversation light and cheerful. Maybe Melissa would relax if everyone else did.

Mindful of the reason for this gathering—and because he was rather obsessed with love and marriage, anyway—he said, "Thirty years. That's a remarkable accomplishment these days. Not many couples are able to keep the fire alive for that long."

He couldn't imagine his passion for Melissa ever burning out, not in thirty years—or fifty, for that matter.

He felt her shift in her seat next to him and her spoon clicked against her dessert dish. He glanced sideways at her, but she was looking down at her dish, her glossy black hair falling forward to hide her face from him.

Frank, at least, seemed pleased with Josh's observation.

"That's it, exactly." Frank pointed his spoon in Josh's direction, almost dripping raspberry jam on the tablecloth. "Keeping the fire alive. Takes work, but it's worth it, right, hon?"

"Absolutely." Diana looked hard at Abby and Greg as she spoke. "All marriages go through challenging times, but with love and patience and mutual effort, the rewards will come."

Abby and Greg shared a startled look, but Frank

spoke again before either of them could respond to what seemed like a sermon aimed directly at them. "I still remember the day I met her, just like it was yesterday."

That sounded like a story worth pursuing. Though everyone else had probably heard it many times, Josh encouraged Frank to continue. "I'd like to hear about it. How did you meet?"

Frank's smile was nostalgic, his eyes distant with the memories. "I was the best man in a college friend's wedding. Diana was the maid of honor. I had a flat tire on the way to the wedding rehearsal, so I was late arriving."

Diana shook her head. Though she still looked worried about something, she was paying attention to her husband's tale. "The bride was fit to be tied that it looked as though the best man wasn't going to show up for the rehearsal. She was a nervous wreck, even though her groom kept assuring her Frank could be counted on to be there."

Frank chuckled. "Anyway, the minute I arrived, all rumpled and dusty from changing the tire, I was rushed straight to a little room off the church sanctuary where the groom's party was gathered getting ready to enter on cue. I didn't have a chance to socialize or meet the other wedding party members before the rehearsal began. Five minutes after I dashed in, I was standing at the front of the church next to my friend Jim. And then the music began and the bridesmaids started their march in. Diana was the third bridesmaid to enter."

"Gretchen was first, Bridget next."

Ignoring the details Diana inserted, Frank continued, "She was wearing a green dress, the same color as her eyes. The minute she walked into the church, I felt my heart flop like a landed fish."

Diana laughed ruefully. "Well, that doesn't sound very romantic."

Frank patted her hand, still lost in his memories. "She stopped halfway down the aisle and informed the organist that she was playing much too slowly and that everyone in the audience would fall asleep before the whole wedding party reached the front of the church."

"Well, she was."

Frank chuckled and winked at Josh. "That was when I knew this was someone I had to meet."

Charmed by the story, Josh remembered the first moment he'd laid eyes on Melissa. He understood that "floppy fish" analogy all too well, though he'd compared his own heart to a runaway train. He could still recall how hard it had raced when Melissa had tossed back her dark hair and laughed up at him for the first time, her green eyes sparkling with humor and warmth. He'd actually wondered for a moment if she could hear it pounding against his chest.

"So it was love at first sight?"

Frank nodded decisively. "That it was."

"And when did you know she was 'the one' for you? That you wanted to marry her?"

"Probably right then. But certainly the next evening during the ceremony, after I'd spent a few hours getting to know Diana. When I found myself mentally saying 'I do' when the preacher asked 'Do you take this woman?' I knew I was hooked."

Josh sighed. This, he thought, was why he wanted to wait for the absolute perfect moment to propose to Melissa. Someday he hoped to tell a story that would make everyone who heard it say "Awww," the way he felt like doing now. "You're a lucky man, Frank. Not every guy is fortunate enough to find a woman he wants to spend the rest of his life with."

Three lucky men sat at this table tonight, he thought happily. Like Frank and Greg, he had found his perfect match.

Melissa dropped her spoon with a clatter and sprang to her feet. "I, uh— Excuse me," she muttered, her voice choked. "I'm not feeling well."

Before Josh or anyone else could ask her what was wrong, she dashed from the room. Concerned, he half rose from his seat, intending to follow her.

"What on earth is wrong with Melissa?" Frank asked in bewilderment.

Words burst from Diana as if she'd held them in as long as she was physically able. "Melissa is pregnant."

His knees turning to gelatin, Josh fell back into his chair with a thump.

After patting her face with a towel, Melissa looked in the bathroom mirror to make sure she'd removed all signs of her bout of tears. She was quite sure Abby would say she was overreacting and being overly dramatic—just like their Mom, Abby would say with a shake of her auburn head—but Melissa couldn't help it. Every time she thought about her life without Josh in it tears welled up behind her eyes and it was all she could do to keep them from gushing out.

Abby had tried to convince her she was only imagining that Josh was trying to find a way to break up with her. As much as she wanted to believe her sister, Melissa was convinced her qualms were well-founded. She knew every expression that crossed Josh's handsome face. Every flicker of emotion that passed through his clear blue eyes. He had grown increasingly nervous and awkward around her during the past few days, when they had always been so close, so connected, so easy together before. Passion was only a part of their relationship—though certainly a major part. But the mental connection between them was even more special—or at least it had been.

She didn't know what had gone wrong. Everything had seemed so perfect until Josh's behavior had suddenly changed. But maybe the questions he had asked her dad tonight had been a clue. Maybe he had concluded that he didn't really want to spend the rest of his life with her. That only a few men were lucky enough to find "the one."

She had so hoped she was Josh's "one."

Feeling tears threaten again, she drew a deep breath and lifted her chin, ordering herself to reclaim her pride. She would survive losing Josh, she assured herself. Maybe.

Forcing herself to leave Abby's guest bathroom, she headed for the dining room, expecting to hear conversation and the clinking of silverware and china. Instead what appeared to be stunned silence gripped the five people sitting at the table. Her gaze went instinctively to Josh, finding him staring back at her. His dark blond hair tumbled almost into his eyes, making him look oddly disheveled and perturbed. She realized suddenly that everyone else was gawking at her, too. Did she see sympathy on her father's face?

Before she could stop herself, she leaped to a stomach-wrenching conclusion. Had Josh told her family that he was breaking up with her? Is that why they were all looking at her like…well, like that?

"What?" she asked apprehensively.

"Why didn't you tell me?" Josh demanded.

It occurred to her that he sounded incongruously hurt, considering he was the one on the verge of breaking her heart. "Tell you what?"

"That you're pregnant."

"I'm—?" Her voice shot up into a squeak of surprise, unable to complete the sentence.

"Don't worry, darling, we'll all be here for you," Diana assured her, wiping her eyes with the corner of a napkin. "Just as we'll be here for you, Abby, after you and Greg split up. Although I sincerely hope you'll try to work everything out before you go your separate ways."

"Wait. What?" Greg's chair scraped against the floor as he spun to stare at his wife. "What is she talking about, Abby?"

Melissa felt as if she'd left a calm, orderly dinner party and returned only minutes later to sheer pandemonium.

"What on earth makes you think I'm pregnant?" she asked Josh, unable to concentrate on her sister's sputtering at the moment.

He looked from her to her mom and back again, growing visibly more confused by the minute. "Your mother told us."

Her mother sighed and nodded. "I've overheard a few snippets of conversation today. Enough to put two and two together about what's going on with both my poor girls. You're giving up caffeine and you're feeling queasy and we've all noticed that you've been upset all evening."

"Mom, I don't know what you heard—" Abby began, but Melissa talked over her sister.

"You're completely off base, Mom," she said firmly, avoiding Josh's eyes until she was sure she could look at him without succumbing to those looming tears again. "I'm giving up caffeine because I think I've been drinking too much of it for my health. I'm not pregnant."

Regret swept through her with the words. Maybe she was being overly dramatic again, but the thought of never having a child with Josh almost sent her bolting for the bathroom with another bout of hot tears.

She risked a quick glance at him, but she couldn't quite read his expression. He sat silently in his chair, his expression completely inscrutable now. She assumed he was deeply relieved to find out she wasn't pregnant, but the relief wasn't evident on his face. Maybe he was thinking about what a close call he'd just escaped.

Her mom searched her face. "You're not?"

Melissa shook her head. "No. I'm not."

"Then why have you been so upset this evening?"

Rattled by this entire confrontation, she blurted, "I'm upset because Josh is breaking up with me."

Josh made a choked sound before pushing a hand through his hair in exasperation. "Why do you think I'm breaking up with you?"

"I just, um, put two and two together," she muttered, all too aware that she sounded as much like her mother as Abby always accused her.

"Well, then you need to work on your math skills,"

Josh shot back with a frustrated shake of his head. "I don't want to break up with you, Melissa. I want to ask you to marry me!"

Chapter Six

by Cindy Kirk

Bedlam followed Josh Wright's announcement that he planned to propose to Melissa Morgan. Everyone at the table started talking in loud excited voices, their hands gesturing wildly.

Family patriarch Frank Morgan had experience with chaotic situations. After all, he and his wife Diana had raised two girls. When things got out of hand, control had to be established. Because his silver referee whistle was in a drawer back home, Frank improvised.

Seconds later, a shrill noise split the air.

His family immediately stopped talking and all turned in his direction.

"Frank?" Shock blanketed Greg DeSena's face. Though he'd been married to Frank's oldest daughter, Abby, for three years, this was a side to his father-in-law he'd obviously never seen.

Frank's youngest daughter, Melissa, slipped into her chair without being asked. She cast furtive glances at her boyfriend, Josh. It had been Josh's unexpected proclamation that he intended to propose to her that had thrown everyone into such a tizzy.

Even though Frank hadn't whistled a family meeting to order in years, his wife and daughters remembered what the blast of air meant.

"Darling." Diana spoke in a low tone, but loud enough for everyone at the table to hear clearly. "This is our anniversary dinner. Can't a family meeting wait until another time?"

Her green eyes looked liked liquid jade in the candlelight. Even after thirty years, one look from her, one touch, was all it took to make Frank fall in love all over again.

If they were at their home—instead of at Greg and Abby's house—he'd grab her hand and they'd trip up the stairs, kissing and shedding clothes with every step. But he was the head of this warm, wonderful, sometimes crazy family and with the position came responsibility.

"I'm sorry, sweetheart. This can't wait." Frank shifted his gaze from his beautiful wife and settled it on the man who'd blurted out his intentions only moments before. "Josh."

His future son-in-law snapped to attention. "Sir."

Though Frank hadn't been a marine in a very long time, Josh's response showed he'd retained his commanding presence. "Sounds like there's something you want to ask my daughter."

"Frank, no. Not now," Diana protested. "Not like this."

"Mr. Morgan is right." Josh pushed back his chair and stood. "There *is* something I want to ask Melissa. From the misunderstanding tonight, it appears I've already waited too long."

Frank nodded approvingly and sat back in his chair. He liked a decisive man. Josh would be a good addition to the family.

"If you want to wait—" Diana began.

Before she could finish, Frank leaned over and did what he'd wanted to do all night. He kissed her.

"Let the man say his piece," he murmured against her lips.

Diana shuddered. Her breathing hitched but predictably she opened her mouth. So he kissed her again. This time deeper, longer, until her eyes lost their focus, until she relaxed against his shoulder with a happy sigh.

Josh held out his hand to Melissa. His heart pounded so hard against his ribs, he felt almost faint. But he was going to do it. Now. Finally.

With a tremulous smile, Melissa placed her slender fingers in his. The lines that had furrowed her pretty brow the past couple of weeks disappeared. His heart clenched as he realized he'd been to blame for her distress. Well, he wouldn't delay a second longer. He promptly dropped to one knee.

"Melissa," Josh began then stopped when his voice broke. He glanced around the table. All eyes were on him, but no one dared to speak. Abby and Greg offered encouraging smiles. His future in-laws nodded approvingly.

His girlfriend's eyes never left his face. The love he saw shining in the emerald depths gave him courage to continue.

"When I first saw you at the office Christmas party, I was struck by your beauty. It wasn't until we began dating that I realized you are as beautiful inside as out."

Melissa blinked back tears. Josh hoped they were tears of happiness.

"This past year I've fallen deeper and deeper in love with you. I can't imagine my life without you in it. I want your face to be the last I see at night and the first I see every morning. I want to have children with you. I want to grow old with you. I promise I'll do everything in my power to make you happy."

He was rambling. Speaking from the heart to be sure, but rambling. For a second Josh wished he had the speech he'd tinkered with over the past couple of months with him now, the one with the pretty words and poetic phrases. But it was across the room in his jacket pocket and too late to be of help now.

Josh slipped a small box from his pocket and snapped open the lid. The diamond he'd seen circled in her bride's magazine was nestled inside. The large stone caught the light and sparkled with an impressive brilliance. "I love you more than I thought it was possible to love someone."

He'd told himself he wasn't going to say another word but surely a declaration of such magnitude couldn't be considered rambling.

Her lips curved upward and she expelled a happy sigh. "I love you, too."

Josh resisted the urge to jump to his feet and do a little home-plate dance. He reminded himself there would be plenty of time for celebration once the ring was on her finger.

With great care, Josh lifted the diamond from the

black velvet. He was primed to slip it on when she pulled her hand back ever-so-slightly.

"Isn't there something you want to ask me?" Melissa whispered.

At first Josh couldn't figure out what she was referring to until he realized with sudden horror that he hadn't actually popped the question. Heat rose up his neck. Thankfully he was still on one knee. "Melissa, will you make me the happiest man in the world and marry me?"

The words came out in one breath and were a bit garbled, but she didn't appear to notice.

"Yes. Oh, yes."

Relief flooded him. He slid the ring in place with trembling fingers. "If you don't like it we can—"

"It's perfect. Absolutely perfect." Tears slipped down her cheeks.

He stood and pulled her close, kissing her soundly. "I wanted this to be special—"

"It is special." Melissa turned toward her family and smiled through happy tears. "I can't imagine anything better than having my family here to celebrate with us."

"This calls for a toast." Flashing a smile that was almost as bright as his daughter's, Frank picked up the nearest bottle of champagne. He filled Diana's glass and then his own before passing the bottle around the table.

Greg filled his glass and those of Josh and Melissa's but Abby, his wife, covered her glass with her hand and shook her head.

Frank stood and raised his glass high. "To Josh and Melissa. May you be as happy together as Diana and I have been for the past thirty years."

Words of congratulations and the sound of clinking glasses filled the air.

Nestled in the crook of her future husband's arm, Melissa giggled. Normally her mom knew everything before everyone else. Not this time.

"You thought I was pregnant because I wanted decaf coffee," she said to her mother, "but yet you don't find it odd that Abby hasn't had a sip of alcohol tonight?"

For a woman like Diana who prided herself on being in the "know," the comment was tantamount to waving a red flag in front of a bull. She whirled and fixed her gaze on her firstborn, who stood with her head resting against her husband's shoulder. "Honey, is there something you and Greg want to tell us?"

Abby's cheeks pinked. She straightened and exchanged a look with her husband. He gave a slight nod. She took one breath. And then another. "Greg and I, well, we're…we're pregnant."

"A baby!" Diana shrieked and moved so suddenly she'd have upset her glass of champagne, if Frank hadn't grabbed it. "I can't believe it. Our two girls, all grown up. One getting married. One having a baby. This is truly a happy day."

Everyone seemed to agree as tears of joy flowed as freely as the champagne, accompanied by much backslapping.

"Have you thought of any names?" Diana asked Abby and Greg then turned to Melissa and Josh. "Any idea on a wedding date?"

Suggestions on both came fast and furious until Abby realized the party had gotten off track. She pulled her sister aside. "The anniversary gift," she said in a low tone to Melissa. "We need to give them their gift."

"I'll get it." In a matter of seconds, Melissa returned, cradling the large basket in her arms.

Josh moved to her side, as if he couldn't bear to be far from his new fiancée. Greg stood behind his wife, his arms around her still slender waist.

"Mom and Dad," Melissa began. "You've shown us what love looks like."

"What it feels like," Abby added.

With a flourish, Melissa presented her parents with a basket overflowing with biscotti, gourmet cappuccino mix, and other items reminiscent of their honeymoon in Italy...along with assorted travel documents. "Congratulations on thirty years of marriage."

"And best wishes for thirty more," Abby and Melissa said in unison, with Josh and Greg chiming in.

"Oh, Frank, isn't this the best evening ever?" Diana's voice bubbled with excitement. "All this good news and gifts, too."

She exclaimed over every item in the basket but grew silent when she got to the tickets, guidebooks and brochures. Diana glanced at her husband. He shrugged, looking equally puzzled.

"It's a trip," Abby explained.

Melissa smiled. "We've booked you on a four-star vacation to Italy, so you can recreate your honeymoon, only this time in comfort and style."

"Oh, my stars." Diana put a hand to her head. When she began to sway, her husband slipped a steadying arm around her shoulders.

"I think your mom has had a bit too much excitement for one day." Frank chuckled. "Or maybe a little too much of the vino."

"I've only had two glasses. Or was it three?" Instead

of elbowing him in the side as he expected, she laughed and refocused on her children. "Regardless, thank you all for such wonderful, thoughtful presents."

Abby exchanged a relieved glance with Melissa. "We wanted to give you and Dad the perfect gift to celebrate your years of happiness together."

"You already have," Frank said, his voice thick with emotion.

He shifted his gaze from Abby and Greg to Melissa and Josh before letting it linger on his beautiful wife, Diana. A wedding in the spring. A grandbaby next summer. A wonderful woman to share his days and nights. Who could ask for more?

* * * * *

After a bad decision—or two—Annie Mendes is determined to succeed as a P.I. But her first assignment could be her last, because one thing is clear: she's not cut out to be a nanny. And Louisiana detective Nate Dufrene seems to know there's more to her than meets the eye!

Read on for an exciting excerpt of the upcoming book WATERS RUN DEEP by Liz Talley...

THE SOUND OF A CAR behind her had Annie scooting off the road and checking over her shoulder.

Nate Dufrene.

Her heart took on a galloping rhythm that had nothing to do with exercise.

He slowed beside her. "Wanna ride?"

"I'm almost there. Besides, I wouldn't want to get your seat sweaty."

His gaze traveled down her body before meeting her eyes. Awareness ignited in her blood. "I don't mind."

Her mind screamed, *get your butt back to the house and leave Nate alone.* Her libido, however, told her to take the candy he offered and climb into his car like a naughty little girl. Damn, it was hard to ignore candy like him.

"If you don't mind." She pulled open the door and climbed inside.

The slight scent of citrus cologne, which suited him, filled the car. She inhaled, sucking in cool air and Nate. Both were good.

"You run often?" he asked.

"Three or four times a week."

"Oh, yeah? Maybe we can go for a run together."

Her body tightened unwillingly as thoughts of other things they could do together flitted through her mind. She

HSREXP0412

shrugged as though his presence wasn't affecting her. Which it *so* was. Lord, what was wrong with her? *He* wasn't her assignment.

"Sure." No way—not if she wanted to keep her job. As he parked, she reached for the door handle, but his hand on her arm stopped her. His touch was warm, even on her heated flesh.

"What did you say you were before becoming a nanny?"

Alarm choked out the weird sexual energy that had been humming in her for the past few minutes. Maybe meeting him on the road wasn't as coincidental as it first seemed. "A real-estate agent."

Will Nate discover Annie's secret?
Find out in WATERS RUN DEEP by Liz Talley,
available May 2012 from Harlequin® Superromance®.

And be sure to look for the other two books
in Liz's THE BOYS OF BAYOU BRIDGE *series,*
available in July and September 2012.

HSREXP0412